NICOLE A OLIVER

RATIONAL MAGIC

DEDICATION

This one's for my dad. Thanks for the "Book Deal" that inspired a lifetime love of reading.

CHAPTER 1
Sophia

Ivy? As in Logan's ex-girlfriend Ivy? I take a step back, shaking my head. This can't be happening. Ivy's supposed to be dead. Mages aren't gods. They can't bring the dead back to life. It must be an illusion or something. My head spins, and my hand flies out, catching me on the wall when I sway.

Logan stands there frozen, but I can't feel his emotions thanks to this stupid cuff. All the joy I was feeling at spending time with him and meeting his family drains from my body, leaving me raw and hollow. We're standing there in awkward silence, gaping at each other, when Liz comes crashing into the room. My bones creak, and I let out a gasp as she pulls me into a painful hug.

"Oops sorry, Sophia, super strength you know, sometimes I forget. Who's at the door?" She releases me and spins toward the door. Her wild energy stills. "Ivy???"

"Hi, Liz. Any chance I can come in?"

Logan's solid form propping the door open doesn't block the soft breeze from whispering through the open front door.

"Let her in, Logan!" Liz says.

He narrows his eyes, and he's clenching the door so hard his knuckles are white. "How can we be sure this isn't some kind of trick or illusion? Ivy is dead, Liz. This can't be her."

Ivy reaches out a slender hand to touch his arm, and her face falls when he jerks away as if she's carrying a contagious disease. The branches on the maple tree to her left rustle with far too much agitation for the light breeze.

"Logan, it's really me. I promise. I can explain everything." Her chin is trembling as she pleads with him.

Shadows darken his face with doubt, but finally he releases his harsh grip on the door and stretches an arm out toward her. I'm surprised his fingers don't leave deep imprints marring the wood. Probably would have if it was Liz. My stomach is rolling around in turmoil as he brushes her cheek with his thumb.

"Ivy, is it really you? Liz, get Mom."

"Uh yeah." She darts off and back in a blur of color. A black cat is chilling in her arms when she returns. "Voodoo will know if it's her."

The sleek cat makes a graceful leap from her arms, landing with a silent thump and padding over to the front door, tail twitching. He approaches Ivy, his nose twitching as he winds himself around her legs in a fuzzy figure eight. A deep rumble vibrates through his slender body.

Her face brightens, and she bends down to scoop the cat up into a snuggle. "Voodoo! You kept him."

A triumphant grin spreads across Liz's face. "See, Voodoo doesn't like anyone except me and Ivy. It's definitely her." She jabs a finger at Logan with a smug look on her face. "He doesn't even like you."

The conflict is apparent in Logan's expression as he flicks his eyes back and forth between the cat and Ivy. "It's a mutual dislike. You can hardly put all your trust in a cat. That proves nothing, Liz."

"It's her, Logan. Let her in." Mrs. Armstrong glides up behind us. Her face is tight with a strained smile, replacing her usual easy warmth.

He hesitates for one more moment before moving aside, letting Ivy pass. My stomach churns at the hopeful look she gives Logan. She pauses as if she's going to lean in for a hug, but he turns away and walks into the living room. The angry beast inside lowers its hackles. What kind of a terrible person am I? Angry that Logan's girlfriend has returned from the dead.

We settle in the living room. Mom ghosts into the doorway and gives the situation an appraising look. "I'll keep an eye on dinner. Call me if you need anything," she says, sending me a sympathetic smile and slipping off. She's always been good at reading a room, and the tension in this one is thick enough to shield a spaceship from cosmic rays.

I rise to follow her into the kitchen, but Logan pulls me back down, settling the comforting weight of his arm over my shoulders. Ivy's eyes widen, and I give him my best 'what the heck?' look. We're still supposed to be keeping this a secret from his dad, right?

"It's fine," he says. As if that's supposed to explain anything. "Okay, what in the Nether is going on?" He swivels his glare between his mother and Ivy. I give a shimmy when his hand tightens painfully on my shoulder, and he immediately eases his hold. The whispered kiss he drops on top of my head sends a shiver down my back.

His mom turns to Ivy. "I think it's your story to tell, sweetie, but first maybe some proper introductions. Sophia, this is Ivy. Ivy, Sophia."

Ivy's chocolate eyes zero in on Logan's arm draped around me. "The Archimage. Nice to meet you."

My eyes widen, and a prickling sensation tickles the back of my neck. How does she know? I thought we were keeping that info on the down low still. If she knows, how many other people do?

Guilt drips from the tight features on Mrs. Armstrong's face. "I told her grandparents. We've been in contact. Let her tell you her story, and then I'll fill you in on my part. I'm so sorry, Logan. You too, Liz."

Logan's whole body is rigid next to me. I may not be able to feel his emotions, but the tension is emanating off him in waves.

Ivy starts her story. "You know how close our families were. After my parents were..." she breaks off twisting her hands in her lap, "killed, my grandparents were very concerned for my welfare. After all, if I had been home that night, I would probably be dead for real. They decided to take me back to Japan with them, but they wanted to make sure no one followed. So they helped me fake my death."

"What?" Liz jumps in.

"I don't understand. Why didn't you tell me?" The anger and suspicion on Logan's face has been replaced by despair and confusion that sends an ache through me.

Her sorrow seems sincere, but what do I know? I don't know this girl.

"My grandparents thought it would be best. They were concerned that someone might go after you. They thought maybe you'd give up my location if you knew."

"I would never…"

"I know that now, but I was terrified. My parents had just been murdered. Everyone knew I was with them on their political views one hundred percent. And I didn't want to put that on you. What if they tortured you or used magical means to get the information out of you? You couldn't have lived with the guilt." She's curled in on herself, her brows pinched together in a pained expression of loss I recognize.

"Ivy. I haven't been able to live with the guilt. I was supposed to be with you that night. I have never stopped blaming myself for your death. Neither has Trey, for that matter. It destroyed our friendship. You have no idea what it's been like. And you. You knew, and you never told me?" I'm glad I'm not the subject of the rage he's directing at his mother.

Ivy's face has crumpled and tears flow from her eyes. "I'm so sorry, Logan. I really am. I didn't know what it would do to you. You'd been pulling away from me, anyway. I know that's not an excuse, but my grandparents told me it was for the best. Safest for everyone. Please, you have to forgive me."

"Why are you suddenly back now?" Logan ignores her plea, and a dark shadow of suspicion creeps onto his face.

"Your mother has been in touch. She asked Chaa-san for some advice about Archimages. You know how sharp my grandmother is. I think she connected one too many dots and your mom told her the whole story. Is that right, Mrs. Armstrong?"

Logan's mother glances at him, her lips pinched together, then drops her gaze to the floor. "That's right, Ivy. Your grandmother's research into archaic magic made her an invaluable resource, and I know I can always trust the Okamuras. I told them about Sophia."

"I can't believe you told them about her while keeping me in the dark about Ivy being alive! You saw how badly it tore me apart. Her death wrecked me."

"I know, and it destroyed me to watch you like that, but you know what would have destroyed me completely? If you died. I couldn't handle that. And yes, maybe it was selfish of me to want to keep you safe, but I would do anything for my children. Anything!" His mom's words come out in an impassioned plea for understanding. Doesn't look like they're landing, though.

Logan's mouth is hanging open. "I never thought you'd keep something like that from me, Mom. I don't even know what to say to you right now." He drags his hand through his hair and turns to Ivy. "You still didn't explain why you came back after all this time."

"I needed to make sure you were safe. After I heard about the bond and the Archimage, I knew you'd be in danger. I wanted to be here for you. To help you fight. I've been hiding for long enough. It was time for me to fight back."

"Well, I don't know if I can trust you now, Ivy. You've been lying to me for the past two years. How do I know you're telling the truth now?" I have to clasp my hands in my lap to avoid reaching up to still the hand he has tearing at his hair.

"I know," Ivy says. "I hope I can earn your trust again. You too, Liz."

"Thanks, Ivy." Liz is the only one in the room who looks remotely comfortable with the situation right now. She's got a floofy gray cat perched in her lap. I don't even know where it came from. I'm pretty sure an earthquake could shake the house on its foundations, and she'd still be chilling with a cat. I'm so shaken that it feels like an earthquake did rock my whole being.

"I think I should get Sophia back to the dorm." Logan drags me up after him.

"You're not staying here?" Ivy directs the question at me.

"No, she's staying at the dorm on the compound. Safer there."

"Ivy where are you staying?" Mrs. Armstrong asks.

"Oh I booked a room at the Riverside."

"You should just stay here sweetie. I know your grandparents would prefer that."

Ivy tilts her head at Logan rather than his mom. "I really shouldn't impose like that."

"Nonsense, you know you're like family to us."

"Yeah, we can get to know each other again," Liz pipes in and the jealous monster inside me starts to rise up again. She gets to stay here so they can all have a nice, cozy sleepover and I'm stuck by myself in an unfamiliar dorm room.

My heart lifts a little when Liz drops the cat and bounces over to give me a bone cracking hug. "I'll miss you, bestie. See you tomorrow, not so bright and early."

Clearly Liz won't let me stay mad at her. "You too."

Logan's already halfway out the front door. "C'mon, Sophia."

"I guess we're not staying for dinner? What about my mom? I at least have to say goodbye to her."

"We can grab something on the way back. Tell your mom I'll see her later."

I guess that means he's not gonna stay with me at the dorm? I was kind of hoping he might. I don't know that I can bear the thought of being alone right now. I'm still questioning this whole 'it's safer at the compound' plan.

The silence stretches on into infinity as the streetlights blink by, but there are so many questions buzzing through my brain I need to break it. "Tell me about Ivy."

His knuckles whiten as his hands clench the wheel a little tighter. "What?"

"Tell me about her. What's she like?"

"She's nice. At least I thought she was." His jaw is popping a little now.

"Nice is not a description. So she's a Bio Mage? Is she trained to fight, too?"

"Yes, the Bio thing is pretty cool. She can make plants grow. From the looks of it, when she was on the porch, the trees were responding to her mood, so her powers have probably grown since I saw her last. And yes, her parents trained her and sent her to the training center when she was older with the rest of us. Not all Mages are, but her family was definitely a part of the warrior class like mine."

Great, she can kick ass magically and she's a trained fighter, too. Not to mention beautiful. I've never missed the bond between Logan and myself more. I really wish I could tell what he's feeling right now.

"And you two were together for how long?"

"You want a burger or a chicken sandwich?" Logan deflects the question as he pulls into the drive-through line.

I tilt my head at him. He knows I don't eat meat. "Veggie burger, but you're not avoiding that question."

He sighs. "Almost two years. We started dating when we were fifteen."

I'm about to open my mouth when he gets to the speaker box. He orders himself a double cheeseburger combo and then we're back to an awkward silence I never remember experiencing with him before. We've always had something to say to one another, even when it was the sharp barbs we flung at each other when our lives first came crashing together.

"I guess I'll just have to get more details from Liz."

"Oh god don't ask her. Who knows what she'll say? Look, we can talk about her, but maybe not right now. I kind of need some time to process this." My stomach clenches at the soft hint of vulnerability that has crept into his usually confident demeanor.

Now I feel like a jerk. Of course he needs time, and here I am only thinking of myself.

"I'm sorry. I shouldn't have pushed you like that."

The car fills up with the greasy scent of fried potatoes as he grabs the bag and thanks the girl at the window. She's definitely checking him out. I can't say I blame her. Those arms.

My thoughts drift to darker things. "We have to think about how to get this thing off. Clearly, time is running out on me learning how to control my magic. Zeus is still out there and god knows who else wants to use me and my magic. What's the plan?"

"I'm not sure where to even start. We could try to find someone powerful enough to break the spell, but it's unlikely. Best bet is to track down the maker. There's always a key that can lift it. But you're never going to get it without talking to them. That or Zeus, since he put it on you, but he'd need to be in your proximity to remove it and no way am I letting him get his hands on you." His face goes dark as he practically growls that out.

We can revisit that protectiveness later, but honestly, I don't really relish the idea of being in the same room as my uncle, either. At least not now when I'm vulnerable without my magic. One day I'll take him down. That vicious thought seeps into my brain. I've never been a violent person before. To be fair, I've never been kidnapped, attacked, or had my mother threatened until this year. Yay for new experiences.

"How do we track her or him down? Is there a way to find out who made it? What about Garrett? He said he can find things, right? That's his specialty."

"We're not going to that guy." Disgust is dripping from the last two words. "Besides, we'd have to track him down first, and as far as I can tell, he's ghosted."

I lift a brow at him. "Uh huh then what do you suggest oh yee Mage of great wisdom?"

"People who create magical objects like this, especially super powerful ones, are obviously proud of their work. And like I said before, it would take an exceptionally powerful Mage to create something like this cuff. There is usually a mark carved into it, kind of their signature. You can bring it out of the design using magic. If I ever designed something kick-ass like that, I'd put my mark right there front and center for all the world to see." Why am I not surprised he'd be a show-off about it?

"I guess you're going to have to be the one to do that, since I am currently non magical once again." I had actually started to enjoy that swell of magic within me for the brief period I had it. It felt like home and even though I didn't have control of it yet, it made me less vulnerable. "And then once we have this mark, will you know who the maker is based on that?"

"Yeah, not quite that easy. I think we're going to have to do some research to figure that out. We can try my parent's book collection, but realistically we're going to have to hit the library at HQ." He certainly doesn't sound thrilled at the prospect whereas my whole being lights up at the thought of spending time at my favorite place.

"Good thing you have me, then. Research is kinda my specialty, if you know what I mean." I bob my eyebrow at him a couple of times.

"Riiight, you're a huge nerd. I like that about you." His lips tilt up in a half smile and my heart sings at the words. "Useful."

"I'm glad you appreciate my skills." At least we seem to have moved away from the earlier awkwardness. "Okay, so we magic the mark into existence, research to find the maker, and then…we have to track down this person? Mage?"

"Uh yeah, road trip, I guess." He stuffs a big bite of burger into his mouth and then turns into the driveway of the NAMC compound. He types in a passcode and the gate guard emerges to talk to him. When she looks over his shoulder at me with a spark of curiosity in her eyes, the car jolts forward as he slams his foot on the gas. I give her a wave before Logan pulls through the massive iron gate sliding aside to grant us entrance.

"What's my story here?" I can't believe I haven't asked this question yet. I don't know how they're explaining my presence at the compound. My life has been caught up in an uncontrollable whirlwind of activity since we rescued Liz and found my mom shaken in the wake of a magical attack. I hate the lack of control over my own life.

"What do you mean?"

"I mean, what are we telling people here? What's my backstory? Why am I suddenly descending on the magical community like this? We're obviously not telling them about the Archimage thing."

"Oh, yeah." he says, as if this is just an insignificant detail. "First off, don't even say that word while you're staying here. My mom told the council that you're an Elemental Mage. You lost control of your power in a public place, and they put a binding spell on your magic while you learned control. They don't know about the cuff, so you'll have to try to keep it hidden. You're from California, but you and your mom are moving here. She's leaving you at the compound to get to know the local community and start training while she looks after the move. No one knows she's actually staying at our house, except Trey and a few other trusted friends of my parents. Since you have your adopted parents' last name, no one will connect you with your biological family. My mom and Liz are going to work with you on your magical training and Trey's going to do the combat training." His face twists in disgust.

"Wait, what about you? Why aren't you going to be training me?"

"I'll do the first couple of sessions, but once we figure out who designed the cuff, I'm going to have to track him or her down. Who knows how long that could take." The few bites of my burger solidify like a lump of dried clay in my guts.

"You're going to just leave me here? Don't I need to…I don't know, be there to get the cuff removed? Seems kind of counterproductive." I'm not loving all of this making decisions for me without my input.

"Yes, but you still have to finish school, right? You can do that remotely from here and then you can also work on your training, so when we get the cuff off, you're better prepared to defend yourself."

He has a point. There's nothing I want more than to be able to fight back and stop relying on others to rescue me, but I'm still not in love with this plan. I'm also surprised he's ok with leaving me here to train with Trey. I know how he feels about that guy. I have no idea how those feelings will change now that Ivy's back. She was, after all, the root of their personal issues.

We've pulled up to the large red brick dormitory graced with white columns and a front porch designed for sipping lemonade on a hot summer night. Not that I'm in the mood for that right now. Logan parks his car right out front and opens my door for me. The night air stings at my cheeks, and I tuck my chin into the collar of my coat.

A long mahogany desk manned by an older guy stretches out to our left. He's immaculate in a dark suit with the NAMC crest embroidered on the left pocket, and his silvering hair is gelled back. He would definitely fit in at the desk of a five-star hotel and this place could pass as one with its rich dark wood floors and tasteful hunter green couches filling the spacious lobby.

After we sign in, we take the winding staircase up to my temporary home. There is no way I'm settling in here for any length of time. I'm willing to stay for now to finish high school, but as soon as my exams are all done, I'm out of here. Regardless of everyone else's plans for me. This is my life we're talking about, after all. It's a good thing I fast tracked through high school. I'll have enough credits to graduate after this semester. I intended to take some extra courses to graduate with my friends, but there's no point now that I can't go to physical school with them.

The room is small and sparsely furnished with a single bed, solid wooden block of a bedside table, and small desk, but we brought my cosmic bedspread and a few framed photos which have been hung up since we dropped my stuff off earlier. A warmth spreads through me. It was sweet of him to get it all set up for me.

We're just standing kind of awkwardly. Logan is tapping his finger on his thigh as if he doesn't know what to do with himself. Well, I'm not letting him go back to his house where his ex is staying without at least something to remember me by.

I take a step closer until mere inches separate our bodies. He's still just staring over my shoulder, so I lean in and brush my lips against his. It's like whatever conflict was racing around behind his eyes vanishes and he takes over the kiss, tempting my mouth open. His tongue slides against my lower lip, sending shivers down my back. I walk him toward my bed, pushing him down and settling in his lap. My skin is hot and agitated as I slide my hands up under his shirt. We're a tangled mess of hands and lips until I start to push him down and he pulls away, holding on to my shoulders to keep me from leaning back in. His eyes are as glassy and hazed over as I'm sure mine are, and confusion pulls at my brow.

"I gotta get back to my house, Sophia, and you should get some sleep." He lifts me gently off his lap and stands up.

Yeah right, like I'm going to be sleeping after that. It's frustrating that I can't read him. Did he pull away because he's thinking about Ivy again? He's smoothed his expression back into the one I call resting-stone-face and it's irritating in the extreme. With the bond gone, I can't feel his emotions anymore.

"Are you coming tomorrow?"

"Yeah, I'll text you to let you know what's up." He turns and leaves without a backward glance. The only telltale sign of his agitation is his hand running through his dark hair.

And with that I'm alone in a strange room with swollen lips, rapidly cooling skin, and strands of hair escaping from my ponytail. I fix my glasses and settle at the desk. Maybe I can get some studying done. Get my mind off that frustrating boy.

CHAPTER 2
Logan

By some miracle, and the use of the basement door, I snuck by everyone when I got back to my parent's house last night. Well, except Liz, of course. I found my nosy little sister lounging on my bed with not one but three cats shedding hair all over it after I snuck up the side staircase to my bedroom. She threatened me with gross bodily harm if I hurt Sophia and then told me she'd be going there to do schoolwork for the day. Knowing she's watching out for Sophia will ease my mind. They can get their studying done and then I'll head over to the compound in the afternoon to do some research in the library.

I guess I can try the library here first, but right now my fists are just itching to punch something. I'll do some training after breakfast. Hopefully, that will help me reassemble my jagged nerves. I used to think that the bond with Sophia was a burden, and I resented my parents for putting that responsibility on me.

That was before I knew her. My traitorous mind drifts back to the thought of her on my lap last night and I grit my teeth so hard my jaw hurts. Thinking about her soft sweet curves is a distraction I can't afford right now. Her safety has to be my number one priority right now. Not my own selfish desires.

I toss my dishes in the dishwasher and stride toward the basement stairs, bumping into Ivy in my haste. I got up crazy early so I could avoid the rest of my family, not to mention sleep was not in the cards for me last night, so I'm surprised to see her up. Although she is probably operating on a different time zone still so that could explain it. My whole body tenses up and I take a step back. Everything is so messed up right now. Too many emotions are fighting for dominance in my head, thanks to Ivy's reappearance. I know I should be happy she's alive, but guilt, anger, relief, and fear are eating at me too. If I let any of these push to the surface, I have no idea what's going to happen, so I'm trying to shove them down for the moment.

"Sorry." My growly tone defies my words.

"Morning." Ivy's gaze drops to her toes. It's not like her to be shy, especially with me. Who am I kidding? Do I even know her at all anymore? "Any chance we can talk?"

"I'm going to do some training." I brush by her. Probably a harsh response, but I'm still all twisted up with thoughts of Sophia and I can't quite harness the small part of myself that's house trained.

Unfortunately, she takes it as an invitation. "Great, I'll join you. I've been slacking off since I got here. My grandmother would be most disappointed in me." She dogs my heels down the stairs to our training room.

Fine, she can train too, but that doesn't mean I have to converse. I don't know why I'm trying to avoid talking to her, but I'm not ready to deal with her. I don't even think I've wrapped my head around the fact that she's still alive. Ivy is alive.

She stops in the doorway, and I turn to catch her staring around our training room. It hasn't changed much since the last time she was here I don't think. Same black mats, and pale grey walls. Her eyes bounce from the heavy bag in the corner to the various blades hanging from the wall, and the black shelves and cabinets hiding more weaponry.

"I've missed this place."

"Really?" I think back to all the days I spent down here getting driven to exhaustion by my father. I guess he was always softer on her, though. He had a surprising soft spot when it came to Ivy.

"Yeah, I've missed so much."

I don't know what to say to that, so I wrap my hands and crank up some heavy rock. I'm not sure if I'm doing it just to piss Ivy off. Maybe better not to analyze my motives that closely. I just let go, bashing the bag along to the pounding rhythm of the guitars until I'm panting and tossing my sweat soaked hair out of my eyes. My frustrations still flood back in once I back off. I grab a pristine towel from the neat stack on the shelf in the corner and take a deep drag from my water bottle.

My eyes land on Ivy as soon as I turn around. She's dancing with her sword. There's no other way to describe it. Her actions are smooth and graceful, and her black hair swirls around her face as she pivots, dips, and spins in an intricate series of movements. My eyes fall to the immaculately polished Katana with the black and gold hilt that she's wielding.

"Your sword." I don't mean to interrupt her concentration, but the surprise at seeing the blade in its rightful owner's hand again startles me. I've kept it polished and cared for these past couple of years, but no one else has used it. It's a shame, really. The beautiful piece of steel deserves to serve its purpose. It just never seemed right for anyone else to use it.

He movements still as her liquid chocolate eyes meet mine. "Oh, you don't mind that I'm using it, do you?" She holds out the sword.

"Of course not, Ivy. It's yours. It's always been yours. I'm glad to see it back in your hands. A blade that fierce deserves to be used." I've tried so hard not to say her name for so long that it feels strange rolling off my tongue. Stiff and unfamiliar like a favorite pair of shoes that are two sizes too small.

"You weren't using it?" She tilts her head with a speculative look.

"No, it would have hurt too much." Her face falls. "I kept it polished and cared for, though. Do you really think I would dishonor you or your grandparents by neglecting it? I did offer to send it to them, but they refused. Said it belonged here. I guess they always knew that you'd come back."

Ivy just stands there, the sword hanging loose in her hand. "I'm so sorry, Logan. I never meant to hurt you like that. Truly. I still want to talk about everything. I can't lose you as a friend, and I want to help with everything that's going on. It sounds like you're facing a lot. That is why I came back, after all."

I feel myself softening as she speaks. Ivy always has been my weakness. Even when I was pulling away from her romantically, I still loved her as a friend. "Okay, Ivy." I eye up the row of shiny blades mounted on the wall and select my preferred blade, sliding it from its holder.

I spin it around my hand as I saunter back over to the mats and drop into a fighting stance. "Let's talk."

She knows me well enough to recognize my need for action when dealing with heavy shit. Coiled energy flows through my body and I slip into a cool, focused zone. She narrows her eyes at me and lunges in a fast as lightning strike. I deflect and back away.

"I understand how you felt when you thought I was killed."

"Can you really?" I dart in, trying and failing to jab under her guard.

"Yes. I always knew you'd be sad, of course, but I didn't realize you'd feel so guilty. It had nothing to do with you."

"Of course it did. I should have protected you!" The crash of metal on metal rings out as our swords connect.

"No. That's where you're wrong. That wasn't your job. I've always been able to protect myself. I wasn't your responsibility then and I'm not your responsibility now."

She slips through with a tap on my shoulder when I falter. I spring back and whip my guard back into place. She doesn't take the time to gloat, twirling away. Her words ring true.

We've been training together since we were kids, so I know how capable she is. I think the guilt has always been more about the fact that I fell out of love with her than about not protecting her.

"You're right. In theory, I know I was never responsible, but I'm still sorry, Ivy. I'm sorry I wasn't there for you. I'm sorry I didn't trust you to protect yourself. Mostly I'm sorry I was pushing you away in the months before you die...well, at least I thought you did."

I almost land a blow, but she moves like her body is made of fluid lightning. She's always been better at this than me.

We've all got our strengths, and what she lacks in size she makes up for in speed and skill and training. She's always been so dedicated to her blade, just like she was dedicated to me. But I let her down.

Her eyes widen as if she's finally getting it. "That's it, isn't it? You feel guilty that you were pulling away. That you were about to break my heart. That's it right? Well, guess what? That does suck, but you know what sucks more? That you didn't trust me enough to tell me outright. You just started avoiding me and going quiet. You stopped making long-term plans, and you avoided any talk of the future. I knew it was coming. I knew you were going to leave me, but maybe I just wanted to cling to you a little while longer. Keep you for myself. Maybe that's part of the reason I never let your parents tell you the truth. Maybe I just wanted a clean break for the both of us." She punctuates each point with a more and more aggressive attack until I land with a thud as she sweeps my legs out from under me and points the tip of her Katana at my heart.

"You're right. I was a coward, but I was young and stupid and afraid to hurt you. Because I loved you, Ivy. I never stopped loving you. It's just that the feelings changed. I wasn't in love with you anymore, and it was eating me up inside. I didn't want to hurt you. I didn't want to destroy our friendship. I regret it now. All of it. I should have manned up and trusted you. I should have let you go. I know that now, and I'm so sorry." Relief crashes over me in a wave as I start letting go of all the guilt that's been tormenting me over the last few years. I know it's not going to be that easy, but at least it's a start. Ivy and I can work on repairing our friendship, and I can attempt to not make the same stupid mistakes with Sophia. Although right now, I realize I've already been acting like an asshole. Pushing her away last night and leaving her alone in that unfamiliar place. With Trey no less.

"I know." She reaches down and grabs my hand to pull me back to my feet. "We've both made mistakes, but I hope we can move past it now. Friends?" She gives me a tentative smile that almost makes it all the way to her eyes.

"Friends," I reply. I shake her hand and then pull her into me for a hug. "I've missed you so much."

"Me too." She mumbles against my sweaty chest. "Me too."

We let the hug linger until she pulls away and drops to the mats cross-legged. I settle down across from her, my elbows resting on my bent knees.

"Tell me what's been happening in your words. I've heard the stories from my grandparents, but I want some firsthand info."

I launch into the story of the whirlwind we've been through over the last couple of weeks after I got the call to come home while I was in Paris. I go over the attack, the kidnappings, and the final showdown where Zeus got the cuff onto Sophia. Ivy just soaks it in with an occasional question or nod until I run out of steam.

"You love her, don't you?" she asks.

"I think I might, but she deserves better than this mess." I gesture at myself.

"Don't do that Logan. Don't pull away from her because you're scared. You both deserve better."

I know she's right. I know I couldn't stay away from Sophia if I tried at this point. "I still have to keep her safe, though."

"She's strong and powerful. Don't forget that. She's an Archimage after all. She can handle herself."

"I know she will be able to, but that's the thing. Right now, she can't. She's not trained yet and she can't use her magic. It's trapped." Sweat flicks off my hair as I run my hand through it. "I need to look out for her. I can't lose her. Not when I've just found her." It's a relief to finally talk to someone about this. I hope I'm not hurting Ivy. It's been a couple of years. I'm not so conceited that I think she's not over me.

"Well, we'll just have to change that. We'll get that cuff off and get her all trained up. She'll be an unstoppable force soon enough."

"You're right. She's amazing. So strong. I said I'd go there this afternoon so we can get some research done. We've got to be able to figure out who made the cuff and where to find them."

"Well then, I'll help. I'm coming with you, and I'm assuming Liz will as well."

"Of course. She's already gone there for the day to do their homework together. They're tight already. You know Liz." I roll my eyes.

"Oh, I know Liz." The smile finally spreads to her eyes, crinkling the sides.

Everyone knows and loves my little sister. And how could you not? She's a bundle of overwhelming energy and enthusiasm for life. I'm probably better off not imagining what she and Sophia are up to right now.

CHAPTER 3
Sophia

"So we're done now, right?" Liz slams her textbook closed without waiting for an answer and springs up off the narrow bed in my dorm room. I'm not sure she read a word of it, to be honest. Love her to death, but finishing my schoolwork would have been much easier without her constant chatter. She definitely does not share my love of learning. Or maybe it's not the learning that's the problem maybe it's the sitting still part. It's like she's in a constant state of potential energy waiting for release. I'm not sure if it's a Phys thing or just a Liz thing.

I gently close my book. Book abuse hurts my soul a little. "Yes, we can finish up now." The twinge in my neck from stooping over the small wooden desk protests when I reach my arms toward the ceiling in a huge stretch.

I roll my eyes at her and then Immortals by Fall Out Boy blasts from my phone. Charlotte. She set her ringtone for me, so I'd always know when she's calling.

"Babe! How are you? How's that hot man of yours?" I pull the phone away from my ear to avoid permanent damage.

"Hey, Char. I'm okay. He's good. Liz and I were just studying." The mattress doesn't offer much give when I flop down on it to talk to my friend. My bed at home is like a warm, comfortable hug from my mom. This one is more like the awkward barely there hug you give a touchy feely distant relative you only see once a year.

"I miss you so much. School is extra lame without you. I don't know if I'm going to survive these last few weeks without you here."

"I'm sure you'll survive. You still have Xander who I miss soooo much, by the way. Plus Anne and Brendon. I've been avoiding Xander's texts because I don't quite know how to explain my disappearance."

"It's fine. I told him everything." She drops this all nonchalant like.

"WHAT?"

Liz whips her head up, eyes wide with alarm. I mouth sorry. "You told him? About the whole...you know." I can't stop my arms from waving around even though she can't see them.

"Yeah, that you went with your mom to help your aunt in Port Grand. Scared you though, right?" I can picture her giving me a smirk on the other end of the line.

"Don't freak me out like that. Last thing I need is to stress about Xander getting whisked off to Mage jail for knowing too much. Or even worse, someone targeting him to get to me. Bad enough they know I'm close with you. At least now I know you can defend yourself. I wish you were here with me or rather that I was there with you."

"Don't think they put humans in Mage jail, babe. They just kill them outright, you know."

I know she's just messing with me, but my heart picks up at the thought of any of my friends in danger because of me. "Not helping the situation."

I'm familiar with Char's habit of blurting things out before thinking them through. She doesn't do it out of malice. Her voice softens to a whisper I can barely hear through the earpiece. "I'm sorry."

"It's okay. How are you doing?"

"I'm good. Can't wait to finish school, then I can come hunt evil with you."

"Really? Like you'd leave your system behind to traipse across the country like the Winchesters." No way would my bestie leave her video games behind.

"Of course not. It's portable. Don't be ridiculous."

"Fair point." I glance around. Liz seems pretty engrossed in her phone as she paces the small room like a caged tiger, so I drop my voice to a whisper. "Have you heard from Garrett?" I know I shouldn't care about him. He pretty much ditched us after I got cuffed, so I shouldn't care but worry has been needling at me.

"Garrett? No. I haven't heard from him. I can ask around if you want me to."

I don't want to stir anything up for either of them. "Nah. I was just wondering."

"I'll let you know if I hear anything."

"Thanks, Char. I miss you, and everyone else at home. Can't wait to see you again." An ache fills my chest and I close my eyes taking a deep breath. I don't want to hang up and lose the connection to home.

"You got it, babe, but if anything happens. If anyone tries to get my girl, call me immediately, and I'll drop everything, including my personalized controller."

"Thanks, Char. Love you." The thing is, I know she means it. She's that kind of friend. Xander too, if I wasn't planning to do everything I can to keep him safely away from this magical world. If only I could see him one more time before everything blows up around me.

"Love you too. Talk soon."

"Bye."

I hang up and turn back to Liz. "What's the plan now?"

"Manis and facials?" She asks hopefully. "Before my bro comes to crash our party."

"Do you know what time he's planning on stopping by?" He said he'd be by in the afternoon to start our research, but I don't recall if he said what time.

"I think he said he'd be here around four, so that leaves us only an hour to enjoy ourselves."

"Cool. One problem. I don't have any nail polish or anything." I point out the obvious. Pretty sure she knows how little I brought with me. Nail polish definitely didn't make the cut.

Liz arches a perfectly shaped brow at me. "Really?" Then she dumps her "schoolbag" onto my empty desk and all manner of non-schoolbooks tumble out. A couple of knives clatter out next to a decent sized cosmetic bag with a kitty face on it and ears sticking out. She grabs it and starts rifling through the contents.

"You are a girl of eclectic tastes, aren't you?" I say, nodding to the knives scattered on the desk. I reach and slide a finger down one of the beautiful rose gold handles.

"Of course. Girls just wanna have fun right? Sometimes it's fun to put on makeup and sometimes it's fun to stab someone."

"There are days when I think you are the scarier one out of the Armstrong siblings. When you say someone, you mean a bad guy, right?"

"Sure, that's what I meant. And of course I'm scarier than him. Hello super strength. I don't even need the knives. They're just an added benefit to living the Mage life."

A dozen colors of nail polish spill from the cosmetics bag along with a handful of face masks. I choose a pomegranate vanilla one and a glittery gold nail polish. She picks a cocoa almond one with an electric blue polish.

"So let's get real. How's my brother really treating you? Cause, you know, I don't mind getting stabby with him if need be. You are my bestie, after all." Her face is set with a stony seriousness that might be a little scary if it weren't for the sparkle of mischief in her eyes.

"No need for that. He was a bit weird last night when he brought me home, but I guess that's no surprise given his girlfriend just came back from the dead." My stomach twists again at the memory of her gorgeous face.

"Ex-girlfriend. You're his girlfriend now, and don't forget it." Her eyes soften with sympathy to an almost aqua color. "I get that you're feeling shook, though. It was a crazy shock seeing Ivy again. He's not getting back with her. That was over even before she faked her death. Honestly, I think he's more angry than anything else right now." That's what I'm afraid of. What happens when the anger dissipates? Will all his old feelings for her come rushing over him in a tsunami that wipes out any chance we had?

"What's Ivy like?"

"She's amazing. Super cool, badass with a sword, and she's got that cool Bio magic thing going on." She must have seen my face fall. "She is cool, but he's not getting back with her. He's totally into you, Sophia. I've never seen him like this. Even when he was with her."

"What if it was just the bond all along though, and he never had real feelings for me?" The way he bolted off last night in the middle of our make out session is causing me some anxiety.

"Well then, I guess you'll find out now that the cuff has stifled it. I really don't think that's the case."

Liz has no reason to lie to me. "It's weird though, right? When I had my magic bound as a kid, he could still feel the bond even though I couldn't? Why can't he feel it now?"

"No clue on how that works, my friend. Magic is weird like that. Maybe the cuff just cuts off all magic within you while the original spell to bind your magic only cut off your personal magic and the bond is something exterior? That's my best guess."

Interesting. I'd like to study all the inner workings of this world. Figure everything out. I wonder if there are any jobs in magical research, cause that would totally be my jam.

Liz is up and crouching with a knife in each hand before I've even registered the knock on my door, which interrupts our girl time. I wake up my phone. It's only 3:45. Too early for Logan, right?

"Who is it?" Liz asks, holding the knives out in front of her.

"It's your brother. Let me in." The words are punctuated with a grumble from the other side of my door.

"How do I know it's really you? The real you would be pissed if I let Sophia get kidnapped."

"The real me is pissed that you won't let me in."

"Yup, sounds like his grouchy ass self." She swings the door open to show Logan standing there. Ivy peeks out over his right shoulder.

"Ivy? I didn't know you were coming," Liz says. Her eyes dart to me and back to Ivy with her brows pinched together.

"I thought maybe I could help with the research." Ivy gives a tentative smile.

"The more the merrier." Liz steps aside, letting the two of them pass through.

I feel like a giant next to Ivy. She's like half the size of Logan. Liz is shorter than me, but Ivy is so tiny.

I control my less stellar urges, like shoving her out the door and return her smile.

"Ivy and I had a chat this morning. Then she offered to help with the research. I figure the more of us delving in, the faster we can get it done and the less musty books I have to look at." Logan shares the info, giving me an assessing look.

He takes a step toward me and leans in for a kiss. It's a little longer and deeper than is appropriate with his sister in the room, but I like the point he's making. He's straight up putting our relationship out there in front of Ivy, and it sends a tingle of warmth through me. I squeeze him tight before letting my hand slide down into his. Without the mental connection of the bond, it's reassuring to have a physical one.

"What is that on your face?" he asks.

Oh crap. Liz and I didn't get around to taking the masks off. Liz's is clear, so it's hardly noticeable, but mine is like bright red. Nice. Not embarrassing at all. I duck into the tiny bathroom and scrub off the mask, leaving me with a damp pink face.

Liz is giggling when I get out. I send her some eye daggers to let her know I blame her for the incident. She just keeps giggling and darts into the bathroom to scrub hers off.

I turn away to root through the desk drawer. I'm looking for a notebook but really just trying to avoid any more embarrassing eye contact. When my hands make contact with my prize, I yank out a new purple notebook along with my pencil case.

"Do we need that?" Logan gives me a questioning look.

"What?" I finally turn around, clutching the spiral notebook to my chest.

"A notebook. Can't we just use a computer or something?"

A laugh escapes. "Of course we'll use that too, but I do all my best organizing in notebooks. With colored pens." I brandish the pencil case at him.

"If you say so. You're the expert."

Liz finally emerges from the bathroom. Did she take the time to apply makeup? I have so many questions about that.

"K let's bust out of here. Lead the way, big bro." Liz links arms with me and Ivy and we're swept off in the whirlwind that she is.

CHAPTER 4
Logan

The library is so big it gets its own building down a winding gravel path a few buildings over from the dorms. Of course, it's more red brick and draped with ivy. That old money feeling infuses every aspect of this place.

I haven't been to the library since I graduated from high school. The main floor is separated into several sections, and there are two more floors full to the brim with books. The musty smell of old paper invades my senses and I catch Sophia's face light up as her eyes sweep the place. I glance around again at the familiar place, trying to see it through her eyes. While I see it as a place where adults forced me to sit still and be quiet while struggling to focus on dry textbooks, she sees it as a place to get lost in other worlds and discover exciting new things.

"Are there computers to locate what we need or is it like old school with card catalogs or some weird magic cataloging system?" Sophia asks.

"Just because we have magic doesn't mean we don't take advantage of technology where necessary. There are computers here. So what are we looking for? Logan, did you bring up the mark on her cuff last night?" Liz turns to me.

I shift on my feet, lust flaring through my core as I remember Sophia's chosen method of distraction last night. "Uh no, I forgot."

"I guess that's the first order of business. Let's see if they have a spell room we can borrow for a bit." Liz strides up to a woman at a circular desk in the middle of the large, open main area we've walked into.

"A spell room? What's that?" asks Sophia. It's so easy to forget how little she knows about our world.

Liz spins around, grabbing Sophia by the shoulders. "Only the coolest place in this building. It's a room where you can practice magic with reinforced walls, doors, and windows. You know, in case things get out of hand." I'm sure my sister would welcome the chaos if things got out of hand.

Ivy still hasn't said anything. It must be weird for her. Being back. Here with us. I'm surprised she hasn't gotten accosted yet by the nosy Mages around here. I guess that's why she's thrown a black ball cap on her head with her silky ponytail hanging out the back. To be fair, she has matured in the last couple of years. Probably more than me.

Liz hops back with a key. "All set, third floor. Let's hit it up. The best part is that Ivy can draw a picture of the mark when it appears. Cause art is definitely not one of my many awesome qualities."

I ruffle her hair, knowing how much it annoys her. "That's like the understatement of the century. Your average kindergartner can draw better than you."

She punches me in the shoulder, knocking me back a step. "You're one to talk."

I groan, rubbing my shoulder. "Why are you so violent, little sister?"

"I dunno. I think maybe it's just something you bring out in me."

Ivy laughs. "You have no idea how much I've missed this."

"You missed it? I guess they are entertaining, but also completely ridiculous. I feel sorry for their parents." Sophia replies to Ivy. It's pretty weird seeing them together. Isn't there some sort of rule about not letting your new girlfriend hang out with your ex? Feels like there should be. I'm kind of terrified they might decide to gang up on me.

"Yeah. They've always driven their father crazy with their fighting. Even their awesome mom gets fed up sometimes, or she did." Ivy trails off as if she's realizing how much she's missed in the last two years.

The elevator lets us out onto the third floor. The center circle is open, looking down over a stunning view of the old library. Hallways branch off from the center in all directions, each labeled with a letter. Sophia lingers at the dark wood banister until I grab her hand and pull her along after Liz, who is marching away at a brisk pace. We follow her down the hall labeled D with a picture of a dragon. Sophia's eyes widen and she glances at me with a question in her golden-brown eyes.

"There are no dragons. Any reports of them in the past were probably based on illusions. A lot of mythology comes from those."

Her lips curve up in a smile and a tingle of warmth shoots up my arm as she squeezes my hand.

We reach an unassuming pine door that's hanging open. Liz and Ivy are already inside. The room is tiny and looks ordinary enough, with beige painted walls and a long table that seats six. I don't miss this place, that's for sure. The endless drills my father used to make me run to practice my magical control are etched into my brain permanently.

I pull out a chair for Sophia and then clasp her right wrist where the shiny silver cuff sits. A slight shiver runs up her spine as my fingers brush the back of her hand. I might not have noticed if I wasn't so attuned to her, even with the bond frustratingly blocked off. I'm kind of wishing Liz and Ivy would vanish into thin air so I could lift her up on the desk and do evil things to her. The thought of pulling her hair out of that slick ponytail in the library is hot. She probably wouldn't be into desecrating the library like that, so I shake my head to clear those thoughts away. I place her palm down on the table and run a finger along the cuff, calling on the current of magic that flows through my body and focusing it into the bracelet. My power activates the magic of the cuff and it emits a bright gleam of white light.

"Got it," I say with a triumphant grin.

Ivy leans in over my shoulder. "Just hold it there for a minute." She opens Sophia's notebook. I guess it came in useful after all.

A mark has risen to the surface that wasn't there before. It's a budding tree with an eye centered in a triangle staring at us from the trunk. Interesting. Looks like a combo of Bio and Psychic Mage symbols. Those must be the primary magical lines within the family. There's also an eagle with wings spread wide rising behind the barren branches. Barbed wire twists around the outline of the shield. I never paid much attention in history class, especially when the teachers droned on and on about this Mage and that Mage. All those names just melted into each other.

Ivy sketches out a remarkable likeness of the design. Her pink tongue pokes out the corner of her mouth as she concentrates. "Okay, I got it," she says, holding up a perfect sketch of the mark.

"That's pretty cool. Was it necessary to do this in the spell room, though? I kinda feel like we could have just done that, um, anywhere?" Sophia voices her confusion.

"We could have if we wanted the whole compound mouthing off about it this afternoon. Bunch of old gossips around here. Nothing better to do than wildly speculate. They're already talking about you. I didn't exactly want any more attention drawn to you." My jaw tightens at the thought of people finding out about her powers.

"Got it. That makes sense. Okay then, where do we start?"

I shrug. "Not my department."

Sophia's mouth turns down in a cute frown. "What exactly is your department then, may I ask?"

I raise a brow at her. "Protection, muscle, intimidation, general badassery, oh and eye candy. Can't forget about that." I list my "skills" off on my fingers and give her my cockiest smirk.

"Should have known better than to ask that. Anyone have any helpful suggestions?" She puts a lot of emphasis on the word helpful. Hey, I can be helpful, just maybe not at this.

"I think we should start in the records room." Ivy chimes in.

"Of course," Liz says, "let's go."

And with that, she bursts out the door. Luckily, she doesn't reach inside and pull out the super speed, otherwise none of us could keep up. Probably not the best idea in a library anyway, but my sister doesn't always make the best decisions, so it wouldn't surprise me. I shrug at the other two and follow along. Sophia twines her fingers with mine.

The massive records room takes up an entire lower basement level. It's like the size of the entire building. Not daunting at all. If I thought the musty smell in the main part of the library was intense, it's so much more down here. It's like the imprint of several centuries of Mages forms a thick coating of dust that coats my lungs as I breathe in the smell.

The books down here range from dusty old tomes to encyclopedia-like reference books in a rainbow of colors with gold lettering embossed on spines.

"This isn't going to take like a year or anything." They all ignore my complaints.

"Are these categorized electronically?" Sophia nods toward the bank of computers grouped in the middle of the room.

"Yes, they are," Ivy says.

Sophia settles in at one of the computers, so the rest of us circle chairs around her until she gives us our next step.

My eyes get caught up in Sophia as she adjusts her glasses and starts typing at a furious rate with the other girls pointing out how to access the records section. The sun coming through the window has lightened her shining eyes to the color of honey, and little lines have popped up on her brow from the intense focus. This girl is way too smart for me. Here's hoping she never realizes it. I'm as engrossed in her soft features as she is in her work, so I'm a little startled when she jumps up and sweeps the room until her eyes fall on the printer in the corner.

She pulls off a long ass list of books and divides it into four sections.

"We've each got a section. Find the books on your list and we'll reconvene and start combing them."

Since I've known her, Sophia has been off balance. Everything she knew was turned upside down and she's had to figure everything out on the fly all while fearing for her life. Here she's in her element. She's in control, and she looks happy, content. What if she can't have that feeling of security back? What will that do to her? I can't let that happen. I've got to eliminate the threat from her uncle. He may have faded into the background for the moment, but he'll be back. That man is hungry for power and revenge against the Mage community and he's not going to stop until he's neutralized. I kind of get where he's coming from. He's had this darkness growing inside since they ripped away his power against his will, but that doesn't give him any right to do the same thing to Sophia. I clench my jaw to keep in the black rage that threatens to take over at the thought of him harming her.

I'm the last to reach the big round table they've convened around. A tower of books I tracked down is threatening to tumble from my arms, so I go with it and let gravity take them to the table. The ensuing crash gets me dirty looks from the two other people in the room. Scholarly types who look like they don't get outside enough. Their gazes fall back to their books at my glare, and I drop into the chair, stretching out my legs.

"Logan, are you trying to terrify the library crowd?" Liz calls me out on my shit. Little sisters are a pain like that.

"What if I am? It's probably better if we have a little privacy for this research project anyway, right?"

"Uh huh. I'm sure that was your intention." She cocks her head to the side with a you-can't-fool-me sisterly eyebrow lift.

I shrug and eye the heap of dry history and records books in front of me with distaste. This is for Sophia, though, so I'll do my part. My knee jiggles under the table as I open the first one, and a puff of dust sends me into a sneezing fit.

The light beaming through the window has gone pinkish, and my jaw stretches in a wide yawn when a loud rumble sounds next to me. I pull my gaze away from the page I've just read five times without absorbing a single word.

I turn to Sophia. "Hungry?"

Unnecessary embarrassment colors her soft cheeks, replacing the deep concentration. "Yes, but I haven't found anything. I need to solve this problem."

My heart hurts for her. She feels out of control. I don't want to know what I'd be like if someone cut me off from my magic. You wouldn't want to be in the same room, that's for sure.

"I know, but we still need to eat. We can come back tomorrow."

"How about after dinner?" She counters my offer.

Liz groans. "Do we have to?"

I'm about to answer when Ivy answers. "We should Liz. This is important."

"I know. Anything for you, Sophia, but as soon as we figure this out, I'm taking a cross-country run. My skin feels almost itchy with all this sitting around." I can see it in her. My sis is practically vibrating in the seat across from me.

Sophia gathers up the meticulous notes she took. Recording each book section and chapter we combed through, plus any notes or ideas she thought would be helpful in our search.

"I may not have found out anything about the maker of the cuff, but at least we have their mark now, and I did manage to find a record of my uncle."

I drop back into my seat, leaning toward her. "What? What did you find?"

"It's not a lot, but something at least." She pulls out a big book of family genealogies. "I found my family tree, which is pretty cool, but weird."

I reach over, running my fingers through the silky ponytail draped over her shoulder to give her some reassurance.

She flips the massive book open to a chapter marked by a crest that features a stag's head with an H on its forehead at the top, a Triskele within a circle, a gladiolus, a five-pointed star, and the psychic eye within a triangle that's the symbol for Psychic Mages. It's an interesting one featuring all the Mage specialties. Most families only have two of them on their crest. The name Hartwin is written in fancy script on a banner across the center. This is her mother's family tree.

She flips forward several pages, then runs her hand down a long family tree that's handwritten in a neat script. Her finger pauses on the name Elora Hartwin - Elemental, and my heart aches at the single tear that escapes. Elora Hartwin is connected to Greyson Tennant - Psychic by marriage, and they have a single branch listing Rose Tennant. All three are listed as deceased.

"That's my middle name. I wonder if they asked Mom to keep it? You know, preserve a bit of them." I reach out to brush away the few hot tears that have slid down her cheek and pull her into my arms. I'd do anything to take away her pain, but I'm helpless here. She never knew her biological family, and she never will. The best I can do is make sure she knows that we're her family now. Her mom will always be there for her too, but she'll never be a part of the magic community, and that's where Sophia's destiny lies.

My eyes close and I inhale her clean, sweet scent as she lets herself relax against my chest for a moment before pushing me away and swiping at her tears.

She refocuses on the book. "That's not the important part. She slides her finger to the left of her mother's name and a line labeled brother connects to Tobias Hartwin - null."

Liz leans in. "So that's Zeus?"

"Yeah." Sophia has shaken off the melancholy and is back to business. "It's only a name, but it's more than we had before. I'll see if I can dig up any more information on him. Is there anyone else we could talk to that might have known him?"

"Our parents are close to him in age, so they would have been kids too when he had his powers stripped. They wouldn't know anything about it. I can ask them if there's anyone we can trust who might have more info," I say, wishing there was anyone I could think of. I don't know who we can trust.

"Ok, we can work on that." Sophia's stomach grumbles again, and I realize mine is begging for food, too.

"Shall we hit the cafeteria?" I ask.

"Yeah." Sophia moves the big genealogy book off to the side with the rest of the stack with one last longing look.

"Yup, let's do this." Liz bounces all the way to the front door and then tosses a wicked look over her shoulder. "Race you!" Then she's off in a blur of color none of us could possibly hope to keep up with. Well, maybe Sophia, if she was in possession of her magic.

When the rest of us reach the old stone building that houses the dining hall, Liz is leaning against the massive stone arch at the entranceway. "What took you so long?"

I roll my eyes at her and give her a friendly shove as we head in.

CHAPTER 5
Sophia

"How late did you stay up last night?" Liz is eyeing the dark circles under my eyes with concern as I catch my head before it drops to my chest.

"Umm. Three." I sort of mumble under my breath, hoping she doesn't catch it. Silly of me, I know. Trying to slip something past someone who has enhanced hearing.

"Are you crazy? Don't you have a training session with Logan today?"

"Yeah." It's not the first time I've stayed up too late studying, but it's definitely the first time I've had to take part in grueling physical training after a late night.

"Well, good luck with that. Let's take a break, anyway. It's for sure break time. Biology holds no wonders that are going to keep me from a snack. We should take a walk around the compound."

That sounds like a great idea. I know Logan thinks I shouldn't be wandering around the grounds and drawing too much attention to myself, but I've got Liz, right? She can totally protect me. And really, when you think about it, won't people think it's more suspicious if I hole up and avoid everyone? No reason to think I have anything to hide if I'm just out there strolling around, mingling with the Mages.

I hit save and shut down my laptop. "Okay, I'm in. This place does have a beautiful property. If I'm going to be stuck here, I may as well enjoy it, and I'm itching to start running again."

"It really does. Let's go."

Liz is bouncing on her heels as she grabs my hand and pulls me up. I fall forward and stumble. "Easy there, Liz."

She giggles. "Oops sorry. Come on, hurry up."

I'm still pulling my shoes on as she drags me out the door and I slam into a person as I'm standing up. Smooth. I glance up under my lashes, meeting a pair of narrowed blue eyes.

"Watch what you're doing." The girl gives me the kind of look I've seen before when someone is trying to make me feel small. I meet her disdainful stare head on, and her gaze turns speculative as she looks me up and down from my messy blonde topknot, past my dark glasses and all the way to my favorite pair of worn-out blue Gazelles.

"You must be, Sophia. I'm Michelle. Nice to meet you." She extends her slender hand toward me.

I'm not sure her words match her thoughts, but I reach out to shake her hand. Liz bats it away.

"Nice try. Don't touch her. She can read your thoughts if you do." I jerk my hand away and take a step back as an extra precaution.

The girl smirks and tosses her long hair over her shoulder. "I heard you couldn't control your powers, so you got sent here."

I suck back the words that want to come out and instead mumble, "Something like that."

"Too bad. Is Logan here? I haven't seen him in forever." She peers over my shoulder as if he might be hiding in there, waiting for her to prowl in.

"No, he's not. Probably at home thinking of everyone but you," Liz says. Wow she can be vicious when she wants to be. I'm glad I've never gotten on her bad side.

"Whatever." The rude girl bumps me hard, brushing my hand as she walks by. She turns around and gives me a startled look that quickly turns even bitchier than before, if that's even possible. Crap, I was thinking about all the ways I could murder her for thinking about Logan like that. Yup, I said it. He's mine. Not Ivy's, not this random girl's. Although it is a little disconcerting to wonder if he's been with this girl before or any of the other women around here. He was honest with me about his past. We just never got around to discussing the details. That's something to file away in the brain vault to never think of again.

I inhale the fresh air deep into my lungs when we make it out the front door without any further run-ins. After spending most of the day cooped up inside, the cool air is energizing.

"Was Logan like, with her?" The question slips out of my mouth against my better judgment.

"Michelle. Ew no. Not that she never tried. She's the same age as Logan. I don't think he actually dated any of the Mages his age other than Ivy...I'm sorry. I didn't mean to say that."

Well, that's a relief. "It's fine. It's weird, obviously, but now I'm just going to have to learn to live with it. So she could read my thoughts?" I ask.

"Only if she's touching you. She's kind of a low-level Psychic Mage. I honestly think that's her only talent, and it's limited since it requires contact. Why, what were you thinking about when she bumped into you? Not the Archimage thing, right?" She hisses that last bit out before glancing around like the worst spy in the secret service, checking for eavesdroppers after she spilled state secrets.

"Ummm. Clawing her eyes out for daring to think about Logan? Maybe." I scrunch up my face.

A wild snort bursts out of Liz and she leans down on her knees laughing until tears are leaking down her cheeks. I join in and we laugh until we collapse on the chilly lawn in front of the dorm.

"Thanks, I needed that," Liz says when she finally calms down. "Oh, and make sure to invite me when you decide to kick her butt. I don't get to see enough hair pulling and slapping in my life."

"Hey, I've got a few skills now. Well, maybe two...one. Never mind, I'm still hopeless. I definitely need to start those training sessions with Logan and Trey, like now."

"And you will, but for now, I'm going to show you around this place. Oooh, they even have stables in the back. Want to go pet some horsies?"

"Sure. Any unicorns in there? Pegasii? Is that the plural for pegasus?" Anything's possible at this point, right? I mean, magic is real. Why not unicorns?

"Uh no. Sorry to break the heart of your inner 8-year-old. They're not real. But the regular old horses are pretty nice."

"That's still cool. I wish my mom could visit. She loves horses." My heart twists when I think of her. I miss her, and the guilt has sunken deep inside that she's been dragged into danger and had to uproot her life for me. I wonder what she told that guy she was dating? The glow of a life enjoyed had just started returning to her eyes. I'll call her this evening. If I wasn't spending all my extra time trying to track down the cuff's maker, I'd insist on visiting the Armstrong's house for dinner tonight.

The grass beside the stone path is so green it looks like they've touched it up with a photo filter. She leads me past several other stately buildings, pointing out their purposes as we pass by. This place is huge. I wonder how much property they actually own here. It's super private too. To get here, we took a road that meandered up the side of a steep hill through a heavily wooded area. Then we turned off on an unassuming private road that eventually opened up to the gates of the compound. No one would ever find it without knowing the location. I guess that's the point, though. Secrecy.

The stable is prettier than a lot of houses I've seen. Gray stone with black trim and a black roof. A patchwork of horses dots the surrounding fields, cropping away at the lush pasture. A few of them poke their heads out of windows in the barn with curious looks. Liz leads me up to a shiny black one who's turned its liquid eyes on us. It snorts and tosses its head up in greeting when Liz runs her hand down its neck in a gentle stroke.

"This is Raven. She can't go outside right now. She hurt her leg."

"Poor baby. It must suck to be stuck in this stable instead of out and about running free like she should be." I can definitely empathize with the horse right now. While this place is beautiful. It's kind of like a beautiful prison. There are still fences keeping me in, and while it's meant to keep me safe, my skin is itching for freedom and I miss my friends already. I reach out a tentative hand and slide it down her long, graceful neck. Her hair is smooth, and the musky, warm smell reminds me of my childhood when my mom still rode. She used to drag my brother and me up to the barn when she went to a lesson. Neither of us caught the bug, unfortunately. It still feels a little like home, though. The comforting time of my childhood, before my dad died and everything crumbled around us. I guess now I'm building a new world.

"Yeah, it's pretty crappy for her. Right, baby?" Liz's voice breaks into my thoughts. "What are you going to do after this semester? You were planning on applying to a biomed program, right?"

I heave out a huge sigh. "I dunno. I mean, I was planning on going to medical school like my dad, but is that even a reasonable goal now? Can I do that?"

"I'm sure you could if that's what you still want. Might have to put it off a bit until we're able to track down Zeus, but I'm sure you still could if that's your dream."

Is it my dream? I don't even know anymore.

I can sense the question behind her eyes, but she doesn't probe. "How are you really holding up under all this change? You're holding it together on the outside, but I know sometimes the outside doesn't match the inside."

Liz's ocean eyes are like x-rays penetrating through all the protective layers to my soul. Somehow, I forgot how insightful she can be. She's so sassy and quirky that you don't expect these deep insights to come out of her. I think over her words.

"I'm ok." She arches a challenging brow at me, and I sigh. "I'm struggling. I'm anxious most of the time now. I'm worried about my family and my friends."

"You know we're all here for you and your family. No one is going to get hurt under our watch. And I'm here for you. If you get anxious you can always talk to me."

The tight ball in my chest eases a little at her words. "Also, I'm wondering if my life will ever be normal again."

She reaches out and squeezes my hand. "You never would have had a normal life, Sophia. You were meant for an extraordinary life, whether it was magical or otherwise."

I pull her in for hug. I always wanted a sister and now I have one.

"Thanks."

A whuff of soft air tickles my forehead, startling me out of my reverie. I forgot where we were for a moment, while I was engrossed in my thoughts and memories. "Ok, girl." I slide my hands down the satiny-smooth neck of the horse one more time. "We should probably get back to the dorm, right? I've got training with Logan in a half hour."

She lets out a sigh. "You're right. Actually, I can't wait to see this. Can I help?" Her eyes sparkle with mischief. That can't be a good thing, right? She's trouble for sure.

"I guess, but you can't make fun of me. I have no clue what I'm doing."

"I'm hurt. Do you really think I would make fun of you?"

"Uh, yeah. I've heard you tease your brother."

"Yes, but that's because he's Logan. He deserves it."

"So him and Ivy..." I trail off. I don't want to seem like a needy girl, but his ex-girlfriend literally just came back from the dead. That's got to do something to you. And as nice as he's been the last few days, there's a distance between us that wasn't there before. It could just be the missing bond, or it could be something more.

"No way am I going there. If you have questions, you need to talk to him about it." She takes a step back throwing her hands up.

I know she's right, but I kinda wouldn't mind the opinion of someone else. As we head back toward the dorm, I nod and link arms with her.

With a shiver, I pull my hoodie tighter around myself. The November air is biting through the fabric as if it's nothing. I stumble as my foot catches on a rock and then a tank crashes into my side as I'm hurled into the space to the right of the path. I bend over, trying to drag air into my lungs and realize we're about twenty feet from where we started. Liz's fingers are like steel traps cutting off the blood flow to my upper arms and is glancing back at the path we were walking on just a moment ago. A huge barrel rocks back and forth against the tree that halted its progress. That would have slammed into us if not for Liz's sensitive senses and her speed.

I finally gasp in a deep breath of air and glance wildly around, trying to figure out where the barrel came from. The stables? I don't see anyone around.

I pry Liz's fingers out of my biceps and wince at the tingle as I try to rub some life back into them.

Concern darkens her eyes. "I'm so sorry. I didn't mean to do that."

"I think you saved me. That barrel could have caused a lot more damage. You definitely don't need to apologize for that."

"But still, I hurt you." She runs her hands down my arm and up my side, and I fail at hiding a wince from her. "That's going to leave a bruise. I am sorry."

"It's fine. Where did that thing come from, though?"

Her eyes narrow. "I don't know."

I nod. Must have been a freak accident.

Her eyes dart from the direction that the barrel came from back toward the dorms we were heading for. "We should get back."

"We can go check it out. See where it came from." I can tell by the way her eyes keep straying back toward the barn that this is what she wants to do, but she's going against her instincts.

"No, we need to get back." She pulls me along behind her.

"You don't think it was an accident, do you?"

"I'm sure it was an accident, but just to be on the safe side."

Dread creeps up my spine. What if it wasn't an accident?

CHAPTER 6
Logan

My head is lolling back, and I've got my feet kicked up on the small desk in Sophia's new room when a rattle at the door yanks me out of my boredom. I'm on my feet before the door swings open revealing my miscreant sister who dragged Sophia off somewhere without telling me. There's dirt smeared on Sophia's cheek, and the messy bun thing on top of her head is all askew. The ashen shade of her skin is freaking me out. I'm in front of her in seconds, engulfing her small frame in a hug. She lets out a pained gasp, and I pull back. Every muscle inside me tightens as I scan her from head to toe.

"What's the matter?"

"There was a bit of an incident..." Sophia trails off, glancing at Liz.

I shoot an accusing look at my sister without releasing Sophia from my arms. "What did you do?"

"It was an accident. She didn't do anything, Logan, leave her be. She saved me." I know how much Sophia likes Liz, so I don't entirely trust her assessment of the situation.

"A feed barrel treated Sophia like its own personal bowling pin. It came out of nowhere. I grabbed her and got her out of the way in time but may have bruised her up a bit in the process."

I don't like the sound of this. It seems awfully coincidental that a feed barrel happens to take aim at Sophia so soon after her arrival. "Did you check it out?"

Liz knows what I'm talking about with no further explanation. A bit of brother/sister telepathy. Nothing magic, just years of living together. "I didn't sense anything magical or physical that raised any alarms. Could have been an accident. I didn't want to leave Sophia out in the open though. Just in case, so I brought her right home."

"You don't think it was an accident do you?" My eyes narrow in accusation at Liz.

She throws her hands up. "It probably was, but it's better to check it out. I can go now." Her gaze flicks to mine.

Frustration is clawing at me. I want to go myself to see if there's any threat, but I also don't want to leave her side. The feel of her soft body tucked under my arm soothes the raging beast inside me that's threatening to burn this place to the ground. I know Liz can handle this. "Do it. We've got training scheduled, anyway. I'll take Sophia down. You can join us at the center when you're done."

Liz's pigtails bounce as she gives me a quick nod before she darts off in a blur. I forgot how good it feels to be on the compound where we can be ourselves without worrying about keeping up appearances.

I turn to Sophia. "You sure you're okay? What were the two of you doing?"

"I'm good. Liz was taking me on a quick tour of the grounds. She took me to the barn and introduced me to some horses. I didn't know you had horses here!" Her face is all lit up, and she's almost bouncing on her toes. I thought books were the only thing that could put that look on her face.

"I could take you for a ride one day if you'd like. I didn't know you were a horse girl."

"I never took lessons or anything, but I'd love that. My mom used to drag us up to the barn all the time when we were younger. She taught me a bit."

I'm satisfied that I'm responsible for the smile that's spread across her face. Who knows when we'll actually have time to do something so carefree? A heaviness settles over my shoulders when my eyes snag on the bracelet glinting at her delicate wrist. We only have so much time before that thing is going to start draining her. I can't let that happen. We've gotta get that dealt with as soon as possible.

"Are you still ok to do some training?" I curve my body around her as I ask.

She looks up at me, shaking her head. "Of course. I didn't actually get hurt. You can stop treating me like one of my mom's China figurines. You better not be pulling all that protective crap on me again. I need to learn how to look after myself." She disentangles herself from my arms. A ghost of doubt floats into my head. It's driving me crazy that I can't tell what she's feeling. I'm beginning to realize how much I've taken the bond for granted.

I let her slide away. "Ok then. Training. Did you need to get changed?"

"I sure do." She gives me a pointed stare.

Right. I swivel around to face the door and give her some privacy. I try to focus on the moves I'm going to work on with her today to push away the thoughts of her slipping out of her clothes. My brain still strays to thoughts of all that smooth skin bared for me. I rub my hands up my thighs. A gasp and the rustle of papers come from behind as a gust of wind whips around the room. Man, did I just lose control of my powers? That hasn't happened since I was a greasy preteen. I'm losing it. What's it going to be like when I have to leave to track down the maker of the cuff? How am I going to leave her behind?

"Was that you?"

"Uh yeah, sorry." I shift on my feet and pull the errant strands of power back inside.

"All good."

I turn around and find her standing there in a pair of gray leggings that hug her curves in all the right places and a hot pink sport top. Her golden hair brushes her bare shoulders as it swings back and forth. Not better. I groan internally and head out into the hall to avoid embarrassing myself while she grabs her winter coat.

Her head pokes out the door, and she waves a pair of running shoes at me. "Should I wear boots and just carry these?"

"Yup. Houston will have your ass if he catches you in the Training Center with outside shoes on. He's fancy like that."

"Who's Houston?" Curiosity gleams in her eyes. I love seeing this place through her eyes. Everything is new and shiny. When I left on my European vacation, I was sick of this place, these people, all the shit that went along with it. Now that I'm back, I'm not sure if it was ever the place that I hated so much as myself for what went down with Ivy. Or what I thought what down. My insides twist a little at the thought of her. Sometimes I catch myself staring at her to make sure she's still there. That she's really alive. It wasn't some crazy dream that I'm going to wake up from one day to find everyone I love is gone. Whatever went down with our relationship, she's been a close friend since we were kids. She left an asteroid sized crater in my life when she disappeared, but now that she's back, I'm not sure where she fits anymore.

I catch Sophia looking at me expectantly as we reach the main level. "Houston manages the Training Center. He's responsible for the physical training of all the future Magical Enforcement officers and young Mages with an interest in honing their fighting skills."

"What's he like?"

"He's a good guy. He takes things pretty seriously, but that's part of his job. I especially like how he keeps my miscreant sister in line. He may be the only one that can."

She smacks my arm at the same time something cold and wet hits my cheek. We make it to the steps leading into the TC just as the sky turns white with flurries. Snowstorms are not unheard of in November, but they're pretty rare. This isn't the work of a Mage though. I'd feel it if anyone put out that much magic. Sophia's chin tilts up as she takes in the snowfall. She looks incredible with her cheeks red from the chill in the air and her brown eyes taking on a golden hue in the light.

I lean down as if I'm drawn to her. She doesn't notice until my lips collide with hers. Her eyes widen for a moment before drifting shut as she leans into my chilly kiss. I pull her in close and tease her lips until she lets me slide in. Her icy hands grasping at my cheeks to pull me down closer don't shake me out my heat fueled fog.

"About time." A gruff voice barks out, dousing the flames immediately.

"Houston." My voice is gravelly, and my lips turn down in a resentful frown. Somehow, the man has the power to make me feel like a high schooler caught making out in the hall on lunch break. I probably shouldn't be making this thing with Sophia public right now. I glance around to make sure no one else saw us. There's no one around, but that doesn't mean anything. I was lost in her. She just does things to me. It's making me careless, and I can't afford to be careless with her safety. I've got to pull myself together.

CHAPTER 7
Sophia

My hands flutter at my sides. I want to smooth out my hair or something, but it's pulled back smooth and sleek. A gruff-looking man towers over me. His black, form-fitting shirt stretches tight over a massive chest, contrasting with loose black athletic pants. He's probably in his fifties, judging by the streaks of gray running through his trimmed beard and caramel colored hair. He looks more like a gracefully aging rock star than a military guy with his hair buzzed on a gradient at the sides, longer and slicked back on top. The intricate tattoos curling out from under his sleeves travel all the way down to his wrists, adding to the look.

"You must be Sophia. It's a pleasure to meet you." The hand he holds out is big enough to swallow both of mine up. "I'm Houston." Is that his first name? Last? A nickname? I have no idea, and I'm not asking.

My sleeve rides up, and I see his eyes pause on the wristband Logan gave me to cover up the cuff that's beginning to feel like a big flashing sign pointing to the Archimage. His midnight blue eyes snag on it curiously as if he can see through the stretchy fabric, but he doesn't comment.

"Hi. Nice to meet you."

"C'mon in. I'll show you around and get you settled in a training room. Logan said he'd be working with you, but maybe I should send someone else on by so you two don't get distracted. Your father emphasized the importance of getting her up to speed and fast." Heat rises up my neck.

"That won't be necessary." Logan's annoyed expression matches his clipped words.

"I don't know Logan. I think he might be right. You might need some supervision."

"I think I'm going to like you!" Houston barks out a husky laugh before gesturing at the cavernous space we've walked into. "This is the main gym."

Music pounds out of huge speakers jutting out from high up on the walls. The musky smell of sweaty bodies and sharp tang of disinfectant surrounds invades my nose. There are mats spread out along the far wall dotted with Mages grappling and throwing kicks. Cardio equipment and weights line the other wall like you'd find at any gym. I'm surprised by what I don't see more than what I do see. "No magic?"

"No magic allowed in this space. This is strictly for physical training. We have another communal gym space to practice magic, plus there are dozens of smaller rooms available for classes or individual sessions. You and Logan will use one of them. Is that wildcat of a sister coming to join you two?"

"She should be along soon," Logan replies.

"Excellent. You two should be good, then. Did you need to use the locker room, Sophia?"

"Nope, I'm good, thanks."

"Okay, I'll show you where it is anyway, in case you need to freshen up after or use the restroom."

We pass by a pair of sweat drenched guys on our way out of the main room, and I smile when the sight of Trey snags my attention. I give him a wave, which he returns with a slow smile that doesn't seem to interrupt his concentration as he carries on with his fight.

Houston gives a grand wave toward a pair of doors immediately inside the narrow hall. "Women's change room is on the right. There are bathrooms in there along with showers and a sauna. There're lockers too and towels if you need. You'll be in TR 5."

I'm impressed with the amenities at their facility. It's huge and well-equipped for a private gym. I'm not sure what I was expecting, but it wasn't this. Although, given that the place has stables, I guess I shouldn't be surprised.

"Did you need to use the washroom or anything?" Logan asks.

"No, but should I hang up my coat in there?"

Logan's eyes narrow and he glances around as if searching for an unknown enemy. "Nah, our room is just up the hall. You can bring it with you."

He steps ahead of me, stopping at a door a few up from the locker rooms. He swings it open, flicking on the light and sweeping his eyes over every corner before he moves aside to let me in.

We walk into the classroom sized room decked out with more free weights, some targets and various other equipment lined up along the wall. My shoelace came undone on the way, so I bend down to tie it up. Logan's eyes have gone hazy, and I'm more than a little happy to catch him staring at me as I straighten up.

He shakes himself out of his stupor. "I thought we'd warm up with some cardio before we work on your stance and a few basic moves."

Cardio I can do. I love running. The freedom of stretching my legs out, feeling the burn in my muscles as I push them to their limits and the wind rushes by. Fighting, on the other hand. Not so appealing, but necessary, definitely necessary. I make a face when he passes me a skipping rope he grabbed from the cupboard but take it from him.

My breath is coming out in rapid pants and there's sweat beaded on my forehead when he finally stops me.

"Time for the good stuff. You need to learn the basics first. Establishing a strong base." It's my turn to ogle as he peels his long sleeve off, revealing a white tank underneath.

"Offer still stands," he says.

"What offer?"

"Go on, take a picture. You know you want to. This is my good side." He tilts his chin at me, and I realize how much his smirk has grown on me when I remember what I thought of him the first time he said that.

"Do you actually remember saying that to me?" I lift a quizzical brow at him as I recall our first "meeting" outside of Arabica Nights.

"Of course, I remember every conversation we've had, princess."

My heart melts a little, but I'm not letting him get away with that. "Well then, you must recall the several where I told you not to call me princess." I give him a playful shove. He doesn't even budge.

"Right. You did say that. Doesn't mean I'm going to stop."

"Whatever. Let's get to work."

He demonstrates a fighting stance, and then I try it out. I think my reaction to his hands sliding to my hips to make a slight adjustment is a pretty good indication that the heat hasn't dimmed with the absence of our bond. I'm still trying to untangle the emotional part of my feelings for him, though. The heat dissipates in a fog of exhaustion after he has me practice it like a thousand times until I'm slipping into it a little more naturally.

"While this is fun and all, I doubt I can evade certain death by standing a certain way. Can we get to the good stuff?" I finally bite this out after the millionth repetition.

"Yes, you're right. We don't have the time you need to master these skills. It's still important, though."

"I get it, but time is not on our side." The fear I've been compartmentalizing in my head pushes against my barriers.

He rubs his hand over his jaw with a pained look in his eyes and a sigh. "It's just the thought of you in danger makes me crazy."

"Well then, teach me. Teach me to defend myself."

"Fine."

We work on a series of kicks, punches, and blocks until my limbs feel like jello that didn't set properly. I lock my eyes on his hands to block an incoming jab, and he sweeps my legs out from under me. He flips me over mid fall, taking the hit himself. I get a soft landing place on top of him.

The fire comes roaring back to life at the feel of his smooth, sweaty body pressed against mine. He ditched the shirt halfway into the workout, so I can see all of his rippling muscles on display. I run a hand down his chest, marveling at each dip and curve that indicates a new muscle. He groans, and I glance up to meet his storm-tossed eyes. My mouth falls open at the naked lust I see there.

I lean down to place a soft kiss on his tempting lips, but before I get there, he lunges up, capturing my mouth. My hands fall to his shoulders, digging in to pull him closer, and he rolls me over. Every part of me burns where it's pressed against his, and we lick and nip at each other's mouths. My hands find the strong lines of his jaw, while his slide around the bare skin around my waist. His hands creep lower when the sound of a throat clearing shatters the bubble of lust we were caught up in.

My eyes widen and my cheeks burn for a different reason as I scrabble out of Logan's embrace. He sits up with me, dropping an arm over my shoulder and leaning down to kiss the sweaty mess of hair that's come loose.

"Taking it easy on your girlfriend? Don't worry, Sophia, I'll take over your training once he heads out. I'll teach you the good stuff." My stomach plummets at the thought of Logan leaving. I know he has to, but that doesn't make it any easier.

I can feel the tension vibrating through Logan's stiff arm.

"You'll keep your hands off her."

"I don't think that's going to be possible. Your dad already has me lined up for the job. You do yours and get that cuff removed."

"Just in case you hadn't noticed, I'm still here and quite capable of speaking for myself. Are we going to work on anything else today, Logan, or were you going to come to blows with Trey?"

"I thought we'd work on that knife throwing if you're up for it?"

"Sounds good. You gonna watch Trey?" Might be a bit awkward practicing my nonexistent skills with an audience, but I guess I'm going to have to get used to Trey watching my performance since he's going to be my trainer while Logan is away.

"Yeah, I'll hang here for a bit. I can probably give you some tips too. I'm better with a knife than your boy here."

"I guess I can give you that, since I'm better at everything else."

My eyes have slid all the way back in my head by now at their ridiculous male posturing. "Enough. You're wasting time we don't have. Pull your heads out of your butts and help me out."

I head to the back left corner of the room dragging my exhausted legs along as they sink into the matted floor. There's a locked cabinet beside the targets which range from a line of dartboard style ones mounted on the wall to a couple of realistic human shaped ones. I'm not sure if the wigs sitting atop the heads make them more or less creepy. Scratch that. More, definitely more creepy.

Logan unlocks the cabinet with a key attached to a red lanyard that he seems to pull out of thin air.

"Where did that even come from?"

"I can't reveal all my secrets."

"Whatever."

He grabs a worn brown belt with a line of knives nestled in sheaths along its length. I reach out to run my fingers along the smooth rope wrapped handles.

"These are a little heavier than the PerfectPoints I got for you, but they'll do for today. Next time I stop by, I'll bring your set so you can get to know them." I give him a weird look. I'm not planning on 'getting to know' a set of knives.

"You got me my own set?" I can't help the smile crinkling my eyes up. It would probably freak the old me out if a guy gave her knives as a gift. New me is touched.

"Yeah. You need something to defend yourself until we get your magic back online."

So true. I pull one from its sheath and stare down the body target with the scary rainbow clown wig on it, closing my eyes for a minute to refocus. My vision comes back, and I haul in a deep breath before releasing it with a quick flick of the wrist. The knife flies out of my hand with a disappointing bounce off the side of the dummy, rattling to the floor.

"I told you his teaching skills are subpar. I can help," Trey says.

"Nobody asked for your opinion," Logan replies.

"Ugh, it's not his fault. This one's on me."

Trey sidles up beside me, placing a new knife in my hand and closing my fingers around it. He steps behind me. "Mind if I adjust your stance a bit?" he asks.

My eyes flick to Logan standing off to the side. His clenched jaw works back and forth, and he's gripping his forearms so tight his knuckles are white, but he doesn't say anything. I don't need his permission, but I also don't want to start a fight between these two idiots. They need to work through their issues and make up. Ivy is back. She's not dead. I know that's not the only problem with their friendship, but I think they need to fix it. They used to be friends and now that we have so few allies we can trust, we're going to need to get along.

"Go ahead."

He bumps my foot with his to shift my stance a little wider. Then his hands fall to my shoulders, adjusting them until they're square to the target, and he runs a hand down my arm to change the angle of my elbow. Luckily, he doesn't linger. Based on how hard Logan's jaw is working, it would only take the slightest slip for him to explode.

Trey leans back, assessing me through narrowed eyes. "Ok, now it's up to you. Focus dead center on its chest. Look where you want it to go. Draw your arm back like this." He pulls my arm back, then forward and a flick. He demonstrates the hand movement and has me practice it several times without a knife.

"Now try it yourself." He takes a couple of steps away and I draw my arm back.

My eyes lock on the target with a laser focus, and this time the knife hits it with a satisfying thunk. I throw my fist in the air. Sure, it's nowhere near the center, but it's progress.

"I did it."

"You sure did. Try it a few more times, then call it a day. I can tell the two of you were working hard before I got here. You're both sweating like pigs. Well, he looks like a pig. Not you, Sophia." A laugh bubbles out of me as the left side of his mouth curves up in a playful grin.

I shake my head and resume my position. I hit the target a few more times and even give it a bit more power, sinking the knife in deeper. I'd like to be proud of my accomplishments, but it doesn't feel like enough. I don't like that I can't study for these physical tasks. I can practice, but I can't just read a book and figure it all out. As this thought drifts across my frantic brain, a glint of light from the knife hurling through the air jogs a stray memory loose from my head.

I'd been studying at the library late, and I decided to look up Ferrebats, but the exhaustion took over, and I nodded off. When I woke up the glint of silver foil on a book caught my attention and I idly flipped through it. That symbol was there. I'd seen it. I'm pretty sure it was the same.

"I've got it! I know how to find the maker. I knew that symbol looked familiar. C'mon, we've got to go now!" The last knife clatters to the ground and I jog toward the door, all remnants of fatigue wiped out by my new mission.

"Wait what?! Wait for me." Logan jogs backward with his eyes on Trey. "Can you?" He tosses a nod at the mess we've left behind.

I pause and glance back at him with a pained expression. I need to go do this now.

Trey unfolds himself from the wall he was leaning on. "I got this. You two head back and figure that shit out, and I'll meet up with you later."

"Thanks, man." I almost stop in my tracks in my surprise. I think that may be the first civilized thing I've heard Logan say to Trey. Now's not the time for a happy reunion, though.

"Come on! Let's go." I pick up the pace without even checking to see if he's following.

CHAPTER 8
Logan

The dark wood doors loom in front of me again. I don't think I've ever spent this much time in the old building. Ever. Even when I was in school. I don't know what idea sparked in that brain of Sophia's, but she's lit up like a stadium at a night game. Not that I watch too many mundane sports. Boring.

"Whoa." My hands fly up to support her as she trips rushing up the stairs two at a time. She doesn't slow her pace at all despite the stumble.

Cool relief flows over me when she bursts through the door onto the second floor. She's like a heat-seeking missile targeting a book stack a few rows in on the left. I glance around the unfamiliar area in confusion. This isn't the section we were in before.

"What are we doing here?" I scan the shelves, looking for some indication of what section we're in. The books all seem to be about animals. Nothing to do with our research.

Her slim fingers run along the spines of a row of books until she pulls one out with a triumphant flourish.

"This, this is the one."

"Help me out here. How did you even know where to look?"

"Oh, I've been doing some side research to learn a little more about Mages and Witches and magic in general."

"Like, in addition to trying to find the maker of the cuff, getting settled in here, oh and doing your schoolwork? When did you even have time?"

Her lashes drop over her gorgeous eyes. "Well, I haven't been sleeping all that well. When I can't sleep, I study."

Guilt punches me as I spot the blue tinge under eyes. I should have known, should have noticed. She's been thrown into this new place, and she's not handling it as well as she's been pretending. Not to mention all the shit she's been dealing with ever since Liz and I arrived in town. I should have noticed. I pride myself on being observant, but I was relying too much on the bond. Now that it's gone, I should have been paying better attention to her. And we really don't know how long it's going to be until the cuff starts draining her energy to fuel itself.

"I'm sorry. Is there anything I can do to help?" I run my hand through my hair wishing there was something, anything I could do for her. This isn't an enemy I can fight, though.

"No, it's just...a lot. It's all for the best, though, because I found this!" She shakes the worn beige book in my face, and I catch the title etched in silver: Mages and Selective Breeding for Magical Ability.

"What's that got to do with anything?"

The back cover falls open easily, hanging loose from its aging, cracked binding. A dark-haired woman peers out from under hooded eyes on the About the Author page. Ingrid Krause. Never heard of her, but apparently, she's on expert on magical biology. The light bulb flashes on, and the weight in my chest lightens as the decorative flourish beneath her name pops off the page. "The symbol. That's the maker's symbol from the cuff. But it can't have been this woman. Doesn't look like she's got anything to do with creating objects of power."

"No, but these symbols are like tied to family crests or something, right? See, if you look closely, it's slightly different." She holds her wrist up in front of my face with an expectant look.

I scope the place out to make sure no one else is around. The place is a ghost town. I pull the tiniest thread of magic from my core and direct it at the cuff. It emits a soft glow, bringing the symbol back to the surface. Our heads bump as we both lean in to compare the symbols. She's right. There's a slight variation, but it's so minor it must be a family member, so if we can contact this woman, we can find out who in her family is a magical forger. I snap a pic with my cell before drawing my magic back inside to allow the mark to sink into hiding again.

"You're right." She squeaks and then laughs when I grab her up, spinning her around. "Good find. What's our next step?"

"Put me down. We're in the library." Her protest is weak, but I put her down. The library is like her sacred space or something, but I leave my hands on her waist, craving her touch. "We're going to send this woman an email. Her website is right here at the bottom. She shouldn't be too hard to find."

"Let's get to it then."

My thumbs dance over my phone as I tap out a quick message to Liz, letting her know we're heading to Sophia's room. I have no idea where she disappeared to, but I guess we'll find out soon enough.

Liz is sprawled out on top of Sophia's galaxy bedspread like she's floating in space, and Ivy is perched on the edge of the desk chair. I texted Liz on the way back, but I'm not sure where she acquired Ivy along the way. My eyes are on my sister as I lurk in the doorway. I still don't know what to say to Ivy. The anger and guilt are easier to shove deep down than deal with, but the feelings still swirl up when I'm in her presence.

"What are you doing here?" It comes out ruder than I intended. I drag my hand through my hair. "I mean, I didn't know you were coming here today, Ivy. And Liz, where'd you disappear to? I thought you were going to meet us at the TC."

"I went down there, but then I ran into Trey on his way to visit you guys and had zero interest in listening to your macho crap, so I bolted the other way. On the way out, I ran into Ivy. She was planning on training, but I convinced her to play hooky and hang with me. We were watching a Housewives marathon in the common room when you texted."

"Not you too, Ivy? You don't watch that shit, do you?"

Her pin straight hair brushes her shoulders as she shrugs. "I'm not into it, but Liz is, and I thought it would be nice to bond."

"Shove over." Sophia pushes at Liz so she can flop down on her bed. She must be exhausted after the day she's had.

"What's your big news?" Liz's mouth gapes open in a slow yawn like one of her cats, as if she has low expectations for any news I have.

Sophia grabs my sister by the shoulders. "We found her, or him, or them. The maker. Or their family, at least. Now we just have to track down the right person."

I throw my hands up in the air. "Hey, don't give me any credit. I didn't do anything. It was all Sophia."

"Of course it was. Don't worry, brother. I have zero faith in your research skills." I roll my eyes at my sister. She does have a point, but I'd never admit that to her. "So who is it? Am I going to have to get creative to extract the information from anyone?"

Sophia darts a concerned look at Liz. "No."

"I'm just teasing." Liz's whole body is vibrating with her laughter.

"You're seriously disturbed. You know that, right?" I eye my sister.

"Anyway. Can I get over there?"

Ivy jumps up to get out of Sophia's way, so she can get to her laptop. Her hand tickles the top of the wilting leaves of the fern sitting on the desk as she moves away, and the plant stretches out, perking up a bit. I swallow hard when a rock forms in my throat at the gesture that takes me back to the past.

Sophia brushes a tendril of escaped hair behind her ear and flips open the laptop, and I pull my gaze from Ivy.

"Did Trey catch up with you?" Liz asks, all innocent cartoon eyes.

"Yes." I grind out between clenched teeth. Ivy takes a couple of tentative steps closer.

"Annnnd..."

"He got all obnoxious and inserted himself into our session."

"He is going to be training her once you leave, right?" My sister is right. The unwelcome image of my former best friend standing behind Sophia with his hands on her intrudes into my brain. I certainly don't love that image. As bad as it has gotten between us, I know he would never make a move on her while we're dating. His smug kiss ass attitude grinds my gears, but he's loyal, I'll give him that.

"Yeah. He is good at throwing. Working with him was helpful."

Ivy has taken a step closer. "You guys really don't get along at all anymore, do you?" Her eyes drop to the ground. "Was it me?"

"It's complicated. You know things were never the same between Trey and I after we started...dating. It wasn't your fault, though. But he thought you died. He blamed me. I blamed me too. That's when it got irreparable. It's between me and him, though. It's not on you, Ivy."

"Maybe. Maybe not, but you guys used to be so close."

We were. He was my best friend for most of my life. I don't really have close friends anymore. Sure I hang out with some of the other Mages we grew up with when I'm in town, but there's no one anymore who has my back to the death.

"I know, but the damage has been done. It's not getting fixed, Ivy. It's just not. We're too different now." I rub at the hollow ache in my chest. Most of the time I don't even think about it, but it's never really gone away. Not since the day I found out she was dead. I lost my two best friends that day, and I've only recently started to come back from that.

Her eyes go liquid. I turn back to Liz. She doesn't get to cry over Trey and me. We both made the choice to date. We both hurt him, but she's the one who lied to us all. She's the one who faked her death and destroyed us. Maybe I do blame her. It doesn't make a difference, though.

"Got it."

Liz's phone buzzes in time with mine as we both receive message notifications. A message has popped up in our group chat. The name Lena Krause is showing next to an address. I Google the address and groan. It's going to be a two-day drive if we drive straight through. Probably three with reasonable stops. I guess it could be worse. Could be across an ocean. At least we know where she is now.

"Why can't we just call her?"

"We can. But the key will be some sort of incantation attached to a physical object. We won't be able to get that over the phone. This is going to require an in-person visit. We should make sure she's home before we leave. Wouldn't make much sense to drive across the country only to find out she's out of town."

"Right. I've got an email address for her here. Let's start there." Her brow furrows in concentration as she settles back over the keyboard and starts tapping away again. I never thought I'd find someone typing so hot.

"Done. I guess we just wait now."

Right, wait. Patience. Not one of my finest qualities. At least not when it comes to Sophia's safety.

CHAPTER 9
Sophia

I quicken my pace to avoid all the eyes burning into me from every corner of the dining hall as we pass by to grab some food. It's a little better once we're settled at a round wooden table. All the attention here has me uneasy. At least no one has approached me to chat, but I guess having Liz and Logan flanking me all the time helps with that. Logan glares a hole in anyone who has the audacity to look for longer than a few minutes. Once he's gone though, who knows what it'll be like here? Anytime I see Liz off by herself, she's chatting to someone. She has an effervescence and magnetism that draw people to her, and she feeds off the energy of other people. Sometimes I think it might be easier to have that kind of extroverted personality, but I'd rather read a book in the corner at a party and fade into the background than be the center of attention.

A notification pops up as I'm about to dig into my omelet. This place has great food. I'll give the Mages that. We went back to the Armstrong's house last night for dinner and it was great to see my mom. She's really settled into the house and is getting along well with Logan's mom. They cooked dinner together, and it was fantastic. I still study her every time we're over there to make sure she's not still in shock, resentful of me, or angry that I've managed to get her life turned upside down overnight. There's nothing there, though. I'm really wondering if she knew something of this before it all came out into the open. I'm too afraid of disturbing the fragile balance that we've reached to bring it up.

Hey Sophy Girl, what's up? How dare you ditch me here alone Can we hang out this wknd

I was hoping it was from Lena Krause. I still don't know how to explain any of this to X or my other friends. I know Charlotte is there to make my excuses, but it's weird having to keep these secrets from Xavier. I've never had secrets from him.

Just having breakfast. I miss you too, X. At least you have Char and the others. I'm not sure if we can meet this weekend, but I'll try.

That's the best I can give him. I can't make any promises, but I really want to see him. There's got to be some way I can sneak out or maybe get him to come to the Armstrong's house. Would that be too weird?

Ok. Well at least send me some texts. So I know ur still alive K?

I will.

I have trouble swallowing down my eggs as I send that last text. Guilt is stealing away my appetite. I have no idea if I'm going to be able to go back home and see my friends anytime soon. Everything is so uncertain right now. There's gotta be a way.

I pull up the inbox on my phone to check if an email came through from Lena. Nothing in my inbox. I idly hit refresh, hoping that something might come up.

There it is. Sitting at the top of my inbox.

"It's here guys. She responded." My voice pitches up as I read the email.

"What does it say?" Liz is bouncing in her seat.

"She's there. She's happy to help you out if you go there, Logan."

"Does she want something from us?" Suspicion tinges his voice.

My eyes scan down the message. "It says you can talk about some sort of exchange when you get there." That doesn't sound ominous at all. What kind of exchange does she want?

Logan just waves that concern away. "That's not a problem. I can deal with that when we get there. I'll start getting ready to head out after breakfast."

My heart sinks to my toes. I know how important this is. The cuff needs to come off, but that doesn't make it any easier to face sending Logan off. At least Liz will still be here. That's comforting. And Trey. Much as Logan can't seem to get along with him, I don't have any issues with the guy. He's been nice enough to me.

"Are you going to come back here before you leave? Or just head out from your house?"

His torn gaze catches on me. "I should probably head out right away. The sooner we get this dealt with, the better."

"You're right. And Ivy is going with you?" I don't know what to think of Ivy yet. She's been nice enough, but I'm not sure if she still has feelings for him. It might be pretty awkward for them to spend a week in a car together after all that's gone down between them. Although I'm glad he has some kind of backup.

"Yeah, she is." His face does that blank thing I hate. It's like a door slamming in my face without the bond in place to read his emotions.

"Okay, I guess we can say goodbye after breakfast and then we can get to our schoolwork, Liz." I've never been less enthusiastic at the thought of doing my schoolwork. Only a few weeks left of this semester and then I'm free forever. I always thought I'd still finish the rest of the year with my friends even though I have enough credits to graduate, but everything has changed now.

She makes a face at me in between shoveling down her breakfast.

Logan gives her a disgusted look. "That's gross, Liz. The food isn't going anywhere. Slow down."

"I'm starving. Mind your business."

"Whatever." He rolls his eyes.

I lingered over my breakfast, trying to draw out the time before this moment. The moment I have to say goodbye to my heart. But you can't slow down time, even if you are a Mage so here it is. We're back in my room. At least, the room I'm staying in while I'm here. I don't know that I'm quite ready to call it my own yet.

"Get out, Liz," Logan says.

"Nice. Feeling that love there, brother." She shoots him some daggers with her eyes but leaves anyway.

"I'll be in the hall, Sophia. Yell if you need to be rescued from his melodrama."

Laughter bursts out in spite of my aching heart. "I'm sure I'll be fine, Liz."

Logan grabs my face before the door has even clicked shut.

His intense eyes have darkened with an aching plea that I can feel in my soul. "Can you please be careful while I'm gone? Stick close to here. Do your schoolwork and training, but don't let my sister convince you to traipse all over the compound. And don't go anywhere without her if you can help it. Or...Trey, I guess. We don't get along, but I trust him to keep you safe, as much as I hate to admit it." His eyes meet mine, searching for a promise.

"I'll be fine. I'm here for a reason after all, right? Nobody knows I'm an Archi...I mean about my powers. I'm safe here, right?" I stop in the middle of the word as his grip tightens on my cheeks.

"I just...I don't know. Shit! I hate having to leave you, but I can't trust this to anyone else. Yes, you should be safe here, but that doesn't mean you can't be careful."

"I will be, I promise." I lean in closer until our noses brush.

He tilts his head and leans in. Our lips meet in a soft, slow kiss that builds in intensity. His hands slip to the back of my neck, tangling in my hair, and I pull him in closer. Our bodies meld together until it's like we're one being. Heat spreads through my entire body and our lips crush together in desperation. It's amazing, but I miss that feeling of our emotions mingling that came along with the bond. None of my feelings have changed, which is good to know. The attraction is still there, even without the bond, but that extra level of connectedness is gone. I never wanted the bond until it was gone and now my heart aches to be closer to him.

He follows me as I drag my lips away from his reluctantly. This could go on forever if one of us doesn't end it.

My breath is coming short pants. "You be careful too. Who knows where Zeus has been hiding out? He could target you if he can track you down. I'll be safe in here, but you're out in the open with a target on your back."

"I'll be fine."

"Well, you should probably say goodbye to Liz as well. You know she's not going to stand out there all day."

"I know. Patience apparently isn't a family trait either of us inherited."

The door swings open before he's even finished his sentence.

"Were you listening to us?" Logan asks.

"Ew no, not on purpose at least. I was scoping out your neighbors. Making sure they're not up to anything nefarious."

"So you were spying on the other Mages in the hall here? That's even worse."

"Hey, you want to keep her safe, right? I was doing you a favor. Nothing interesting anyway. People are so dull."

"Ok, I'm going to head out. Please stay in touch. Let me know what's going on and if anything else sketchy happens."

"We will. Now get out of here. We'll be fine without you. Bye, Logan."

"Bye, Liz." He turns to me, and his voice softens. "Goodbye, Sophia."

"Bye."

He drops one extra kiss on my forehead before turning away.

A sense of foreboding settles over me as I watch him disappear through the door that leads downstairs and away from me. I'm being silly. He'll be fine. He can look after himself.

CHAPTER 10
Logan

"I'm heading out to the car, Ivy. Hurry up." I call over my shoulder as I'm walking out the front door. I toss my bag in the trunk and leave it open for her. My car gleams with a thin layer of condensation, and the sky is a dull gray that paints everything in a dreary light.

I glance over my shoulder and contemplate honking, but my mother would never let that one go. Ivy was hanging out with Mom when I got back to the house. I told her to hurry and pack her shit, but she's taking her sweet time. I want to get out and back to Sophia as soon as possible.

Wearing that cuff for too long is going to have negative effects on her. It's a question of when, not if. They're only meant to be worn for a day or two max.

The lack of news from the Zeus department is a little unsettling as well. I haven't heard of any more Mages disappearing, which is a good thing, but not knowing anything about his whereabouts is disturbing. He's plotting something. That's for sure. I've kept our departure on the down low. Nobody else at HQ knows that I'll be gone for the next week, but if they start seeing Sophia around the compound without me, people will figure something is up. After all, I've been pretty much glued to her side since she got there. Liz's presence is both a relief and a worry. My sister can be a bit unpredictable on the best of days. She cares about Sophia too much to let something happen to her. I've gotta have faith in that.

I'm about to grab Ivy and drag her out to the car when her slight form appears in the doorway with Mom.

My hand is drumming out a fast rhythm on the steering wheel as I hear the trunk slam, and then Ivy settles into the seat next to me. The engine is purring to life and I've given a wave to Mom before she's gotten her seatbelt on.

"I've got the navigation set up." I nod at my phone mounted on the dash. "Can you keep an eye on it for me? Hopefully, we can push on until lunch, but let me know if you need a quick break." I make sure to emphasize quick. I'm not a complete asshole. If she needs to stop to use the restroom we can, but we're eating meals on the road as much as possible.

"I will." Her response comes out in almost a whisper, and I glance at her. She's sitting all hunched over, curled in around her phone. I've never seen her look so unsure of herself. I'm used to a quietly confident Ivy.

"You know you don't have to come if you don't want to, right? I can do this on my own. This is your last chance. If you want out, let me know." It's not that I don't want her here. Trey and Liz are looking out for Sophia, so if Ivy hadn't come back, I would have done this alone. It's better to have help, though. I have no idea what we're driving into. It could be a trap, and I'd rather have back up. I glance over at her again. In addition, there's still a seed of doubt that's taken root in my mind about her sudden return. Why did she come back? And why now? It's better she's here with me, so I can keep an eye on her rather than back with Sophia.

She looks up. "No, I want to be there for you, Logan."

I nod and refocus on the road. I can't be worrying about whether she wants to be here this whole time. If she says she's in, then she's in.

The silence hangs in the air like a heavy curtain between us. I'm torn between trying to make conversation to ease the awkwardness or leaving it be. I don't have any obligation to her, do I? No. That's on her. If she wants to talk or to apologize, that's on her. I have nothing else to say to her, so I crank up the radio. I put on my favorite road trip playlist. It's all hard driving classic rock. She used to like stuff like this, but I don't know Ivy anymore. Her tastes may have changed. My car, my music, though. She can just deal if she doesn't like it.

I focus on the road, the beat, and the mission, trying not to let my thoughts stray to Sophia and what she must be up to right now.

CHAPTER 11
Sophia

I crammed all my homework and studying into the morning so I could do some training with Liz and Trey after lunch. The familiar gym stank hits me as we pass through the front doors. Houston is nowhere to be found today, but I spot Trey's long, lean body folded over the reception desk as we get in. He's wearing red track pants and his biceps are straining the sleeves of his white t shirt as he props his elbows on the desk to lean in and talk to (flirt with) the girl working there. She's probably around the same age as Logan and Trey and she's flashing a commercial worthy white smile at him.

I clear my throat when Liz and I get close. He takes his time unfolding himself and turning around.

"Good afternoon, ladies."

"Hi." Liz and I chorus out.

"We've got the same training room as yesterday." He runs his eyes over us. "You need to use the locker room, or are you good to go?"

"We're good," I reply.

"Yeah, let's get to it." Liz is back to bouncing on her heels.

In the training room, I stand awkwardly in the middle of the mats waiting for some instruction from Trey. Liz is loosening up her muscles with a slow jog around the outside of the room.

"Should we work on my stance first?"

"Nah, let's get to the good stuff. We'll do a bit of stretching first, then we can do some kicks and holds."

I like the sound of that. I think Logan was maybe being a bit too cautious and taking things too slow. It might be a good thing to have a new trainer. "Sounds good."

Liz joins in on the basic stretches and then heads over to a punching bag in the corner. "Let me know if you need anything." She calls out before wailing on the bag. I'm kind of expecting smoke to start rising from the poor thing like you see in cartoons.

"Ok, since you're probably going to be shorter than a lot of your opponents, you're going to have to learn to get in under the holes in someone's guard while keeping yourself out of their reach. I'll teach you how to get out of some holds, but your best strategy is going to be to avoid getting caught in the first place."

I nod as if I get it. His words make sense, but I don't have a lot of context to put them in based on my life experience.

We work through enough moves to send my head spinning before he eases up on me. One of his first lessons was teaching me how to fall properly and man did I practice the heck out of that one. After the millionth time hitting the mats, I shut my eyes and throw my arms over my head in exhaustion. I'm not sure I'm going to be able to peel myself off the floor after this.

Trey reaches a hand down to help me up and laughs when I shake my head.

"Just leave me here in peace. I'm one with the floor now."

"Come on, we can practice with the knives now. You like that, right?"

I groan, but the knives are fun. Never thought I'd add throwing sharp objects to my list of fun things to do, but here we are. I reach out and let his solid hand close around mine to pull me back up on my feet, groaning as my burning muscles protest being vertical again.

"Where's Liz?" She's been doing her own thing, but she's been here the whole time. I didn't even notice her leaving the room.

"She darted out of here. Said she wanted to go do some cardio with a few friends."

"How did I miss that?" Are my powers of observation that bad?

"Well, she is fast."

Right. Super speed.

Trey sets me up with the knives and goes over his lesson from yesterday before letting me at it. This doesn't seem dangerous at all. Me, a bunch of knives. I mean, he is still here, but that might be worse. What if I really screw up and hit him with one? That wouldn't be mortifying at all.

"You can do this," he says, almost as if he read my mind. He's not a Psychic Mage, is he? No Elemental like Logan.

The first one flies off in a wild arc. He resets me, and I try again, enjoying the feel of the rope handle sliding from my palm. I'm determined to get this down. Throwing the knives is very precise and mathematical. It's all about balance and aim and I can break that all down into angles and force. I know I can get this.

"What really happened between you and Logan?" I'm curious to hear his side of the story. I've heard Logan's, but it seems to me Trey is the one who got hurt when Ivy chose his friend. I'd kind of like to hear what he thinks really tore them apart.

I could have mistaken him for a mannequin when I peek at him out of the corner of my eye.

"Uh, well, what have you heard?" He unfreezes, shifting on his feet and avoiding eye contact.

"You guys grew apart after he started dating Ivy, and then you blamed him for her death."

"I guess that's the gist of it. The three of us were tight. And I was into Ivy, but I could have forgiven that. Them dating. I wanted her to be happy, and if he's what made her happy, then I was just going to deal with it. And I did. We weren't as close as before, but we were still friends."

I refocus on throwing the daggers. He seems more inclined to talk when I'm not looking at him. I'm surprised he's being this open. We don't know each other that well, and I kinda thought he might be more closed off, like Logan.

"I could tell, though. When Logan started pulling back. He didn't care for her like he should have. And fine, these things happen, but he wasn't upfront with her. I gave him hell about it, and he got mad. Then all that bullshit went down with the council, and Ivy wound up dead. He should have been there for her. I would have been there. But he wasn't."

"How do you feel now? Now that you know she never died. She's here, and she's ok. Can you forgive him?"

"I dunno. It's been a long time and I'm still pretty angry about a lot of things. Maybe though. Maybe we can work together. Maybe things will get better." That's something. I think it would be good for both of them to let go of all the animosity between them. As much as I want to help them, it's not my problem to fix. They're going to need to figure it out together, and I know how stubborn Logan can be.

"What went down with the council? I never heard all the details." We've been running from danger nonstop since I got swept up in this world, so there hasn't exactly been time for a history lesson. I've heard some vague things, but it sounds like there's a story here.

"Half the council is stuck in the dark ages. Like your uncle. They stripped his powers, right? That's a terrible thing to do to someone, especially a child, and that was only a few decades ago. In spite of some forward progress, there are still members that are old school. This group wants revenge on the Witches and won't let go of the past. They started targeting them for small things, locking them up. Ivy's family was staunchly against this, and they were trying to get support from the Mages. They were lobbying to allow the Witches representation on the council, so we could all work together."

I narrowed my gaze at the target, drew my arm back and let fly. Every time it hits the target is a win in my books. "Why do they hate the Witches so much?"

"We've got a dark history with them. A long time ago, the Mages used the Witches as lackeys. They never recognized their abilities but would still use them to perform spells and wards. And it was not for fair pay, let me tell you."

"Sounds like the Mages were the ones in the wrong."

"Well they were, but the Witches got sick of this and a group of them splintered off and revolted. Problem is they didn't fight with words. They started turning the Mages over to the mundanes. They hid in the shadows and let Mages get burned at the stake or drowned."

"Salem?" I ask, my curiosity piqued. "Couldn't the Mages escape?"

"This group of Witches went dark. They called on help from the spirits in the Nether Realm and started using black magic to dampen or steal the Mages' power. Death magic, blood magic. Really nasty shit."

"The Mages hunted this sect of Witches down and we all signed a truce, but it's been an uneasy alliance since then. If anyone gets caught doing any black magic, they're punished instantly and severely. The council has zero tolerance for that shit."

Interesting. I'm going to have to do some more research into the history of the Witches and Mages. It sounds like there's a lot of bad blood between the two groups.

A squeal escapes when my knife lands solidly in the middle of the dummy's chest. A rush of excitement floods through me. I've got a long way to go, but I'm definitely improving.

"Good job. Did you want to end our session on a high note?" he asks.

"Probably a good idea. I'd like to hit the shower and make a call before dinner, anyway. We should probably track Liz down."

Liz is happy to leave with us. She chatters away on our way back to the dorm, but my mind isn't with her. It's wandering off to the dark ages and the Witch/Mage issues. Liz seems to notice my preoccupation.

"Did you want some time to yourself? I'm happy to hang in the common room and watch some trash."

"Yeah, that sounds good. Enjoy yourself," I say, still lost in my own thoughts.

I make it to my floor without even thinking about it and I'm so lost in my head that I don't notice someone else is coming through the door until I crash into them, I reach up instinctively to steady myself and my hand clasps a bare arm.

"Oh." An unfamiliar voice chirps out. I look up to meet the eyes of that girl I ran into earlier. Michelle? I think. Crap, I'm not supposed to touch her, am I? I yank my hand back like her skin is coated in molten lava, but it's too late.

"Interesting," she says. I look up and catch a malicious smirk twisting her lips.

What did she see? She can't see everything, right? Just what I was thinking about at the moment of contact. I was thinking about the Witches and Mages and…Charlotte. I think that's it. None of that is going to get me in trouble. She can't use that against me. I hope there was nothing else going on in there subconsciously that she could read. Like the "A" word. She reaches a hand back toward me, brushing my wrist as I dance back, quickly slipping by her into the hall.

"Catch you later." I stare at the door swinging shut behind me. I can't do anything about it if she saw something she shouldn't have, so I'm going to have to let it go for now. What's done is done.

I sigh and head back to my room. A shower and then a chat with Char should help.

I flop back on my bed, wet hair splayed out on my pillow. My phone is ringing in my ear as I wait for my best friend to answer. I want her take on the Witch situation.

"Soph! I miss you, girl." Her familiar voice caresses my ear, easing the tension that's been building since my conversation with Trey.

"Hey, Char, miss you too."

"What's going on? How's that hot Mage of yours?"

"He left this morning. With Ivy. They're going to find the maker of the cuff to get the key to removing it."

"That sucks. What have you been doing to keep yourself busy?" That's the thing about friends you've had forever. They know you and they know how you deal with issues. I'll take on five new tasks to distract myself if anything is weighing on my mind.

"I don't have to try too hard to keep myself busy around here. I'm spending half the day doing a day's worth of school, so I can spend the afternoon training."

"Of course. Who are you training with now that hottie is gone?"

"Charlotte, please. He has a name."

"I know, but that suits him."

"Whatever. I trained with Liz and Trey today. Mostly Trey. Liz did her own thing as usual."

"He's nice to look at, too. How did that go?"

"It was good. He said some stuff though, and I kind of wanted your take on it." I'm not sure how to broach the subject. Are the Witches sensitive about this? Do they talk about it? I have no idea.

"Well you know I'm always happy to share my opinion. What's it about?"

I run my free hand up and down my leg. "I asked him some things, and he was telling me about the problems between the Witches and Mages."

"Oh, did he? Did he tell you the Mages persecuted the Witches for centuries and then acted surprised when they rebelled?" There's some heat in her voice.

"Yeah, actually he did."

"Oh." She pauses in surprise for a moment. "I guess he's more enlightened than some of the Mages around."

"I guess. He seems like a good guy. I can see why Logan used to be such good friends with him."

"I get that."

"So what's your take on the most recent situation with the Witches? Trey said some of the council members were targeting Witches. Were they breaking the rules? Doing dark magic? Or was it unwarranted?"

"It was totally not cool. I knew some of those Witches. No way were they practicing black magic. They were good people. They locked my friend's dad up for some miniscule display of magic in an empty store. There were no mundanes around. He didn't out the magic community. Simon just caught wind of it and that was it."

"Who's Simon?" I haven't heard this name before from anyone.

"He's a jerk with an influential family. The Montgomery family has had a seat on the NAMC for decades. They don't like the idea of sharing power with Witches or anyone else they consider lesser, so they'd been working against Ivy's family."

"Good to know. I'm going to do some more research into this history and the council, too." I'm sure I can fit that into my already crammed schedule.

"Of course you are. I know how my girl works. Also…" she pauses for a minute, "there are rumors going around among our community that some of the Witches have been working with Zeus. They might be working with him to try to seize power from the Mages. Not my family obviously, but there's talk going around."

"Thanks for the info. That's something to look into for sure. So what else have you been up to? Anything interesting?"

"Nothing new. Games, school. X has been a pain in the butt since you left. He's so needy. Always begging for attention."

"Be nice to him," I chide her. We're all friends, but I've always been the glue that binds the three of us together. I need to know my friends are going to be okay when I can't be there.

"I will. Don't worry. I love X too. But we need to get all your crap sorted so you can come back. I wish I could come out there, but Mom and Grams would throw a fit if I skipped out on school."

"More than usual?" I ask. Charlotte, after all, has no problem skipping school to play video games.

"What they don't know won't hurt."

"Uh huh. Ok, I gotta go. I should hit the library one more time to figure out more of these details."

"Kk darlin' Talk to you soon. Smooches."

"Bye, Char."

I disconnect and sit up, pondering the information Charlotte shared. That gave me some things to think about and research. The pieces are falling into place. I didn't know the Witches and Mages had such bad blood. The ones I've met have seemed to get along alright, but that is too small of a sample size to draw any conclusions from.

I should probably grab Liz to take me to the library on my way, even though it's only a short walk. Hopefully, I can avoid any more run-ins with Michelle. Hopefully, she didn't see anything she shouldn't have.

CHAPTER 12
Logan

A soft, rhythmic snore comes from beside me. Ivy fell asleep after we stopped and grabbed lunch to go at a rest stop. I scarfed my burger while driving, since I want to push through as far as I can on this first day, but the scenery is flying by in a blur and fatigue is dragging my brain into a foggy haze. I avoided talking to Ivy the entire morning. She made a couple attempts at conversation, but I just replied with a yes or no or noncommittal grunt. She got the hint pretty quickly and put her earbuds in.

Restlessness is itching at my skin. I hate being trapped in a car this long. A yawn sounds from my side.

"What time is it?" Ivy's voice comes out in a sleepy rasp.

I give another grunt and nod at the dashboard clock.

"Enough. Enough of this crap, Logan." My head whips toward her.

"We can't survive a multiple day drive without talking at all. We need to sort things out between us. This is killing me."

My fingers tighten on the wheel, and a flare of heat races through me. "Wouldn't be the first time you got killed. Oh wait, that was a lie." She provokes the angry response out of me. How dare she try to act like she has any right to force a conversation between us.

"Logan, I'm sorry. I should have told you, but I thought it would be better that way."

"How is that better? How did you think leaving me in the dark, thinking you were dead, was better for me?" My mind is dragged back to the night I found out about her death.

I walked in the door, still laughing about some stupid thing one of the guys had said. The smile fell off my face when I caught sight of Mom waiting for me with swollen, red eyes brimming with sympathy.

"Logan, come here and sit down."

I shook my head. "I'm good. What's wrong? Is Liz, ok?"

"Liz is fine, honey. It's..." she broke off, hugging her arms to her chest, "the Okamura's." The tears that were building up in her eyes spilled over.

"Ivy's parents? What happened? I've gotta call her." I pulled my phone out of my pocket.

My mom reached out and stilled my hand before I could dial Ivy. "I'm so sorry. You can't call Ivy. Her and her parents...they were killed."

The tears were flowing freely down my mother's face. I shook my head again and dialed Ivy's number. It rang and rang before going to voicemail. I heard a thump in the back of my mind as the phone tumbled from my shaking hand.

I was vaguely aware of my mom wrapping her arms around my numb body as a strangled sob escaped and I crumpled to the floor.

The nightmares of that night are less frequent now than they were, but the memory is seared into my brain. I don't know if it was the worst night of my life or if that came later after the numbness wore off.

"Do you know what that felt like?" I immediately regret the question at her stricken look. Of course she does. She lost her parents for real that night. "I'm sorry, of course you do."

"You were already pulling away, Logan. You know it, I know it. Everyone knows it. I had so many friends who told me to just give up on you. You weren't worth it, but I loved you so much. I loved you so much, I let you go. The clean break was supposed to be better for both of us. I was going to fake my death, anyway. Not telling you about it. It made sense at the time."

"It killed me, Ivy. You have no idea. You have no idea what I did to try to get over it or just bury the pain and guilt." My voice has deepened as all the emotions I've been bottling up begin to leak out.

"I know that now. At the time, I didn't think you cared anymore."

"You didn't think I cared?" I give her an incredulous look. "How could you think that? You, me, Trey. We were best friends. Just because the romance stuff was waning didn't mean I cared any less about you as one of my best friends. That's what made the whole thing so hard."

"Sure didn't seem like it from where I was standing. If you really cared so much about me as a friend, you would never have left me wondering and waiting. Friends are honest with each other. You were never honest. You didn't tell me that your feelings had changed, you just avoided me. Like a coward."

Her words take my breath away like a punch to the gut. She's not wrong. I was a coward. That's one of the things I've worked so hard to bury in a locked box nine feet under. I knew the massive amount of guilt over everything that went down with Ivy would overwhelm me if I let it make an appearance.

I lift a shaky hand to my hair. "You're right. I was a coward. I know I was a coward, but you were, too. Letting everyone who cares about you believe you were dead. We were both cowards."

"I know. I was, Logan. I was angry and scared and so many other things. But when I heard what was going on back here. I came back. I'm here for you now, and I just hope we can repair some of the damage between us. Do you think that's possible?"

The confined air in the car is stifling. Can we fix this? I don't know, but maybe we need to at least try. "We can try. I honestly don't know if things will ever be the same between us, Ivy, but we can have something. We can at least call a truce for the next few days. Then we'll see what happens."

"Truce," she says, a tentative smile spreads her lips and brings out the dimple in her right cheek. I missed that smile. I realize now how much I've been missing Ivy and Trey in my life. Ugh Trey, that asshole. I don't know what I'm going to do with him. One step at a time.

I know I'm not ready to forgive and forget, and I don't know where we'll end up after this trip, but I don't think either of us can handle that level of tension for the rest of the journey. We need to at least be on speaking terms. Especially since we have no idea what's waiting for us at the end of the road.

Towns blur by one after another as my thigh cramps up from driving for so long. The sky in front of us has gone pink as the sun fades into the night.

Ivy has been quiet for a while as we each wrestled with our own thoughts when a startled gasp escapes.

"What, what is it?" My body goes on high alert, fearing the worst.

"Another Mage has gone missing."

"Who is it? Someone we know. My words come out fast in my urgency.

"Dexter Grant."

My shoulders relax a little. I know Dexter, but not well. He lives up North, so he's in a different branch of the NAMC. I've met him a few times at events, though. The image of a middle-aged man with a thick beard and dark hair flash into my mind. I can't remember what type of Mage he is. Consciously, I know I should be more guilty about my relief, but I can't muster it up. I'm too relieved that it wasn't someone I care about.

"Does it say where he disappeared from?"

"It says he left his house to go to work and never made it there. They found his car parked in the lot, but no sign of him."

"So this could be something else entirely, not Zeus resurfacing?"

"It could be." Ivy says the words I want to hear, but her tone is laden with doubt. "Looks like there were no signs that he was unhappy or that he would disappear for no reason. It also says there were scorch marks found next to his car. I wonder what that's about."

Scorch marks. I don't remember hearing about that with any of the other disappearances. Where are you hiding, Zeus? "The last disappearance was out West. That's a long way to travel to kidnap a Mage. I wonder if he still has someone with teleportation abilities." That doesn't seem quite right, but it is possible. We locked up his own thug that kidnapped Sophia and it's not a very common power, especially over long distances.

"Could be. Could be something else." I can almost hear her brain whirring. Ivy has always loved puzzles and solving mysteries. This must drive her crazy.

"Something else to think about. I'm going to stop for the night. I should probably get some sleep, so I don't drive us both off the road."

"Gee thanks." It's good to hear her razzing me again. Small steps, I guess.

"Can you find the nearest motel and we'll stop there?"

Turns out there's one a few miles up. My hand taps impatiently at the steering wheel until we pull into the lot of the shady motel. Definitely looks like somewhere a serial killer would take up residence. Broken boards hang loose beside the front doors. The peeling red paint has seen better days and the rusted balconies are a safety violation if I ever saw one. There's an empty pool out front filled with dead leaves and junk.

"Nice choice," Ivy chirps up.

"Whatever." I'm exhausted. Driving can be physically tiring, but it's my mental state that's worse. Dragging out all those memories and hashing it out with Ivy has left me drained.

It's not like we have to worry about getting robbed or anything. I'd like to see anyone try to catch a couple of Mages unaware. Good luck to them.

CHAPTER 13
Sophia

I peeked in the common room on my way to the library, but Liz had her arm wrapped around another girl's shoulder and their heads were together, laughing as they watched whatever ridiculous show was on. I didn't have the heart to interrupt her. There's nothing to worry about. Logan is being ridiculously overprotective. He wouldn't have left me here if he was that worried about my safety.

A yawn stretches my jaw after I catch myself doing another head nod. I glance around. The library has emptied while I was in here researching. There's a lot to take in with the whole Witch/Mage history. They've got a pretty ugly past between them. I'm surprised they've even managed even this uneasy alliance. The remaining strife seems to be among fringe groups, but who knows how many people are hiding deep grudges under polite exteriors.

My shoulders and legs protest as I drag myself up and start collecting the array of books scattered across the big library table. It was busy in here earlier, but my towering piles of books kept everyone else away from the round table like a fort of knowledge.

I grab the few I'm planning to check out and my backpack digs into my shoulder as I sling it on.

Dora smiles at me when I hand her the books to check out. The librarian with the messy brown top knot and serious blue eyes is the one person I've actually gotten to know at this place. No surprise, really. I spend so much time holed up here. Liz must still be in the common room. I haven't heard from her, so I head back out on my own. The sky darkened while my nose was stuck in a pile of books, and it's almost eerie in the dim light of dusk. I don't see anyone else out and about the grounds.

My ear twitches at a rustle coming from the wooded area on my left. I eye the area up and down but don't see anything. Must be a squirrel or something. The uneasiness doesn't dissipate at my rationalization, so I step up my pace kinda wishing I had called Liz.

A sharp burst of pain between my shoulder blades accompanies a hit that forces me to my knees. Get up, get up! My brain screams at me. All the training I've been doing lately has taught me I can't stay on the ground. I'm way too vulnerable here. I shove myself up onto unsteady feet and whirl around, only to receive a blow to my shoulder that spins me off to the side. Run. I have to run. I'm not going to win this fight.

I dig in and launch myself forward. I don't even know what direction I'm going. Away. Tears fill up my eyes at the wind stinging my face. I push faster. Footsteps pound behind me. I realize I've run into the woods when tree branches start clawing at my face. Great. If I'm going to hide, this is the best place, but I'm just as likely to get lost. The figure catches up to me and I put on the brakes abruptly, allowing the person to slam into me. It hurts, but it also throws them off balance, not expecting the collision. I spin around slamming my hand into their face. Something crunches under my hand and hot blood spurts over my palm. Gross.

I start running again now that I've temporarily incapacitated my foe. The crackling sounds of someone crunching on the carpet of fallen leaves trails after me. I must be that loud, too. I need to figure out how to be quieter. I dart off the path, weaving around until I find a trail that's soft underfoot. Mossy undergrowth rather than fallen leaves lines this path. I edge along, my hearing on overdrive as I listen intently.

I need to get out of here and back to a crowded place. Liz. I need Liz. My hands close on my cell phone when I see a couple beams of light scanning the woods. They'll spot me if they get close enough. I abandon the idea of a phone call and pick up the pace again, winding my way deeper into the forest until I can't see the beams of light anymore. The rich smell of damp earth and plant life surrounds me as I try to get my bearings.

My heart is still racing, and I'm dragging my feet when moonlight breaks through the treeline. I creep behind a thick tree trunk and peer out around it. I'm at the edge of the property. The big iron gate looms to my right. I don't see anyone. I'm about to head for the long driveway to walk back up to the dorm building, but a terrifying thought seeps in. What if they're waiting for me up the road? There was definitely more than one person after me, and I have no clue who they were. The first attacker was dressed all in black with a hood shadowing their face. I couldn't even tell if it was a guy or a girl. And there was more than one beam of light in the woods. Who was it? Am I even safe here anymore? I don't know who to trust.

With my decision made, I don't hesitate. I've got to get out of here. The massive front gates loom in front of me. I'm not getting out that way. They have cameras and a guard at the gate. My eyes fall on the fence surrounding the property. Can I get over that thing? No idea, but I'm going to try. The perimeter stretches out to both sides. I keep just inside the treeline and make my way around, keeping an eye on the fence searching for a suitable place to make my attempt.

After walking for what feels like an hour to my tired body, but it's probably only been ten minutes, I spot a weakness. There's a pile of old crates stacked up next to the fence. I can use those to get over and then...I don't know. I'll deal with that after.

I drag the crates into some semblance of steps. The first one is stable enough when I lean a little weight on it to test it out, so I cautiously climb up the rest. I stretch out to reach the top of the fence when I'm perched on the top crate. My stomach drops when the crate wobbles and my hands shoots out to grab hold of the rail. The smooth metal is cold under my fingers, but I ignore the bite and pull myself up. I swing my leg a few times until my foot settles next to my hands. It's gotten darker since I ran. I wonder if Liz is worried about me or if she's still hanging out with her friends and hasn't noticed I'm missing. I'll text her as soon as I'm out. As I look down, I cringe at the distance to the ground. Wind whirls loose strands of hair into my face, but I'm too scared to let go to brush them away. I'm just going to have to let this happen. My body drops heavily on the outside of the fence, my shoulders protest the strain of holding me up.

Don't look down, don't look down is the chant running through my head when I close my eyes and let go. I bend my knees, trying to absorb some of the shock, but it still feels like shards of glass are stabbing my ankles and knees as I hit the ground. My hands land on my knees as I bend over and gulp in a few lungfuls of cool air, trying to slow down my breathing.

Okay, I'm out. Now what? I'm on a main road. I can call the Armstrongs to come pick me up. That's the most sensible thing to do, right? I'll text Liz as well and tell her to come meet me here but keep it on the down low.

I shoot a quick text to Liz to let her know where to find me, and also to be quiet about it. I don't want my pursuers to find me that easily. My hands are shaking so hard it takes a couple of attempts to type in Mrs. Armstrong's number. Mom was the first one to cross my mind, but she'll freak out and worry. I'd rather have the Armstrongs come pick me up and take me back to their house. Mom will be easier to deal with once I'm safe.

My eyes keep scanning the area, searching for any signs of pursuit as the phone rings.

"Sophia, is something wrong?" Relief floods me at the sound of her concerned voice on the other end of the line.

"Mrs. Armstrong, I need you to come pick me up." I don't even recognize the broken whisper that comes out of me.

"Of course. Where are you?" The concern has stepped up to alarm.

"I'm outside the fence. I'm not sure exactly, but I'm near the road, not too far from the gates."

"I'm leaving now. Are you hurt? Do I need to bring anything? Where's Liz?"

"I'll be ok. I texted Liz."

A car door slams in the background of the call and an engine starts up. "I'm putting the phone on speaker, dear. I'll leave it on."

I nod and sink to the ground in the shadow of the trees beside the road, clutching the phone to my ear like a life preserver. The cold ground sends chills through me and dampness seeps through my clothes, but everything is sore, and I can't muster the strength to stand right now. How did this day come to this?

A soft thump from behind has me springing to my feet in spite of the exhaustion. I'm ready to run at the slightest sign of danger until a breeze kisses my cheek, and I see Liz's face next to mine. She must have used a speed boost to get here. I wrap my shaking arms around her shoulders in relief. A few strangled sobs escape.

"Where were you? How did you get out here? What happened?"

I explain to her how I went to the library and got attacked on the way back.

"I would have come to the library with you. Why didn't you come get me?"

I shrug. "I didn't want to bother you. You looked so cozy and happy in there. Plus, it was only the library. I didn't think anything would happen. I thought I was safe here."

She gives me a stern look before her face softens. "I would have come. You're not a bother. I wouldn't have even been at the compound if you weren't here. Sure, I was having fun with my friends, but that doesn't change anything. Not only do I care about you, but my brother would literally murder me if I let anything happen to you. Well, he'd try anyway." A wobbly smile pulls up my mouth at her assessment.

"I know. Maybe this is better, though. Now we know I'm not safe there."

"This is true. Who's coming to get us? Please say my mom."

"She's the one I called so hopefully."

"Good. If my dad comes, he'll ream us both out."

Blinding headlights hit us as a car pulls off the road. I hesitate before I approach it, but Liz grabs my hand to pull me along behind her.

"It's fine. That's my dad's car. Ugh. Prepare yourself."

The worry on Mrs. Armstrong's face almost has me dissolving into tears, but I squeeze Liz's arm to hold it together. A soothing wave of her sweet, floral perfume surrounds me when she gathers me up in her arms. She pulls away, her eyes running over me, checking for damage.

"I'm ok, can we get back to your house?" I'm sure I'll lose it completely once I see my own mother, but I just want to hold it together until we get back.

Instead of the lecture Liz was preparing me for, we're met with a stony silence from the driver's seat that reverberates through the vehicle as we settle back on the leather seats. We definitely enraged Mr. Armstrong.

"We'll talk about this after we get back to the house." These are the only words he bites out the entire drive, while Liz distracts her mom with idle conversation. I think she knows I'm not ready to share my story yet if I'm going to maintain the fragile control I have over my emotions.

Mom is standing in the door wringing her hands when we get back. I hurl myself into her arms, dropping my head onto her shoulder. Her hand leaves a comforting tingle where she strokes my hair.

"I thought you said she was safe there." There's a hint of steel behind her wavering tone.

"She should have been." The growl that comes out reminds me a lot of his son when he's really pissed off. "There must be someone in there who knows. Who did you tell, Sophia?"

"I didn't tell anyone. I haven't really talked to anyone there aside from Liz, Logan, and Trey." I don't think it's worth mentioning the librarian since I've hardly talked about my deepest, darkest secrets with her.

"Well, it wasn't Trey. I trust him. Someone else must have found out. The question is who."

While he ponders the very question that's been eating at me, Mrs. Armstrong comes in. "We can figure that out. For now, we need to make sure Sophia is ok. Can you tell us exactly what happened?"

I go through my story one more time. Their features are in stark contrast. Mr. Armstrong's face darkens even as his wife's grows more sympathetic.

"You should have been there, Liz," he barks out.

"I know," she says, not even trying to throw me under the bus.

"It's not her fault. I left without telling her." My mom gasps.

"That's irrelevant. She knows her duty. She shouldn't have left you."

"Leave them alone. They've had a rough night already. Now hon, are you hurt anywhere?"

My mom's hands smooth over me as if to seek out any injuries at Mrs. Armstrong's words.

I assess my various aches and pains. A lot of them are from the training I've been doing, so it's hard to tell which ones result from the attack. There's a definite deep ache between my shoulder blades where I got hit with who knows what. The front of my right shoulder is also causing me some grief after getting slammed into. My shoulders and arms are a little sore from hanging off the fence and minor scratches sting my face.

"I think it's just bruises. Nothing feels broken or anything."

"Are you sure?" Mom asks.

"Yes, Mom. I'm fine, or I will be."

"You let us know if anything changes. I think you girls should go to bed, get some rest. We can talk about this more in the morning," says Mrs. Armstrong.

The mere mention of bed is enough to have me yawning. I should call Logan though, before I go to sleep. Make sure everything is good with him and Ivy.

Mom fusses around me until I give her one last hug and practically force her out the door of the guestroom they put me in. I get it. She's worried. We've had to deal with more craziness in the last few weeks than ever before. I'm sure I'm safe here, though. I only wish they had let me stay here in the first place. Although I might not have had so much library time. I've learned a lot of information that might prove useful.

Logan's phone rings and rings with no answer. I frown and glance at the clock. It's only nine o'clock. I guess he could still be driving if he's trying to push through. I scroll my contacts to find Ivy. She gave me her number before they left in case of emergencies. Each unanswered ring puts me a little more on edge. I shoot them both texts and pace back and forth a couple of times before heading over to Liz's room. She answers my soft knock.

"What's up, Soph?"

"I called Logan, and he didn't answer. Neither did Ivy."

"Maybe they're still driving. Or sleeping. I'm sure they're fine. I wouldn't worry about it. You should get some sleep."

I gnaw on my lower lip. She's probably right. I'm overreacting. It was one phone call. They're probably exhausted from driving all day. I can call them in the morning.

CHAPTER 14
Logan

My lip curls in distaste as I cram a last soggy handful of fries down my throat at the sad motel diner and reach for my phone. I should check in with Sophia. My hand comes up empty. Must have left it in the car.

"Ivy, can I borrow your phone for a sec?"

"Um, sure." She pats down her pocket, then dumps the contents of her purse on the table. How she fits that much crap in her bag blows my mind. Her shoulders lift in a shrug as she tilts her empty palms toward the ceiling. "I guess I left it in the car."

I groan. Well, our bags are out there, anyway.

"I'll go grab our bags. You can wait here if you'd like."

Ivy eyes the trucker in the corner with the Santa Claus beard. That's where the resemblance ends. He's got a mean look in his beady eyes, and he's been leering at Ivy in a way that's had me clenching my jaw since we got here.

"Never mind. You come with me." I throw some money down on the table to pay for the crappy meal and crappier service and head for the door.

Movement out of the corner of my eye grabs my attention as I'm reaching for the car's door handle.

A shriek comes from behind me, and I whip around. Someone grabbed Ivy. The guy has one hand wrapped around her waist and one covering her mouth. It's not some useless trucker. Elemental magic is crackling in the air. I'm calculating if I can use my magic without hurting Ivy when a vine creeps out from the weeds at the edge of the parking lot. It wraps around the man's ankles, pulling him down. He swears and shoots an errant lightning bolt at the vine. I laugh when it singes his ankle just a bit, but the vine withdraws. Ivy took advantage of the distraction to break his hold and now we're both facing the Mage.

Not good odds for him. An evergreen tree rains needles down over the man as the vines creep back up and start sliding up his legs. I'd pull out a weapon, but I just want to end this. I harness the wind into a small tornado, whipping around the man until he's spinning. He shoots some fireballs erratically at us. I don't want either of us getting hit by one of those blasts, so I ease up on the wind.

"Ivy, get his hands locked down with those vines. We need to immobilize him, then I can knock him out and we can call for a cleanup."

As if she was already anticipating my request, her vines slither around the man's torso, reaching for his hands. Before they quite get there, he sends off another volley of fireballs. The flaming projectiles are heading straight for Ivy, so I hurl myself to the right. My body collides with Ivy's, and I take us both to the ground. I wince and throw my arm over my eyes as intense heat crashes over us in a wave, but neither of us gets hit. Before I can breathe a sigh of relief, a blast rocks us back and the sky lights up with an explosion of flames. A loud ringing sound steals my hearing and sends and ache through my eardrums.

He must have hit a car. Realization dawns on me, and I swivel my head toward my car as if in slow motion. My car. Flames are licking up the sides of my car. Metal warping and twisting under the blaze. All of our shit and our phones were in there. My thigh screams as I pound my fist into it.

The acrid smell of burning rubber slices down my throat like a knife dipped in acid.

I jump up to face off with the Mage who got us into this. I don't see him anywhere.

"You ok, Ivy?"

"Yeah, other than the imprint your body made." She groans, rubbing her side.

"You're welcome."

"Uh huh, where is he?"

We split up and search the area, but there's no sign of the Mage. It's like he vanished into thin air. The only odd thing that catches my eye is a perfect scorched circle marring the ground in the spot I last saw him. I scuff it with my booted foot, but nothing comes off. My lip curls up at a sharp scent lingering in the air.

"What in Hades is this?"

Ivy's hair swings from side to side as she shakes her head. Her puzzled look probably matches mine.

The urge to get out of here is itching at my skin. I don't want the delay from dealing with the mundane police. The car is in my name, though. They're going to get suspicious if we flee the scene.

We're going to have to find a phone to get the nearest RED team out to clean up this mess and handle the police. I turn toward the motel diner behind us. The hostile locals are hardly going to welcome us back in after this incident. You can tell what kind of place it is based on the fact that not a single person emerged from the motel or diner to help after a car literally exploded in the parking lot.

"I'm going to head up to use the hotel room phone. You should probably come with in case anyone else decides to stop by for another unwelcome visit."

My nose wrinkles at the stale stench of despair and cigarettes that wafts over us as we open the door. I scope out the room to make sure no one is lying in wait.

My father answers on the first ring, and I wince as his voice shouts at me. "I thought I could trust you two!"

What? Why is he yelling at me already? I haven't even told him what happened here.

"Dad, ease up. Something happened here and I need a cleanup team asap." I hesitate and run my hands through my hair, closing my eyes. "And a new vehicle."

"What happened? Where are you? Who do I need to call?" He snaps right into business mode.

I explain the situation, then hang up and drum my fingers on my knee. I'm still not sure why he was raging about Liz and me before I got a single word out, but I don't have time to think about that right now. Sirens blare with increasing volume as they get closer.

Someone's going to be dropping a car off any minute and then we can get out of here. We can drive for a little while longer and stop at another depressing motel a little farther down the road.

CHAPTER 15
Sophia

The warm comfort of Mom and Mrs. Armstrong in the big kitchen isn't enough to chase away my exhaustion after a restless sleep, but it is comforting. Seems like restless sleeps are all I get anymore. I had this heavy feeling of foreboding pressing down like a weight on my chest all night. And my mind kept racing with worst case scenarios to explain why I couldn't get ahold of Logan or Ivy.

A cup of coffee and bowl of oatmeal waits for me at the big modern looking kitchen table. Mom reaches over to pat my knee, and I narrow my eyes at the don't-freak-out expression plastered all over her face. My heart picks up as all the scenarios I thought up last night come charging back.

"What's wrong?"

"Nothing is wrong, honey. Eat your breakfast."

Something is definitely up. I lean back into my chair. "I'm not eating until you tell me what's going on."

Not a great sign when Mom shoots a look at Mrs. Armstrong, seeking help with the explanation.

"Everything is fine. Logan and Ivy just ran into a minor problem."

I sit up straighter as alarm puts my senses on high alert. "How minor?"

"They got into a fight with another Mage. Logan's car got destroyed. They're both fine, though." She must have noticed the panicked look on my face, because she rushes that last bit out.

I shoot to my feet. "I need to call him."

"Their phones were in the car, unfortunately."

At least that explains why I couldn't get a hold of him last night. "Are they coming home?"

"No. Robert sent a new car, so they've continued on their trip. It's extremely important we get that cuff off of you."

"How exactly was his car destroyed? Was it an accident?"

Mrs. Armstrong looks at my mom again. "Apparently, the fight was with an Elemental Mage, and he hit the car with fireballs. It...exploded."

"His car exploded!!! They didn't get seriously hurt, but they could have been. They could have been killed. I have to go there. This is my fault. I'm the one who got this cuff on. Now they're in danger trying to get it removed."

My mom looks terrified at my statement. "You can't go. It's too dangerous. Not to mention you've got school. You're safest here."

"Am I though? Am I really safe here? Look what happened last night." A connection sparks in my head. Last night.

Probably around the same time as I was attacked, Logan was also targeted. Maybe someone is trying to keep us separated.

"You're safe here. You can't go after them. Don't get any ideas about running." The blue-green eyes she shares with her children narrow in suspicion at me. Right, she can read my mind, can't she? I blank out my mind and go to the white room that helps me prepare for tests and competitions. She's not in the habit of invading people's privacy, but if she thinks I'm up to something, she has easy access to my brain. I haven't learned how to shield my mind from Psychic Mages.

"Fine. I'm going to read or something."

"We're here for you, Sophia. If you need anything, let me know." The way she drops her head to give me a searching look adds a hint of a threat to her friendly offer. I'm watching you and I'll know if you try anything.

Our heads all turn to the door in suspicion when the doorbell breaks through our thoughts.

Mrs. Armstrong answers it with a pleasant greeting.

"Hi, is Sophia here?" A familiar voice warms my heart.

I fly to the door and throw myself at Xavier. He laughs and catches me.

"Miss me much, Sophy girl?"

"So much." I pull away and give him a long look. "Did you skip school today?"

He gives me a guilty smirk. "Maybe, but it was totally worth it. I thought maybe pod people took over your body. Had to make sure that it was really you, and I could only do that in person."

My palm glances off his shoulder. "What if I was a pod person? What would you do then?"

"I'd exorcise it from your body, of course." The gleam of mischief in his eyes turns serious. "I just needed to see for myself that you were ok."

"I'm so glad you came. Are you hungry?"

He gives me an incredulous look. "Do you even know me anymore? What kind of question is that?"

"Yeah, yeah. Let's go fill that endless void that is your stomach. You can say hi to my mom while you're here."

A bright smile spreads over Mom's face at the sight of my friend. Mrs. Armstrong looks pleased as well.

"Ok, I'm heading in to work. You two have fun." Fantastic. Xavier's appearance is actually perfect. Couldn't have come up with a better distraction if I tried. She can't spy on my thoughts from work.

Xavier chats with my mom for a few minutes before she says, "I have to head into work now, too. Will you be ok?" Worry clouds her face again.

"I'll be fine, Mom. I've got X here now, and Liz."

The pinched lines between her eyes ease a little as she gathers up her things before pulling me into a hug. I close my eyes and squeeze her tighter than usual.

"Bye, Mom." I give her one last squeeze.

"I'll see you later, darling."

"What's really going on here? Is it that guy? Are you in some kind of trouble?" Xavier turns his narrowed gaze on me as soon as Mom leaves. "I thought you were helping your mom's aunt, but here you are staying with his family.

"How did you find me, anyway?"

He shifts from one foot to the other. "Don't get mad at her."

"Charlotte? She told you?"

"I dragged it out of her. I threatened to come here and bang on every door until I tracked you down. She caved and told me you were staying here, because your great-aunt is in a facility. The thing is, I never remember you talking about an aunt here, so I know you're both lying to me. The thing I can't figure out is why."

I struggle with a reason to explain my presence here. "Look, X. I can't tell you the exact reason I'm here, but I am fine. Nothing is wrong. I'm still finishing my schoolwork online. I'm going to graduate."

He drops his voice to a whisper, and his eyes dart from side to side as if he's checking to make sure no one can overhear him. "Are you…pregnant?"

I can't help the laugh from exploding out. "What?! No. Seriously, Xavier. This isn't the dark ages. Even if I was, which I categorically am not, I wouldn't get sent off to live in some aunt's house like a dirty little secret."

His features relax in relief. "Then what is it?"

Liz bounces in to save the day. "Hey, Xavier. What's up?" she asks.

His lips lift in a tight smile. "Hi, Liz. I came to figure out what's going on with Sophia here."

"My family said they could stay here while her mom looks after her aunt. What else could it be?"

He opens his mouth and closes it again, shaking his head. "You're going to lie to me, too?"

I study the face of my friend that I know as well as my own. I wish I didn't have to keep secrets from him. He's my best friend. He can't know about the magic world, though. Not only is it forbidden, but he could end up in danger.

"X, I just can't talk about it. I wish I could, but I can't. You know how much I care about you. That's why. I don't want you getting hurt because of me."

"Right. So that's it? You're done with me? They're your new friends now? Logan and Liz. Even Charlotte knows something she won't tell me. I thought I was your bestie. I guess not."

"It's not that."

"Well then, what is it?"

"I can't talk about it."

"You can't talk about it with me. That's what you're saying. Fine. I'm out of here. Call me when you're ready to talk."

I grab his arm as he spins around to leave. "Wait, Xavier. Don't leave like this, please?"

His voice comes out gruff. "You ready to talk?"

"N..no."

He shakes my arm off then heads for the door. "Then I'm out. You know how to reach me, but don't bother unless you're ready to share."

Heat burns behind my eyes as my friend walks out of my life. Magic has taken so much from me already. I start to let him know I love him, but the door frame vibrates as he slams the door, cutting off my declaration.

"I'm sorry." Liz's eyes are wide with sorrow at my loss.

"What are you sorry for? It's not your fault." I sniff.

I turn around and hustle up the stairs so she can't see the tears starting to escape. She leaves me alone while I slump at the desk in my borrowed room and get myself back together.

After the briefest of breaks to compose myself, it's time to start making a plan. I need to track down Logan and Ivy, so I can be there for them. It can't be a coincidence that we were both attacked at the same time. I have to get to him.

Liz seemed to understand that I needed some time to myself after Xavier's visit, so she left me alone until I hear a loud rap on the bedroom day that startles me out of my reverie.

She's got my backpack and a pile of books in her arms. "Mom thought you'd want these, so she had someone drop them off."

"Oh, that's great. Thanks."

She dumps them in a haphazard pile on the desk that wobbles precariously until I straighten them out.

"Want to work together at the kitchen table?" I tilt my head and eye her with suspicion. Our moms clearly sent her to spy on me.

"I'm good up here." I'm going to get no plotting done if she's glued to my side for the rest of the day.

"Ok, I'll get to my own work too."

She blurs out in a move I'm still not used to returning a moment later with some books. She proves my suspicions when she slides down the wall next to my door, pulling her knees up to her chest and flipping a textbook open. "I'll work in here with you." Her smile is brighter than the midday sun.

A sigh accompanies my rolling eyes. I definitely can't count on her for help, and it's going to be harder than I thought to get out of here without escaping someone's notice. I'm sure I can figure this out, though.

My mind is racing on everything but math work as I plot. Who can I ask for help? Xavier doesn't have a clue what's going on here. Not to mention he probably hates me now. He's a no. Charlotte would probably help me, but she is also likely to turn me in to the parental units. With my car back home I need a ride, and I need to figure out how to track down Logan and Ivy without a way to contact them.

Possibilities flit through my mind, and I bat them all away until one snags in my mind. Nooo. That won't work. But what if it did?

I wait impatiently for Liz to get bored. I can't make the call while she's nearby. She's got the super hearing to back up the super speed. She'll hear any phone conversation.

I'm practically crawling out of my skin to get out of here, but I hold out until after we finish up our lunch. Liz raises a brow at the mangled pile of crumbled bread that I turned my sandwich into, but she doesn't comment on it. I know she's worried about Logan, too.

"I got my schoolwork done." Lie. "I'm going to do some training after lunch. Wanna join?" I think my nonchalant tone is pretty good. I'm getting better at lying. Seriously, what is my life now?

She looks relieved. "Nah, I'll let you into the training room, though."

This is working out better than I thought it would. The Armstrong house has a similar training room to the house Liz and Logan were staying in back home. My mind drifts back to my real home. I rub at my chest to ease the hollowness that's taken up residence there. I miss my house. My friends. My old life. Nothing I can do about that now, so I try to shake it off.

I was banking on Liz turning her nose up at a training session. There's no way I could sneak out of there from under her nose, so she won't feel the need to spy on me.

The training room here is bigger and better stocked than the one I was in at the other place. Makes sense. This is their permanent home. I had wondered why they kept that second house at all in my hometown, but Logan explained they'd gotten it to have a place close to me.

My eyes widen at all the space and equipment down here. I don't waste any time though once the door shuts behind Liz. Music fills the room from every direction once I crank up the tunes.

Please let him still have the same number. Please. If this doesn't work out, I don't know what other options I have.

I'm about to hang up after five rings when his voice comes through. "Hello." It sounds deeper than I remember.

"Hi, is this Garrett?"

CHAPTER 16
Logan

We've made good time in spite of the incident last night. We got a nondescript beige sedan for the rest of the trip. There's no way anyone can connect it to us, so they can't track us that way. Without our cell phones, we're pretty much untraceable via technological means. Now we have to remain vigilant. It's just as likely they're tracking us using some sort of magical means. There's nothing we can do about that except stay on guard.

The lack of a phone is more irritating than I thought it would be. I really need to hear Sophia's voice to make sure she's actually ok. I didn't think this would be as hard as it is. Being away from her. Plus, we can't look up anything online. I'll make sure to call her when we stop for the night.

"That last article about Dexter disappearing mentioned a charred black area, right?" Ivy asks.

"It did." I've had the same thought circling my head. "The question is, what could have caused it, and why didn't anyone notice this at any of the previous sites where Mages have gone missing?"

"That and also where did that Mage go?" Ivy adds in a contemplative tone.

"Well, what can cause that kind of thing? There was a distinct smell lingering around the circle. Smoke and ash along with burning metal and rubber from the car, but there was something else." I zone out on the road ahead, searching for the memory. Everything was a bit of a blur after the fight, and I was all hyped up on adrenaline. I snap my fingers. "Sulfur! It was sulfur."

"Right. That's it. Sulfur. Someone created a portal there."

"A portal?" Portals don't cause that sort of thing.

"Not on this plane. A portal to the Nether Realm."

"The Nether Realm. I've never heard of anyone using a portal to get there." The appeal of going to a realm full of evil spirits escapes me.

"No, me either, but it's theoretically possible. Someone could open a portal down there. The kind you'd use to summon a spirit and bring it up here. Only instead of bringing something up, they're sending people through it."

"I guess." Zeus. It's why the locations of the disappearances have been all over the map. It's how he's been able to hide from everyone. "Zeus is hiding out down there. That's why we can't find him."

Ivy snaps her fingers. "Yes! That makes sense."

The brief moment of hope I had at having a little more information is immediately squashed. This doesn't help us at all. Knowing that Zeus can appear anywhere he wants without notice is freaking terrifying. He could snatch Sophia out from under our noses. Plus, who knows what he's doing down there? Not a place I'd like to visit for a vacation, that's for sure.

"That explains a lot. I'm not sure what we can do with this information, though. We need to figure out who he's got working for him up here. There's no way he's tracked us from down there. He has people up here working for him."

"He for sure does."

Ivy offers to take over driving, but I'm in the zone, so I push myself until my hunger threatens to spill over into my mood. I don't want to start snapping at Ivy given the current fragile state of our truce, so I give in to its demands and pull over at another flea infested motel.

I send Ivy off to check the diner/gas station area for anything suspicious and I swing around to do a full perimeter sweep and check the motel building. There's not even a whiff of magic in the air. No signs of anything untoward. That means nothing if Zeus and his lackeys are traveling by a portal through the Nether Realm. We'll have to keep an overnight watch. Take turns.

I park the car in a spot right below the balcony of our room after we check in, so we can keep an eye on it. Losing one car on this trip is more than enough. I can only imagine what my father would say about that. Even though it is in no way my fault, I'm sure he can find a way to blame it on me.

CHAPTER 17
Sophia

"You shouldn't be calling me." Gone is the polite, friendly Garrett I thought I knew. He sounds wary, but he did answer the phone, so that's got to mean something, right?

"Garrett, I need your help." I think back to the boy I met at debate with the floppy sandy hair and the sweet smile and compare him to the one who came with Charlotte to help rescue me from Zeus. Debate Garrett was nice, but he was a fraud. It's Witch Garrett with the sword and the attitude that I need to back me up on this journey.

The silence ticks by and I'm about convinced that he's hung up when he replies. "I told you I don't want to be involved in this mess you've got yourself tangled up in." As if the mess is of my own making and not a circumstance of birth.

"I don't have anyone else. I need you. Plus, you kind of owe me." He did track me down and insert himself into my life to turn me over to Zeus before switching sides.

His sigh vibrates through the earpiece. "I came to help. I paid my debt."

"What's going on in the Mage world is going to affect us all, Garrett. It's not just about the Mages. The Witches are going to be affected too." I'm not above begging to gain his help. The stakes are way too high for misplaced pride.

"The Witches aren't my concern any more than the Mages are. I've got my own thing going on."

"Why'd you answer the phone then? Why did you keep the same number?"

"Fine, tell me what's up and I'll let you know if I can help." Got him. If he really wanted to never talk to me again, it would have been quite easy to get a new number or cell phone and disappear. I know there's a good guy buried in there somewhere. I don't know why I trust him after everything he did and everything he lied about, but I do. Maybe it's the fact that he risked his own skin to defy Zeus and came with Charlotte to save me. Maybe it's the fact that the Garrett I first met seemed way more authentic than the one he changed into. Whatever it is, I don't think he'd do anything to hurt me. He had his chance, and he didn't.

He listens without adding any input while I go through the events of the last few days. "I need to find Logan and Ivy to meet up with them. I need your help to track them down. And I need a ride. My car got left back home."

"Whoa, whoa, whoa. You need a chauffeur? That's not a little help. You want to drag me on some hazardous expedition? Why can't you get one of your friends or Liz to go with you?"

"Because you can track them, Garrett. I know what your witchy specialty is. I can't track them any other way. They lost their cell phones in the car explosion."

"Explosion? Well, why didn't you mention that right away? How could I turn down a chance to get blown up? That'll be a hard no."

"Please, Garrett. Please. I need to find them, and I need to get this cuff off. There's too much at stake. Hasn't there ever been anyone you cared enough about that you'd do anything for them?"

Another long pause. "Yeah, that's kinda the problem." His voice has a rough edge to it, like sandpaper scraping an old piece of wood.

"You understand how I feel then."

"Ok. I'll do this, but that's it. I'll track them. I'll drive you and once we catch up with them, I'm out of there. For good. Don't call me. Don't try to find me."

"That's all I need. Thank you so much."

"Don't thank me. You're probably just going to get killed in the process and me along with you. Man, I know I'm going to regret this."

"You're going to have to meet me tonight after everyone's gone to bed. They've got me on a close watch here."

"Will eleven work?" he asks.

"That'll be fine. I'll meet you up the street at Hillside Park." I give him the address and hang up, hoping he'll actually come through for me.

I hit the treadmill to clear my thoughts and work up a sweat so Liz doesn't get suspicious.

The bright moon hanging in the inky sky has cast foreboding shadows in the corners of my borrowed room. My pacing is going to wear a path in the light gray carpet at this rate, but I can't seem to keep myself still while I wait for the rest of the household to go quiet for the night. I've had my headphones on all evening trying to keep my mind on the music rather than my plans, so Mrs. Armstrong doesn't figure out what I'm up to and spoil my plans.

For the hundredth time, I check my phone. It's finally 10:45. I check my bag one more time. I packed a few extra pairs of clothes, my bathroom stuff, and a bit of cash I had in my unicorn bank at home. It's not a lot, but hopefully we won't need too much money to get through the next few days.

I peer cautiously out of the room into the silent hall. I'm sure everyone is at least in bed if not asleep. Liz is likely awake, so I'll have to be extra quiet. I steal through the big house on my tiptoes and breathe a sigh of relief when I make it out the front door without getting caught.

I'm halfway down the street when Liz catches up. She didn't turn on her super speed, though. Must not have wanted her parents to sense her using her magic. Crap. I should have known I couldn't keep it a secret from her.

"Where do you think you're going?"

"I'm going to track down Logan and Ivy. Please don't stop me, Liz." She can definitely stop me if she wants to. There's no question about that.

"I'm not going to stop you. I'm going to come." I can tell by the sly grin curving up her lips that she has no intention of missing out on the chance to go on an adventure.

"You can't come. You need to stay here and make sure my mom is ok. Not to mention, your parents will never forgive me if I put both of their kids in danger." I can't let her come with me. Logan's already out there in danger. What if both of them got hurt? My entire being shudders away from the thought of the worst-case scenario. In the brief time that we've known each other, Liz has become like a sister to me. "Please, Liz. Don't try to follow me."

"How are you getting there? How do you think you're going to find them?"

I wince and keep walking. "I've got a plan." Sort of.

She keeps pace with me until we're almost at the park. "Really? What exactly is your plan?" She interrogates me.

"I've got help." I try to deflect her question, but I know she's not going to leave it alone. She'll know I'm going to rely on Garrett's tracking skills to find Logan and Ivy.

"Uh huh. I'm not leaving until I can trust you'll be safe," she says as we reach the park.

Garrett melts out of the shadows in front of us. "Thought you were coming alone?"

"HIM?!? This is your brilliant plan? I thought you were the smart one, Sophia."

"Hey, I'm hurt." His posture and casual tone say otherwise as he leans back against a tree with one ankle crossed and his arms folded across his chest.

"He can track them, Liz."

"But you can't trust him. He was going to turn you over to Zeus." A chill snakes up my spine at the mention of my uncle.

"But he didn't. He could have, but he didn't." It's the action that means the most, right? And he answered the phone. I can tell he wants to help. He just doesn't know it yet. "When he came with Charlotte to find me, he put a target on his own back."

Doubt and disapproval cover Liz from her pinched lips to her arms crossed over her chest. "Sophia, I can't let you go off with him."

"You have to, Liz. Don't turn on me. I need to go. And I'm obviously not safe around here either. Please, please don't tell our parents. I left a note. They don't need to know you had any knowledge of it. Please. I can't stay here knowing Logan is in danger."

The expression in her eyes wavers. "But they're two days ahead of you. You're not going to catch up to them."

"At least I can meet up with them after they get the key, though. I can get this off sooner, and then I'll have a way to defend myself. This is what I need, Liz. I can't just keep relying on everyone else to save me. You probably don't know what it's like to be powerless, but that's how I feel right now."

I know I'm getting through to her when I see her azure eyes soften. "Ok, Sophia. I'll keep your secret for the day." She turns to Garrett. "You though, I don't like you, and I don't trust you. You look after my friend or the biggest piece of you anyone will find is a toe. The little one. That's a promise."

Liz is scary when she wants to be. The dark look on her face is enough to shake Garrett up a bit. He straightens up with a serious look on his face. "You are one terrifying little thing. I knew I should stay a mile away from this situation. Now that I'm in it, I'm sticking with it. I might be a liar and a thief, but I don't go back on my word. Besides, I haven't got anything better to do right now. Jobs have been hard to come by after I ditched my last one."

"Fine." She turns back to me and yanks me in for a hug that squeezes a groan out of me. "Stay safe and call me if he puts one single finger out of line. One finger and I'll be there. With knives."

"I got it, Liz. This will be fine. I promise."

She gives me a doubtful look, but lets me follow Garrett.

"Later, psycho." He calls over his shoulder.

I study him through narrowed eyes. This is not the boy I hung out with at Arabica Nights. It's like he's let down a shield, and a dangerous vibe emanates from him. Gone are the soft smile and shy comments. He's all casual confidence that borders on arrogance. Even his features look harder as if they're chiseled from ice. There's something different in his hazel eyes, too. Sadness maybe? Longing? I'm not sure. He does still open the car door up for me, though. I guess the gentlemanly politeness is ingrained.

I settle into the passenger seat and fiddle with my backpack, suddenly nervous that I'm in the car with someone who is pretty much a stranger. I'm going to have to get to know him all over again, since I'm not sure how much of his personality was a mask.

"Did you bring something of Logan's?" he asks.

"Yeah." I hand him the knife that I brought along at his request.

I watch, fascinated, as he pulls a necklace out from under his black long-sleeved shirt. Gone are the preppy button ups along with the rest of the smart, academic facade. A pear-shaped green crystal the size of a ping-pong ball dangles from a leather cord. He holds Logan's knife in the palm of one hand while he dangles the crystal over top. A line pinches his brows together, and he recites a few sentences in a language I don't recognize. Maybe Latin? I blink as the crystal starts to glow, brighter and brighter. My gaze strays to Garrett. His lashes have dropped down to protect his eyes from the nuclear luminescence.

"Got it."

"That's it? Couldn't a Mage do that? Why is that a Witch thing?"

The crystal swings like a pendulum when he dangles it in front of my face. "This is a family heirloom. It's keyed to my family's bloodline, so it would be useless to anybody else."

"That's cool. So does your whole family have one, or do they have other talents?"

His face looks like he's thrown the shutters closed to keep out a hurricane, and his voice drops even lower. "I don't have any family."

"Oh, I'm sorry. Are they...?" There aren't any right questions here. I know what it's like when people ask me about my dad. It reopens the deep wounds every time I have to tell someone he died. Even thinking about it disturbs the shard of glass that's permanently wedged in my heart, sending a fresh shock of pain through me.

"It doesn't matter." And that's the end of that conversation. I understand where he's coming from. If he's suffered a loss and he doesn't want to talk about it, I'm not going to push him. I rub at the hollow ache in my chest as memories of my dad flood me.

We fall into an awkward silence for the next couple of hours. I try to amuse myself with a book, but I can't stop thinking about the dark look that came over Garrett's face before he shut down. There's a story there and it may be the reason he's chosen this life.

"I can drive part of the way if you need a break." I offer, while hoping he says no. I don't love driving. I don't trust other drivers and don't relish the loss of control that comes with putting your life in the hands of random strangers. Unfortunately, that seems to be my entire existence at the moment. That's why I need to get this cuff off as soon as possible. I need to get some control back over my own life.

"It's fine."

All his answers so far have been one or two words. I don't think I can handle an entire drive with the air hanging heavy with tension between us. I need a safe topic of conversation.

"You were fantastic at debate, but that must have been fake, right? Have you done debate before?"

"Yeah, I used to." Maybe that stirred up old memories of his past. I don't want to cause him pain.

"What kind of music do you like?" That's a safe topic, right?

"Why are you trying so hard?"

"I'm not trying so hard. I'm not sure I can handle a multi-day drive in awkward silence. Honestly, Garrett, I kind of feel like I'm driving with a stranger, since the guy you were before isn't really you. I want to get to know you a little better, so I'm not actually on a road trip with a complete stranger."

He grumbles and runs a hand through his blond hair. "I'm sorry. I wanted to make it up to you, but I don't exactly know how."

"Well, maybe try talking to me. That's a start. Maybe you can tell me why you decided to help." I flit my eyes away from the road to settle on his tense shoulders.

"Honestly, I'm not even sure. I've been feeling bad ever since I ditched you after you faced down with Zeus. Over the last few years, I've done some bad things, but I never felt guilty about it. I mean, stealing stuff from rich assholes who have no real claim to it certainly doesn't bother me. Then I started hanging out with you, lying about who I am to get information. Once I started getting to know you, there was no way I could turn you over. You never did anything wrong. So I came to help when Charlotte asked. I thought that would appease my guilt and I could get on with my life."

He pauses for so long I give him a nudge. "But..."

"I couldn't. I haven't stopped thinking about you and everything that's going down in the magic community right now. It's not sitting right with me."

"Ok. See, there's a start."

"I am curious about something, though. Why'd you call me? What made you think I'd come?" His eyes lock on mine with a laser focus.

"I didn't know for sure you would, but like I said. I trust you, Garrett. Even if you didn't turn me over to Zeus, you could have ditched the job and run. Never looked back. But you didn't. You helped Charlotte find me. A bad guy wouldn't do that. You're not a bad guy."

"Don't go trying to make me out to be some noble rescuer or anything like that. You'll be disappointed. There's no shining armor under these clothes. I'm just a thief, and once I help you find your real knight, I'm out of here." Something tells me he's trying to convince himself just as much as he's trying to convince me.

He turns back to the road and rubs his hand down the back of his neck, falling into silence again. Sharing time must be over for the moment, but I feel a little better knowing this has all been weighing on his mind and he's fully committed, at least for the time being. Maybe longer.

139

CHAPTER 18
Logan

You have got to be kidding me! Pain reverberates through my hand as it sinks into the steaming hood of the piece of crap car the MED gave us. Time is not our friend at the moment. I can't deal with another delay. Particularly this garbage problem. Rage balls up inside me with no outlet. At least if there was someone to fight, I could let it out that way. There's nothing I can do about this.

I pace back and forth at the side of the road, waiting for a car to pass by. We don't even have a cell phone to call a tow truck and this country road leading into a nowhere town is not exactly a hub of activity.

A small hand lands on my arm. "Want a snack?"

"What?" I glance back at Ivy.

"Well, the only way I remember to calm you down when you're all worked up is a distraction. And food is always a distraction." A laugh slips out. Ivy knows me so well. My stomach drops all over again at all the shared memories we have that got washed away by everything that's gone down between us. It's a little unsettling to think that maybe I was a better person when I was with her. Sometimes I don't recognize who I've become in the last couple of years. Hard, bitter, and careless with the feelings of other people. But I'm trying to change that.

"Too true. What have you got?" I raise a questioning brow at her.

"There are some grapes." I give her a look. "No, how about a granola bar? I got it." She roots through her backpack in the backseat, which is guaranteed to be just as messy as her purse. If we had ended up together, our house would have been a nightmare. I think about Sophia's immaculate desk and her precise handwriting. She definitely balances out my chaos better than Ivy ever did. "PB & J." She pulls out a sandwich with the fillings spilling out from the middle of the squished bread jammed into a too small container. "Your favorite."

I just stare at her.

"Or is it not your favorite anymore?" Her face falls and I laugh. "Oh, you're messing with me."

"I'll take your sandwich."

As I'm reaching for it, a car rumbling in the distance has me pulling back and scanning the road. I take a couple of steps forward and wave down the dusty black pickup as it gets closer.

"Hey folks, need some help?" The driver pokes his bearded face out the window.

"Yes, please." Ivy pipes up. Probably better to let her do the talking. "Our car broke down here and he let our cell phone die." I shoot her a dirty look at the blame, and she smirks at me.

It was smart of her to not reveal to this random guy that we're completely cut off from contact.

"I've got a phone. I can call for a tow. Bobby's probably around. He can pick it up and drop it at the shop for you." Right, because this is the sort of town that has one tow truck and everyone knows the driver.

"Thank you so much, sir," Ivy says.

"Alright, he's on his way. Did you want me to give you a ride into town? He hasn't got room in his tow for both of you."

"That would be great."

I can't shake my suspicion, but I'm not leaving Ivy here by herself, or letting her go off with some random farmer by herself.

"I'm Merrill, by the way."

"Nice to meet you." Ivy smiles politely. Her small hand disappears in his huge, rough paw. "I'm Ivy, this is Logan."

"Good to meet ya both."

I offer a hand to help Ivy clamber up into the truck, but she avoids it, hopping in on her own and I follow. The inside of the truck is the polar opposite of the mud-caked exterior. It's clean and tidy. Like too clean for a middle of nowhere farmer. I'm already eying the door for escape before he pulls away from the shoulder. As if Ivy knows how twitchy I'm getting, she lays a hand on my shoulder. I settle down when I realize the air in the truck is devoid of magic. He's as mundane as they come.

"Where are you folks headed?"

I narrow my eyes, not wanting to give away our destination.

"We're just on a road trip. No particular destination. Driving. Stopping where we want."

"Ah, you young people. Things sure have changed since I was your age. We don't have too much to offer you here in

Valmont, but Sally's got good grub at her diner if you want to grab something to eat while you wait for your car to be fixed."

It better not take long for the car to get fixed. I want out of here as soon as possible.

I make my best effort to turn the frown on my face into some semblance of a pleasant smile. "Would I be able to use your phone, Merrill?"

I shoot a dirty look at Ivy's stifled snort. Apparently, she saw through my forced civility.

"Of course. Have to check in with your parents?"

How old does this guy think I am? "Yeah."

"Help yourself. It's not locked." He points a thick finger at the cup holder where his shiny smart phone is resting.

"Thanks." I grab it and dial Sophia's number. I'm pleased and also surprised that I memorized it. I would have been screwed, otherwise, after losing my cell.

I frown at the phone as it rings and rings before going to voicemail. She must be training or something. I could try Liz or my parents, but I don't want to get sucked into a conversation with them right now. I'll try her again later.

"No answer?"

"No."

I lose myself in my thoughts. Luckily, Ivy and Merrill fall into a friendly conversation that lets me check out without looking too rude. This Nether Realm thing is driving me crazy. How is Zeus traveling there? How long has he been hiding out? What's his next move? The lack of contact with the rest of the Mage world is frustrating. I try to put myself in his shoes. What would I do if I were him? Where would I strike next? When Sophia is alone and vulnerable. When I'm not around. That's the point I keep circling back to. At least she's safe at the

NAMC dorms. That's why I left her there. Surrounded by other Mages, but hidden in plain sight where no one knows she's an Archimage. That's all going to change once we get that cuff removed. I know it's necessary. It will only hurt her if it stays on too long. The thought of her powers loose again for anyone to track makes me edgy.

"I'll leave you here, folks. Hopefully, everything works out and you get back on the road quickly. Sally's diner is just up the road if you need to grab a bite. Good luck and have fun." His booming voice cuts into my thoughts.

A dusty garage with two bays sits in front of us. It has definitely seen better days. The faded sign gracing the top says Fitzgerald's Auto in peeling red paint and is hanging crookedly. Promising.

"Thank you so much," Ivy says, giving the man a warm smile. "Can we pay you for the gas?"

His laugh bounces off the inside of the truck. "My momma taught me better than to expect payment for helping a stranger in need. You go on."

A thick layer of dust coating the front door prevents me from seeing inside. I don't like walking into a place blind like this. It creaks as I push it open. The small reception area is about as welcoming as the exterior, with a cheap-looking desk and an overflowing pile of papers balanced on it. Nobody is at the desk when we get in, but there's one of those silver hotel desk looking bells with a handwritten ring for service sign beside it. I slam my hand on it and Ivy gives me a dirty look at my impatience.

It seems like about an hour before a slim guy in a grease-streaked coverall walks in. He's chewing on a toothpick, and I don't like the look in his eyes as he runs his gaze over Ivy from head to toe.

"I'm going to go wait outside, in case the tow truck comes," Ivy says, brushing my hand with hers. That sketchy guy is probably making her uncomfortable the way he's looking at her. I don't blame her. I nod as she slips away.

"What do you want?" Customer service is clearly not the specialty here.

"We got a ride here from Merill. He called to have our car picked up off the side of the road. It's on its way here now," I say.

"And what's wrong with it?"

I shake my head. "Not sure. It just stopped. There was steam coming out of the hood." The thought of my father teaching me about car repair is laughable.

"I've got two cars to work on this morning. I can fit your car in at four." He's about to turn away.

"Look man. We need to get on the road sooner rather than later. We're in a bit of a rush. Any chance you can get to it sooner?"

"Nope."

"I can pay extra?" I don't like the idea that he's going to squeeze extra money out of me for this job, but I'll do anything to get this situation dealt with and get back to Sophia.

His sharp eyes narrow and I can tell he's assessed me as a sucker, but whatever. I'm never going to see him again after this. "I can take a look at it after lunch if you pay the premium."

"Sure."

"Just need the make and plate number and your phone number." I scribble the info down on the scrap piece of paper he plops on the desk.

"We don't have a phone at the moment. How about if we come back here at one?"

"Works for me." He turns away and saunters off. Maybe he could get more cars looked after if he picked up the pace a bit.

I burst out the front door and panic for a moment when I don't see Ivy in the dusty parking lot.

"Ivy?" I call out and stride along the side of the building.

She's pulling her backpack over her shoulder as I round the corner brandishing a granola bar at me. "How about we find that diner Merill was talking about? I'm getting hungry and we can figure out our next steps."

I give her a confused look. "You can't wait until we get there for a snack?"

She looks at the bar in her hand. "Don't be ridiculous. This is an appetizer."

True enough. She has always had a good appetite. Not Liz level, but she can eat.

"Fine." I'm not going to hang around this place anymore, that's for sure.

CHAPTER 19
Sophia

Garrett has been driving all night and all morning when I beg him to pull over. We made one quick rest stop this morning and grabbed some food for the road, but that's it. It's like he's hellbent on getting this over with and getting rid of me as soon as possible.

We pull into one of those big rest stops that has several restaurant choices and use the bathroom. It's huge and clean, but only a few stalls are occupied.

The large dining area is occupied by a variety of families, couples, and some single men scattered among the beige plastic tables. Assorted food kiosks surround the eating zone.

I'm wavering between a slice of gooey pizza or noodles cooked to order, but my brain is on overload and I can't decide, so I follow Garrett to the sub chain and grab a veggie sub instead. We settle down at a table in the corner. Garrett's mouth gapes in a wide yawn after he inhales his sub without taking a breath, while I nibble at mine. The bread has that bland cardboard flavor of big chain sub shops, and the shredded lettuce is pale and a little brown. It looks as ragged as I feel.

"Maybe you need to take a longer break, Garrett. I'm in a hurry, because I really want to catch up with Logan and Ivy. I'm not sure why you're in such a rush." I'm anxious to get back on the road, but it won't do anyone any good if Garrett falls asleep at the wheel.

"I'll just grab a coffee," he says, nodding at the line twisting away from the coffee shop.

"Seriously, I appreciate you taking me Garrett, but you don't need to kill yourself over this."

"I'm fine, Sophia. I said I'd help you and I will, but I don't want to get any more involved in this situation than I have to. Under the radar, remember?" I do remember him saying that, but I think helping me at all will probably not help him in his quest to keep a low profile.

"Ok. Mind if I make a phone call before we head out?"

"No problem. I'll get you a coffee. You can meet me back by the car in a bit. That line is pretty long anyway, so I'll probably be a little while."

"Awesome. See you soon."

I need a little privacy for this conversation, so I head out of the rest stop into the crowded parking lot. After almost getting hit twice by distracted drivers, I head for the big, empty field stretching out behind the station before I make the call.

"Sophia! Where are you?" I pull the phone away from my ear as Charlotte's anxious voice pierces my eardrums.

"I'm not going to tell you where I am, but I'm fine. I'm safe. I'm going after Logan."

"You're what? Are you by yourself? Your mom is freaking out. Nobody knows where you are."

"I'm fine, seriously. I'm safe. I'm actually not alone. I'm with..." The sky doesn't provide me with any assistance when I glance up and press my lips together. This is not going to go over well. "Garrett." I squeak that last bit out, almost hoping she doesn't catch it.

"What?!? You're with Garrett! I can't have heard you right."

"Calm down. You're the one who brought him to help us the last time. You must trust him on some level. That's actually why I called you. That and to let you know I'm safe."

"Yeah, I trusted him to help on that mission, because I was there. I was just relying on his tracking skills."

"Well me too. I need him to help me find Logan. His and Ivy's cell phones got wrecked in an explosion. A freaking explosion, Charlotte. I need to find him."

"True, but you're also alone with him. That's a lot more trust than a simple mission."

"You know he could have turned me over at any time if that was his plan. He came to rescue me with you, he answered my call and came to help me again now. I do trust him. What I need to know is if that's completely unfounded or not. You said you knew him and his family. What happened? Why did he go all lone wolf thief?"

I lift the phone off my ear and double check Charlotte is still there after the long pause. "I don't know if I should be the one telling you this. It's really personal stuff."

"It's not like you have any loyalty to him, Char. I'm your best friend and I'm stuck in a car with him for at least a couple of days. I need to know that I'm safe. Or as safe as I can get these days." A little guilt creeps in at my ulterior motive. I already trust him. Maybe I shouldn't be digging for information about Garrett from Charlotte, but I know she has some knowledge of his past.

"Okay, Sophia. I'm telling you and you can be the judge of whether or not this makes him someone you can trust. You shouldn't stay with him too long, though. He seems to feel some sort of obligation to you that's keeping him on the straight and narrow, but who knows how far that will go. It could be gone when a higher bidder offers something up for him."

"I got it. It's only until we catch up with Ivy and Logan."

"Hang on, I'm at school. I'm going to go find somewhere private where no one will overhear me."

I hear a rustling sound and pace around the open field as I wait for her to come back on the line.

"Ok, so Garrett and his family were tight members of the Witch community. They lived a a ways away, so I didn't see them often, but I've heard Gran talk about them and we'd occasionally meet up at events. He had one sister who was about our age. Leonore. She was a sweetie."

"What happened to them?" I can't contain my curiosity.

"There was a fire at his family's house. He was away at some school event at the time, but the rest of his family..." A small gasp escapes me.

"That's so sad, poor Garrett." I know the deep pain of losing a parent that never goes away, but I can't imagine what it would be like if my entire family was gone like that. The guilt of not being there, the loss. It would screw anyone up.

"Yes, it's terrible. That's not the worst part, though. They ruled it an accident, but there were definite signs that it could have been foul play of the magical variety. There was an investigation by the MEDs, but they don't always concern themselves with problems in the Witch community as much as they should. They followed a couple of leads, hit some dead ends, and eventually gave up. They never found out who did it."

That explains a lot. "And after that? What happened to Garrett?"

"Another member of the community took him in, but he was acting out hardcore, so he got kicked out. He disappeared from the area and then we only heard stories. It was like he stopped caring about everyone else. We'd hear about some valuable object of power being stolen and him being connected to it, but no one's ever caught him."

"And you still trusted him to come help that day we faced off with Zeus?"

"Yeah, like I said. He came from good people, and his tracking magic is off the charts good. I only needed him to find you, and he was reluctant to even do that. Like I said, there's something about you he likes or he wouldn't have done any of it. If I didn't know better, I might have thought he was like, into you."

"I don't think that's true. He's barely spoken to me over this trip and he's driving as if there are hellhounds after him." Are hellhounds a real thing? God, I hope not. There's enough to deal with without adding demonic dogs to the mix.

"Whatever you say, Soph. These are my observations. Take 'em or leave 'em."

"Thanks for that chat and the info, but I should let you go." It was nice to hear her voice, but she's given me a lot to think about and we should get back on the road.

"Keep in touch. I need to make sure you're safe."

"I will. Bye."

I hang up and slide my phone into my jeans pocket. The rest stop buildings have become mere specks in the distance. I didn't realize I had wandered so far while I was on the phone with Char. I glance around. The sweeping expanse of dead grass around me is all I can see except for the dark shapes of a few birds beating their wings as they glide through the air. At least I'd see it coming if anyone tried to attack here. A brief shiver rocks me and I pick up my pace to head back toward Garrett's car.

A gust of wind at my back interrupts the rhythmic crunch of my feet hitting the frosty grass. A heavy weight slams into my back, throwing me off balance. I trip over my own feet and when I spin around to see what it was, I'm met with a pair of luminescent green globes protruding from a furry face. It might be cute if it wasn't for the malicious intent in its eyes as it swoops at me again with its claws out. My hand twitches reflexively toward the scar on my neck. I am not looking for a repeat of the last time those claws tore a chunk out of me. My mind races through my options. Run. That's my first instinct. I gauge the distance to the closest building, ducking and flinging my arm out as the Ferrebat attacks again, but I'll never make it in time. I dart away and slip my hand under my shirt to grab one of the daggers Logan gave me, hoping I don't stab myself in the process. As soon as I left the compound, I started wearing the set. I only wish I had it with me when I got attacked there. Not sure if it would have made a difference given my current limited skills, but it wouldn't have hurt.

No way is my aim good enough to hit that thing with a throw. I take a deep breath and fling my arm out so it doesn't get my face. When it hits its mark, sinking its claws into my arm, I shriek at the fiery sting that shoots up the limb. I swallow down the pain and bring my good arm down, slicing at the creature. My stomach drops and I have to stifle the gag that rises at the sickening squelch and feel of flesh giving way to my steel. But it works, and the vicious thing retracts its claws, releasing my arm. I don't ease up though as the bat thing tries to fly away. I throw my body weight at it, taking us both down. Pain radiates up my side as I hit the ground, but the creature looks like it got knocked out.

I struggle to yank the knife out, but it's in there good. "Get out!"

I drag myself to a crouch, placing one sneakered foot on the creature. It comes out in a rush that sends me toppling backward jarring my tailbone as I land on my butt. I shudder as something hot and wet splashes me. Prickles of heat spread through my skin and a ringing starts up in my head before everything goes black.

"Sophia, Sophia!"

My eyes flutter open, and I blink for a minute. A pair of concerned eyes meet mine. They've gone dark like the mossy undergrowth in a shadowed wood. With his hair escaping its gel prison over his forehead, Garrett looks more like the guy I met at debate. He's not, though. A glint of steel catches my eye and I spot a knife dangling from his hand.

"Sophia, what the hell happened?"

It's pretty obvious, isn't it? I give him a confused look. "Ever heard of a Ferrebat?" I look over at the creature lying on the ground and notice that its head and body have parted ways. Sour bile rises up my throat, but I swallow it down.

"Yes, I have. I've never seen one in person, though. They're pretty rare."

"Well, this one really likes me. Or...it did." I shudder again, realizing I killed it. Or mostly killed it? I've never killed anything bigger than a centipede. Those things are gross.

"Where were you hurt?"

His brows are drawn together in concern and he reaches out to me before pulling back, as if he's afraid to touch me.

"It got me in the arm with its filthy claws." I shudder and my mouth twists in disgust when I show him my torn jacket. "Then I hit the ground on my side when I took the thing down. Nothing major." I sit up and wince as I stretch out my side. I'm going to have a solid bruise there, but nothing feels seriously damaged.

His eyes rake over me. "Ok. We'll still need to check everything out, though. What did you do to it?"

I grope around until my fingers grasp the handle of the dagger I dropped when I passed out. His eyes light up with admiration when they fall on the knife.

"Nice. I didn't know you had any weapons on you." He searches me as if he's looking for more hidden weaponry.

I pat my side where the knife holster runs under my shirt. "Just this set. I've been working on my knife throwing. I didn't think my skills were up to the level of hitting a moving target hard enough to incapacitate it, so I let it get close and stabbed it."

"Impressive. Next time we have an argument, I'll keep that in mind."

"I wouldn't stab you over a trifling argument," I say. "Stabbing things hasn't exactly been necessary in my pre-Mage life. I've never killed an animal, that's for sure." A greasy feeling flows through me, and I wonder if the feeling of a blade sinking into flesh ever gets any easier. Not that I'd want it too. I need to go have a shower to wash the feeling of death off.

"Good to know. We should get you back to the car. We can check out those wounds and clean them up."

I give him a quizzical look when he pulls off his coat. "Um, whatcha doing?"

"Can't leave that for the mundanes to find." He drops his coat carelessly on top of the dead Ferrebat and gathers it up. My stomach flips again, but I push myself to my feet unsteadily.

"How come they've never discovered these things before? Logan never explained that one to me the last time I got attacked by one. The same one, maybe? He said they can track people." I started doing research about magical creatures in the library, but got distracted when I found the mark of the person who made the cuff, so I never got to the Ferrebats.

Garrett offers me a hand to help me up and his firm hold on my elbow supports my wobbly legs as we walk back to his car. I try not to look at the gruesome bundle in his other arm.

He gives me a curious look. "When did you get attacked by one before?"

"Remember the night we went on that date?" It's weird to talk about this.

"Yeah, I do." His words are almost carried away on the wind.

"That night. At my house. It was scratching at my window, and me being completely clueless went outside to see if I could scare it away. I thought it was a bat or something." I pause for a second, remembering what it was like before I knew about the Mages and my magical blood. "Obviously that didn't work. The thing bit my neck and Logan chased it off. It got away while he was trying to kill it. He was super pissed about that."

"I bet. He was at your house that night?"

"He was keeping watch." I bring the conversation back to my question. "Why do regular people not know about these things?"

"Oh, yeah. They're not natural wild creatures. Mages created them, and there's only a limited number, so they're all captive. And in addition to the tracking skills, they're kinda of like homing pigeons. They always return to their owner."

"Ok. Gotcha." Still seems a little weird to me that no human has caught one on film or seen one before, but it would probably be pretty easy to brush off or explain away as a bat or bird or something.

The trunk of his car pops up and he drops the dead animal in there with a sickening thud. He reaches to the back and pulls out a big red first aid kit.

"I didn't know you were such a boy scout."

He looks away. "I've had to learn to be prepared for anything. I don't stay in one place too long and I travel alone. I have to look after myself if anything happens."

Right. That reminds me of the revelations Charlotte told me about his past, and I look at him with fresh eyes. Sadness washes over me at the thought of him all alone.

"What?"

I look away, guilty that I dug up this personal information about him. I doubt he wants me to know. "Nothing."

The sun has lightened his eyes, bringing out golden specks that are currently piercing my soul. I shift under his gaze. "Get in the back seat. It'll be easier to fix you up back there."

We both slide into opposite sides and then he turns to face me. "Can I?" he asks, gesturing at my coat.

"Oh, yeah." I wince as I try to shrug out of my coat, and he helps me slide it off my arms.

He lets out a whistle. "Mind if I cut this?"

I look down at the sleeve of my favorite long sleeve shirt. It's one of those extra soft ones that feels like a hug when you wear it. The arm has several slashes where the claws tore it, and crimson bloodstains are seeping through. I guess it's a goner, anyway.

I shrug and give him a nod but turn my head so I don't have to watch the desecration.

A sense of déjà vu settles over me as Garrett wipes a swab over the puncture wounds on my arm. I dig my nails into the seat to avoid crying out at the sting. At least it's just my arm this time. Not like the vicious rip out of my neck from my last encounter with one of those things.

"Is that ok?"

"I'll survive." I'm trying to keep still and avoid eye contact while enduring the painful burn from the disinfectant. It's weird being this close to him. Even though we've been stuck inside a car together for the last day and a half, this is way more intimate.

I eye the small brown container he pulls out of the first aid bag. Looks like some sort of homemade remedy. My science brain balks at the idea of using natural medicine of any sort.

"What's that?"

"It's a healing paste."

"Did you make it?"

He snorts. "No. Not my specialty at all, but I know a healing Witch. It comes in handy in my line of work." He must catch the doubt in my eyes. "What?"

"I've never believed in any sort of natural remedies. Do you know what's in it? What's it supposed to do?"

"Right. It's easy to forget you didn't grow up with magic. I'm sorry. I don't know what's in it. I have used it before, though. It speeds up healing a bit and prevents infection. Who knows what germs were on those claws. I don't have to use it if you don't want me to."

I appreciate his concern for my feelings, but I've seen so many things that I would have thought were impossible by this point I guess a little healing potion won't hurt. "No, it's fine."

A sweet, and smoky smell with a slight hint of mint wafts out from the jar. I didn't even know how tight my shoulders were until they relax as the scent slides down my throat.

A cooling sensation spreads through me as he scoops a generous dollop of the milky paste onto my wounds before pulling out a roll of gauze wrap.

He finishes wrapping my arm up. "Can I take a look at your side?"

I hesitate a moment before lifting my shirt with my good arm. Goosebumps rise as the chilly air hits my bare skin. He lets out a low whistle and I jerk back when his freezing hand meets my rib cage.

"I'm sorry. Didn't mean to hurt you."

"No, it didn't hurt. Your hand was just cold."

"Well, sorry for that, too." He rubs his hands together and blows on them before he places it back on my side.

I wince at his touch in a couple of places.

"This is going to leave a nasty bruise. Any particularly painful spots, though?" he asks during his gentle probing.

"There are definitely some tender places, but nothing's broken."

"We'll get you some ice to put on there, but there're no cuts or anything, so I don't need to wrap it."

He drops my shirt back down and lifts his head to look at me. His eyes have darkened to the color of the woods in twilight, and I can't quite pull my gaze away. Some fleeting looking I can't decipher crosses his face before he pulls back.

"We should get out of here. Even though that thing won't be returning to its owner, they could be close by. I don't like staying in the same place for too long." He's got the door open before he even finishes his sentence.

I blink for a minute to catch up and take a minute to get myself out of the car. Not sure what happened there, but he's right. We need to keep going. My side protests as I bend down to get back in the front seat. His eyes dart to me once more but don't linger.

We're back on the road before I remember he was going to grab ice.

The silence is back to the level of awkward from the beginning of our trip and I'm not sure how to break it, so I jam my earbuds in and turn on my favorite science podcast.

CHAPTER 20
Logan

"You have got to be kidding me!" I kick the side of the old building as we leave. I know it's not going to do me any good, but that doesn't take away the satisfaction that accompanies the sharp pain in my foot.

"That's mature." I catch a look of judgement on Ivy's face before it flickers away, and I'm reminded of how long it's been since we spent time together. She's right. I should probably stop kicking and punching things to let out my frustrations. But all my pent up energy usually gets burned through my daily training schedule, so I'm buzzing with energy all the time right now.

My eyes run up and down her length, lingering for the first time since her return from the dead. I've spent a lot of time with her lately but have never let myself look at her for too long. As if I let my eyes linger on her, she'll evaporate into the mist like the ghost I thought she was. She's always been strong, but her softer edges have hardened to steel. The form fitting jeans that encase her legs show off the wiry definition she's gained. I wonder if I look different to her. Apparently, I don't act it.

"It's just..." The frustration is a tight ball threatening to explode out of my chest.

"I know. But there's nothing we can do about it, Logan. Unless you have some sort of mysterious access to car parts. The guy said he can't get it until tomorrow. We'll be on the road as soon as we can after that."

"Maybe my dad could..." I hate asking my dad for favors he'll only throw back in my face at some indeterminate future date, but this isn't for me. This is for Sophia. I'm not sure when or how she burrowed in so deep under my skin in such a short time, but there it is.

Ivy gives me a long look of understanding only a friend you've known forever is capable of. She knows all about my complicated relationship with my father. "Is that what you want to do?"

I shake my head. No. It will be fine. Sophia will be fine. As long as I keep repeating that to myself, maybe it will be true.

I start for the sidewalk at the edge of the shop's parking lot. The one good thing about this place is that it's right on the main road of this farm town. And by main road, I mean only road. Looks like this is about it. One strip of basic shops with handwritten signs in the windows and dusty panes surrounded by a whole lot of nothing. I don't even know where I'm going, but I let my long legs eat up the pavement. At the very least, we've got to find a hotel or whatever passes for one in this place.

"I saw a library when we were at the cafe. They can at least help us find a place to stay. Who knows? They might even have a computer we can use."

I glance dubiously around. We'll be lucky if this town even has telephone access. It is a good idea, though. I let Ivy lap me so she can lead me to this library. The rhythm of my stride is interrupted when I collide with Ivy's back.

"Whoa there." She throws a hand behind her to steady herself on me. "We're here."

"What? Where?" I squint against the sun glaring down on us and look around. There's a tiny red brick house to our right and another strip of storefronts, none of which have a library sign out front.

"Right there? Did your vision deteriorate while I was gone?"

I follow her hand that's pointing to the tiny house beside us. This time I notice the lettering above the front door that proclaims it as the Valmont Public Library. It's a joke compared to the public library back home and looks like a child's playhouse when I compare it to the massive, graceful building that houses the library on the NAMC compound. Thankfully, we live in an age where you can access all the world's information in one spot. It's called the internet and would be available at my fingertips if our phones hadn't gotten destroyed.

"Well, I guess you better hope they have a computer in there, because they sure can't fit more than a dozen books."

"Even if they had a large collection, I highly doubt they'd be useful to us. I'm sure we'll be fine here. If we can't find a place to stay, I'll make us a nice fort in the woods."

"As much fun as your forts are, Ivy, I doubt they'd be great shelter for us two grown adults to stay in overnight." When we were kids, she used to bend the plants to her will to create intricate leafy green shelters to play in. Definitely a dream come true for us back then. Not so practical for an overnight stay.

"I think you might be surprised." A gleam shines out of her melted chocolate eyes and her lips quirk up in a smile that issues me a challenge.

Right, her magic has grown in power. I had noticed a hint of that at my house when she first appeared back in my life. However, I was a little busy trying to grapple with her coming back to life to give that too much more brain space in the moment. Her vine action with the Mage back at the motel was also quite impressive.

A young woman with brown curls bouncing around her shoulders greets us at the small desk near the front of the library. I guess not all hot librarians hide behind severe buns and glasses.

"Hello." Her eyes travel my length in appreciation. "Where did you come from?"

Ivy inserts herself between us. "Hi, we're passing through, but we had some car trouble. Did you happen to have internet we could use?"

The librarian's red-lipsticked smile doesn't falter. "Of course we do, hon. Let me show you."

I scan the small room and spot a single computer perched in a cubicle in the back right corner of the empty library but follow her anyway. Maybe you need a special password or something to log on.

The beige desktop looks like it belongs a decade or two back, but it whirs to life when she touches a key. A lock screen comes up to enter a username and password, but there's a faded note taped to the top of the monitor that lists them in neat black marker, so it would not have been a problem to figure it out on our own. Top security here, for sure. Ivy slides into the wooden chair and types in the info.

"You got yourselves all set up. Anything else I can help you with today?"

I'm about to wave her away. "Actually, we need a place to stay tonight. Our car's not going to be ready until tomorrow. Is there a hotel around here anywhere?" I don't have a lot of hope. We may need to catch a ride to another town to find a place to stay.

She brightens up. "Of course. My sister owns a little B&B. She probably has a room for you." I'm sure she does. Who would come to a town like this willingly? "I can give her a call if you'd like."

"That would be great." My lips tilt up in a smile I've been told is charming. There hasn't been much use for it lately. I was getting crusty and closed off before I met Sophia, and she strangely finds my smirk just as intriguing as my charm. I think she can see right past the surface.

"Excellent. I'm Cindy..." She pauses and gives me a long look.

"I'm Logan. This is Ivy."

"Pleasure to meet you."

Ivy's been engrossed in her search while we chatted. "Whatcha got, Ivy?"

"Well, I did a search on this Lena we're meeting up with. I wanted to make sure it looks like she's on the up and up. Plus, I don't exactly want Cindy seeing the other stuff we'll be looking up. I can search for that after you're done with her. Oh, and don't mind me. I'll be here ignoring your flirting."

"Hey, I'm taking one for the team. If she wanted to flirt with you, I'd be all for that. She's going to find us a place to stay that's not on the ground. No offense, I'm sure your fort would provide ample shelter, but I'd rather have a bed and let's be honest, it is November. I don't want to wake up with frosty toes."

"True, proceed," Ivy says without glancing back at me. I can see Cindy's red dress approaching in my peripheral vision.

"Good news. She's got a room for you. It's got two beds, so you and your...friend should be ok." She glances at Ivy for a moment. Wow, she's pretty presumptuous, but I gotta give her credit. She's not afraid to go after what she wants.

"Great. Where's her place?"

I listen as she goes over the directions, which are basically two turns. It'll only take us a half hour to walk it, so we're good on that point. Not really a surprise, given the size of the town.

"If you're looking for some company for dinner, let me know." I fight the urge to jerk away when she places a neatly manicured hand on my biceps. I don't want to offend the woman, but I also don't want her touching me.

"We're good, but thanks for the offer. Ivy and I have some stuff we're working on."

"Ok, let me know if you need any help to find a specific book or section." I wonder what this woman would do if we actually told her what we were searching for. She'd call her sister, the police, who knows. On the plus side might hurry up that slow mechanic. They'd all want us out of town quick if we started talking spirits of dead Mages and portals to the Nether Realm.

"Will do." I turn back to Ivy until I feel her presence retreating.

"What's up with Lena? Anything shady? You think she might have been responsible for sending the wolves after us?"

"Nah, she looks shiny. Doesn't look like she even has any family that Zeus could threaten to force her hand." She pulls her lips together in a thin line.

"Right. We know Zeus has a habit of doing that. Look at Helena. So if she didn't give us away, who could it have been?" I don't like the other options. Not too many people know where we went and the few that do are back home where Sophia is. If anyone was going to go after her, now would be the prime time. While I'm away and she's cut off from her magic.

Ivy sighs. "I don't know Logan. Can you think of anyone back home who would betray you?"

My mind settles on Trey's face for an instant, but nah, he's way too squeaky clean for that. I still throw it out there for Ivy. "Trey?"

Her eyes widen. "Logan, no. He would never. I know you guys don't get along anymore, but he would never do that."

"I know." I run my hand through my hair and rock back on my heels. "Who else knows about Sophia, though? My family, your family. Sophia's Witch friend Charlotte." My eyes narrow. "That floppy haired coward."

She whirls around. "Who?"

"Garrett. That thief for hire. He knows about Sophia. He saw the whole thing go down before he performed his disappearing act. He knows she's cuffed and everything. It's gotta be him."

"Ok." Ivy knows the story of what happened when we rescued Liz and he took Sophia. She's heard of Garrett. I used to think he was merely a useless coward, then I learned he was a shady thief, too. "He took off, though, right? How would he know we went on this trip?"

"He's a tracker. A powerful one. He has an old family heirloom amulet he uses to track people and things. That's what makes him such a good thief, and that's why Charlotte brought him the last time. I didn't really think he would turn on Sophia. Maybe it was stupid of me, but I thought he actually had a thing for her. I should have known better."

Doubt muddies her eyes. "That still doesn't explain how he would know you left Sophia."

She's right. Unless. "What if he's working with someone on the inside? Maybe he shared her secret with someone on the compound? Maybe he has Mage friends." It doesn't fit quite right, though. I know he had a thing for her. I could see it in the way his eyes followed her when she was nearby. I didn't imagine that. Not to mention he's a loner. I don't even think he has any Witch friends, much less Mages.

"I don't know, Logan. It would be a problem if it was the case. If he can track us, there's no hiding from them."

"Yeah. I guess we just need to get this done and go back home as fast as possible. No stops after this unfortunate one. I'm going to shoot emails off to Sophia and Liz while we're here."

Ivy pushes away from the desk, letting me take a seat. "It's all yours. I'm going to see if this place has a bathroom I can use."

Once my account is open, I stare at the blank email trying to figure out what to write to Sophia. I can't express all the things I want to say so I keep it short and bland.

I hope everything is going ok there. Stay safe and look after yourself. Be home soon. Watch out and stay away from Garrett if he tries to contact you. I think someone may have betrayed our location and I'm worried about you there by yourself. He knows about your

secret too. We're fine, though. I don't want you to worry. Miss you.
Logan

I write and delete and rewrite the message way more times than I should have for that handful of inadequate sentences. Finally, I give in and hit send not having said any of the words I really wanted to say.

CHAPTER 21
Sophia

I stare out the window of the motel we stayed in last night watching a pinkish beam of light through the yellowed gauzy curtain. I don't want to touch it to shift it all the way open. Who knows what microbes make their home on it? Gross.

My phone is resting in my hand while I contemplate calling Mom to let her know I'm alive when its tinkling ring makes the decision for me. Yup, it's her.

"Hi, Mom."

I wince at the shrill tone that blasts me. "What do you think you're doing out there? Alone. In danger. These people have done everything to help you and keep you safe and here you are running off. Not to mention giving me a heart attack. I thought I raised you better than that. To be logical and sensible and to make reasoned decisions."

I jump in when she pauses to take a breath. "You did, Mom. And I know they were trying to keep me safe, but it obviously wasn't working. They got to me at the compound and they got to Logan, and I need to get to him and I need to get this cuff off sooner rather than later. It's vital. I'm sorry I left like that, but I am safe and I'm not alone."

"You're not alone? Who are you with? Don't tell me Charlotte came with you. Her grandmother will never let her see you again if you convinced her to come with you." I'm shocked to hear my mother's usually measured voice come out in such a jumble.

"Mom, it's not Charlotte."

"Xavier? It wouldn't surprise me if you convinced that boy to come with you, but he's not a part of your world." It hurts that she's already thinking of my world being separate from hers, but it's true. She's not a Mage or a Witch. She has no role in my new community. And while I guess that is the ultimate goal for all parents to raise their kids to be independent and then set off on their own to live their own lives, it's a little different in our case.

"No, not Xavier." The thought of him saddens me. I love, X. He's one of my best friends, and I've hardly talked to him since all this magic stuff went down.

"Well, then who? Did you make a new friend at the dorms you were staying in? Can you trust them?"

"No, Mom. Not from there." I hesitate for a moment, steeling myself for her reaction. "Remember Garrett?"

"Garrett? That boy you started dating? You went off alone with a boy you barely know? What's he got to do with any of this?"

"He's a Witch, Mom. Like Charlotte. He came out with her to track me down when I got...taken. He left after he dropped us off at the house. You know, after you were attacked." It's hard to even get those words out. I don't want to think about what could have happened to her. What could still happen to her, because of me and the danger I've brought into her life.

"You shouldn't be alone with him. You need to come home now, honey. Please." Her tone has gone pleading as she begs me.

"I can't, Mom. I love you, but I can't come home yet. I talked to Charlotte about Garrett. Don't tell her mom." I add in not wanting to get my friend in trouble. "He's had a lot of grief in his past, but I can trust him. When it came down to it, he came through for me." Luckily Mom doesn't know about the circumstances that brought us together initially or she'd lose her mind.

She sighs. "Please be safe. Call me if anything happens. Anything at all. I need to know right away. The Armstrongs will come right away. They'll drop everything. They said so." Her voice wavers and I know I need to hang up before she starts crying. I can't handle her tears right now. I need to keep myself together.

"I gotta go, Mom. I love you, but I have to do this. I promise I'll call if anything happens." No need for her to know about the Ferrebat incident. She's already worried enough. And what I learned from my research on them was that Ferrebats can only track you after they've had a taste of your blood. That one must have been the same one that attacked me before. At least it won't be coming after me again. I shudder, thinking about the dirt hitting the thing as we buried it in the woods off the side of the highway. Not sure if that thought is scarier or if it's that

Garrett had a shovel in his trunk. I guess it could be for the snowy weather we get here in the winter, but he didn't seem to be phased at all by the whole thing.

"Bye, sweetie."

"Bye, Mom."

I stare out the window for one more minute before I place my paltry items back in my backpack to go knock on Garrett's door. The door swings in before my fist can make contact, and I get a whiff of piney soap as I stumble into him. His hazel eyes meet mine and I watch as his Adam's apple bobs.

"We should get going. Wanna grab something quick to eat on the road?" His voice is gruff.

I nod, glad that he's ready to go. We agreed to an early start and didn't stop until close to midnight last night. He's got to be running on fumes at this point.

"I can drive for a bit if you'd like. You can nap in the car."

"Nah, I don't sleep in cars. I'll be fine. I'll grab a coffee at that diner, and we can grab a few snacks for the road." He points to the diner across the parking lot from the hotel

"If you say so, but let me know if you want me to take over." I've never driven for any length of time, but I imagine it must be difficult.

I take a tentative sip of the diner sludge once I'm settled in the car. Smells like the fumes from a diesel truck. "Mmm, this must be what burnt toast tastes like in liquid form." I make a face as the ashy flavor lingers on my tongue.

"Yeah, it sucks. Maybe I'll grab an energy drink at our next stop." He grimaces but takes another gulp. "I need to check the tracking before we get on the road. Make sure we're still on the right track."

He pulls out his crystal—amulet, is that what it is?—and does his Witchy magic thing. I watch in fascination as the thing lights up again before closing my eyes to avoid burning my retinas out. Fear twists my insides when I open them back up to find him scrunching his face in confusion.

"What? What is it? Is something wrong?"

"No, it's weird. It's like they haven't moved at all." My stomach drops out at his words and a ringing starts up in my head.

"Whoa, whoa. Deep breaths." His warm hand rubs my back, and he counts in and out with me. "I didn't mean to freak you out. He's not dead or anything, if that's where your mind went. I'd be able to tell."

Relief floods over me and the warmth returns to my fingers. "Oh. That's good."

"Maybe they got stuck somewhere. Unless that was their destination," he says.

"No, it should be another day and a half to get to the Mage."

"Well, it's good news for you. We should get there before lunch if they don't get a move on."

I note how he said good news for me. Since he never really wanted to be on this adventure with me in the first place, I would have thought it was good news for him, too. I don't want to invade his privacy, but this might be the last time I see him, since he has a habit of disappearing when things get dangerous, and I'm pretty sure they're about to get real dangerous. I study his profile. He looks like a mixture of the Garrett I met at debate and the Garrett who came to help rescue me. He's wearing the thief-on-a-day-off casual long-sleeved black shirt and black track pants rather than preppy clothes, but his hair isn't slicked back, so the beachy mix of blond and brown falls over his forehead in a wave. He looks more natural like this. Like this is the guy he was meant to be, before his life was interrupted by sorrow. I know the feeling. I can't understand the depths of anguish he must have gone through, but it clearly changed him.

Once we're on the road, I can't hold it in anymore. "Garrett, I know."

"What? What do you know?"

"About your family."

His already chiseled features harden to stone, and his knuckles on the steering wheel whiten. He doesn't say a word, though, and I leave him alone. He needs time to process this information, and if he decides he doesn't want to talk about it, I'm not going to push him. I probably shouldn't have said anything at all, but I know how important it is to talk about your grief. It took me a long time and lots of therapy to come to that place myself, and I'd be willing to bet he hasn't talked to anyone about his losses ever.

I don't know how much time has passed, but I'm about to put my earbuds back in when he speaks. His voice comes out so low I almost don't catch it. "They're all gone, Sophia. It's in the past. It happened and there's nothing I can do about it. This is my life now."

"I wasn't trying to get you to change your life. I just wanted to let you know that I'm here for you if you want to talk. I know my experience is nothing like yours, but I know how much it hurts to lose a parent and I'm here for you if you want to talk."

I lift a hand to reach out for him, pulling it back before it connects.

The car shudders as he pulls over to the side of the road and yanks the emergency brake on. His shoulders tense and I jump when he slams his hand into the steering wheel, setting off the blaring car horn.

A vein pulses in his temple as he sits there, stiff and still, as if he's made of clay. I stare at him until it looks like he's not going to explode, and then I unsnap the seatbelt. I wince at the loud click that breaks the silence, but he doesn't even twitch, so I slide a little closer, wrapping an arm around his shoulder.

He swallows hard. "My little sister...she had her whole life ahead of her and it was all ripped away. So stupid, so useless. And I wasn't there for them. Sometimes I wish I had been there with them. It couldn't be worse than this." He's staring blankly through the windshield.

"I know it changes nothing and the words don't mean much, but you couldn't have done anything. You couldn't have saved them. It was horrible and senseless, but it's not your fault."

"I know. I know it, but I still feel guilty. Every day. So I do what I do. My mom. She'd be disappointed in me, but she isn't here, is she?" His features twist and his voice rises in anger at his mom. I get it. She left him. It wasn't her fault either, but he still sometimes blames them for leaving him behind. I feel the same way about my dad, and then guilt rides me for feeling that way at all.

"It won't ever be ok. We both know that, but you can still be whoever you want to be. Whoever you were meant to be. You shouldn't let their deaths dictate the course of the rest of your life."

His death grip on the steering wheel eases up, and he finally turns to look at me. The weight of grief is still heavy in his eyes, but the anger seems to have burnt itself out.

He gives me a nod. "We should head out now. We can still catch up to them in a couple of hours if we make good time. And I'm going to come all the way with you. I'll come with you to the Mage to get the cuff removed. It's the least I can do." He turns back to the road and falls silent not seeming to expect a reply after his declaration.

I nod, pull my seatbelt back in front of me, and we hit the road in a silence that isn't quite so weighty.

CHAPTER 22
Logan

This place is messed up. Apparently, they couldn't get the part in like they promised. I almost pull the guy over the counter to give him a shake, but I don't think that'll make a part appear out of thin air. The guy is oily and not in the works-under-greasy-cars kinda way. He makes me feel dirty just looking at him, so I can't imagine Ivy is appreciating his lecherous stares. She could have waited outside, but she chose to come in. Probably wise, since her presence reminds me not to pull a knife on the sleazy mechanic.

I know I'll regret it before I even pick up the phone, but I'm going to have to call Dad. I've destroyed two cars in the last few weeks. While neither was my fault, it won't stop him from blaming me. "I have to call for a new vehicle."

"Want me to call for you?" Ivy asks putting a tentative hand on my shoulder. Since she came back into my life, she's been careful about avoiding physical contact. She knows I've moved on and I don't know how she's feeling, but I imagine she's well over my stupid ass. She deserves better than me and my ghosting, anyway. Sophia does as well, but I don't think I could force myself to let her go. I hope I've at least learned a few things from the way I handled things with Ivy, and I'll have an easier time being straight up about my feelings now. My father didn't exactly set the example of a man who could express his feelings. Vulnerability was a weakness to him, but I don't want to spend the rest of my life like that.

"That would only make it worse," I say as we walk out the front door.

"Um, should we ask to use his phone?" Her neat bob brushes her shoulders when she looks back at the shop.

I bark out a laugh. "Don't think he's going to be too into doing me any favors."

"I guess we should walk back into town then to find a phone we can use."

"Yeah."

Frustration is building with each obstacle that gets in our way. I hope Sophia got my email. I don't know what exactly possessed me to send that warning. When I was younger, the random awareness of her used to itch at me and drove me nuts. I was so angry our parents tied us together. Now, now I'd give anything to feel that tingle at the back of my neck, letting me know she's close. It wouldn't help me from this far away but knowing that it was there would be reassuring.

The surroundings are starting to become familiar as we travel along the dusty sidewalk. Some small towns are all cutesy and manicured. This one looks like someone left it to fade away. There are a couple of faded wreaths hanging from dented lampposts, but that seems to be the extent of the effort they've made to celebrate the season. Makes no difference to me either way, but it would be nice if we could have some sort of normalcy celebrate the holidays with our families. Not looking promising at this point.

A car approaches a little too fast from behind us and it trips my alarm, sending me into fight mode. Ivy squares up beside me as we turn to face the potential enemy in the car that's squealed to a stop next to us. I've got a dagger ready to fly from my hand before the passenger door flies open. I jerk out of the throw at the last minute and instead of slicing cleanly through the air toward its target, it flies wildly to the side, clattering to the ground. My heart leaps in hope for a moment before suspicion takes over. This has to be an illusion. No way is Sophia here. My Sophia.

I've never hesitated like this, and fear grabs hold. She makes me vulnerable. The small body hurtles into my arms, and I'm knocked back a step, but my arms come up automatically to grab her. Her body is solid under my hands. She feels real. A hint of vanilla drifts to me and I can't help myself. I lean in and inhale her hair. Smells like her. Everything is right and everything is wrong all at the same time. What is she doing here?

"Sophia?"

"Logan! You're ok. I was so worried when Garrett said you hadn't moved." Wait a minute. Did she just say Garrett? I pull my nose out of her hair. Over her shoulder I can see the car she showed up in and sure enough, there he is leaning against it with one leg crossed over the other. He gives me an insolent smile and wave.

"What's he doing here?" I force the words out between clenched teeth.

"He gave me a ride."

"Sophia, he could be the one who gave us away. Didn't you get my email?"

"No, what email?"

Flames ignite within me as I let her slide down my body, but I try to shove those thoughts out of my head. Not the time or place. I'm reluctant to let go of her now that I have her back with me, so I keep her hands clasped in mine. "Ivy and I were trying to figure out who could have given away our location. Since hardly anyone knows about your powers or where we were heading, there's a limited choice of traitors. He's on that list. Top of it if you ask me."

She arches a brow at me. "If he was planning to betray me, I wouldn't be here. He could have already given me up."

She has a point that I'm not quite willing to accept yet, because if it wasn't him, then I don't know who it was. It has to be someone close to us since her Archimage status is a closely guarded secret. "Maybe he's going to give us all up."

"He's not like that. He helped me. He helped me get here. He helped me find you. He didn't even have to answer my phone call, but he did."

I'm letting the presence of that sneaky thief cloud my thoughts. Sophia is here. She's here, out of the safety of the compound. A target for anyone to find. "What are you doing here? Why aren't you safe back at the NAMC?"

A shadow clouds her amber eyes and her brow pinches together. "That's the thing. It wasn't safe there. I got attacked, and I ran."

"WHAT?" I wince when she jumps at my shout. "Where was, Liz?"

"Someone attacked me when I was leaving the library. It wasn't her fault. I snuck out on her, but honestly, if you thought it was so safe there, why did I have a bodyguard?"

"That was just a precaution, but apparently a necessary one." How could that have happened, and who am I going to have to kill? "So you ran, and you called this guy?" I look over at Garrett with disdain.

"No, I called your mom and texted Liz. She picked the two of us up and took us back to your house. But when I heard what happened, I knew this was where I needed to be. Especially since no one could get a hold of you since your phone exploded along with your car!"

"You should have stayed there, Sophia."

A hint of steel enters her gaze. "Would you have stayed, Logan?"

"No, but..."

"There are no buts. Someone attacked us both on the same night. They're trying to get to us when we're apart. We're better and safer together. I knew I couldn't ask Liz to take me, or Charlotte. They're still in school. I couldn't do that to their parents. Plus I couldn't deal with the thought of putting them in danger."

"But you have no problem doing it to your own mother? And my parents. You may not have known them for very long, but they've been looking out for you since you were born. My mom cares about you like you're another daughter. Think of how they're feeling right now? Not to mention you're still in school, too." Should I feel bad about trying to lay the guilt on her? Maybe. Am I going to do it, anyway? Yes.

"Yeah, kind of like I felt having no idea where you were or if you were ok. I get it. Mom is freaking out and I feel bad enough about that, but this is where I needed to be. She's safer when I'm away from her. And school doesn't matter at this point. I only need a couple of credits to graduate. I've been fast tracking and taking extra courses all through high school. If I have to delay finishing a little bit, it will be fine." I don't like the wistful look that's tinged her eyes with sadness. She's smart and driven. At least she was until she fell into this whole magical mess. I want to make everything right for her and I can't. I ache for her.

"Still doesn't explain how you ended up here with him." I toss my head at Garrett.

"I didn't have any other way of finding you. He could track you." The light bulb flashes on. With no way of contacting me, this was her solution. I have to give her points for creativity. I don't love how she went off with him, but she seems to have arrived unharmed. It looks like my suspicions were accurate. He does have a thing for her, and he probably didn't betray us to Zeus.

I don't know what to do. We're closer to the Mage than home. It's better she stays here with us, but I don't love the idea of her out in the open.

I melt into her as she slides her arms around my waist and tilts her chin up. The light is bringing out the sparkle of gold in her eyes and her lips are slightly parted, inviting me in for a kiss. I'm about to act on my desire when she speaks up. "It's fine. He's already helped me bury a body."

I pull away from her. Her lips have twisted up into a playful smile. How does she look playful after dropping that bomb on me? "What are you talking about?"

"Oops, um yeah. I got attacked by a Ferrebat at a rest stop. But you would have been so proud of me. I fought it off!" She bounces on her toes.

"You fought it off?"

"Yeah, with my mad knife skills." She whips out a dagger, and the sunlight bounces off it as she brandishes it at me.

I close my hand over her delicate wrist. I'd like to avoid an accidental stabbing if I can help it. "Be careful with that thing. So you killed it?"

"Well, I knocked it out. Garrett finished it off. Then we had to bury it in the woods. That was kind of awful."

Who is this girl? "Fighting it off, no problem, but burying it was beyond you?" I laugh. "I think I'm impressed and terrified at the same time."

"Yeah. Not my thing. To be fair I passed out after I stabbed it. The blood." Her lip curls up as she shudders.

A picture of her lying alone and vulnerable sucker punches me in the gut. I glance at Garrett still leaning on the car. "Where was Floppy while this was going down?"

"He was getting us coffee. I wanted some privacy to call Charlotte. Also stop being a jerk. He has a name. When he found me, he sliced the thing's head off." Great, now they're road trip best friends and he came to her rescue. Unfortunately, I can't be mad at him for that.

"What do I care about his name? This is the last time I'm going to see him. Hopefully forever." I give him a wave. "Not so nice seeing you. Hope to never repeat the experience."

"You're going to have to get over it. He's coming with us. He wants to help."

"No."

"Not your decision. This is a democracy, not a dictatorship. Hi, Ivy. Sorry if I was ignoring you."

Ivy was standing off to the side letting us have our catch up and conversation while giving Garrett the side eye. She's probably been influenced by my opinions, but she takes a step closer at Sophia's greeting. "Hi, Sophia."

"Ivy, this is Garrett, he's a..." she looks around as if to make sure no one is listening, but still drops her voice to a whisper. "Witch. Garrett, Ivy."

"Nice to meet you." Ivy gives me a searching look.

"Ah, the infamous Ivy, come back to life. Nice to meet you." He takes a few strides over to our group and encloses Ivy's hand in his for a shake. "How's that working out for you?" He looks at me after he takes a step back.

"None of your business."

"Logan, enough. And you," she turns to Garrett, "don't wind him up. Garrett offered to help. He's going to come with us the rest of the way."

"That's a hard no. I'm not going anywhere with him," I say.

"The feeling is mutual, bro, but I told Sophia I'd help, so I'm going to."

Did he just call me bro? This is not the preppy guy that had the nerve to take Sophia out on a date. "Like I said, hard no."

"Logan, don't be unreasonable. An extra pair of hands will help in any fights we get into. You can fight, can't you?" Ivy asks.

"Of course. I've got many skills." His bobs an eyebrow at Ivy.

"We can't trust him. He'll sell us out to the highest bidder at the first chance he gets. That's what he does." How is no one else getting this?

"I can trust him, and you can trust me. That's going to have to be enough, Logan. He wants to come with us, and I want him to come. This is happening whether you like it or not." Sophia sure can be stubborn when she wants to be.

"Plus, there's the whole car situation." Ivy pipes in with that useful information.

Right, the car. Our car is stuck. Who knows how long that shifty mechanic is going to take to fix it. I hate to admit it, but this would solve that problem. The thought of getting into a car with him is not a good one, but Sophia seems determined to adopt the stray and form some sort of ragtag superhero team or something.

"Is that why you've been here? I freaked out when Garrett said you hadn't moved for so long. I thought you were..." Sophia trails off, and I pull her back in rubbing her back in soothing circles to wipe the fear off her face.

"Our replacement car broke down. The mechanic said he could get the part today, but he was stalling us again this morning. I was about to call Dad to get another ride sent here." That lifts one weight off my shoulder. If I don't have to call him to get a new car, then he'll be none the wiser about our third car incident.

"Fine." I force the words out through my teeth.

"Fine, what?" Garrett asks. I want to punch the smug look off his face, but the girls both seem to be onboard with this situation, so I exercise the steely self-control that my father tried to instill in me.

"You can come."

Garrett opens his mouth like he's about to poke at me again but squeezes his lips together after he gets a dirty look from Sophia. Instead, he slides into the driver's seat. My head swings from Ivy to Sophia. I need Sophia next to me, so I can reassure myself she's really here, but Ivy has never even met Garrett before. I'd hate to subject her to his presence for the long drive ahead. We've got at least a day of driving left if we make a stop to sleep somewhere. I'm surprised how fast Sophia and Garrett got here. If she got attacked the same night as us and then went to my parents' house for a bit, they must have driven well into the night to catch up to us. At least that means they didn't stay long in a hotel. Red rage spreads through me at the thought of the two of them in a hotel room together.

Ivy's dark chocolate eyes soften as she looks at me. "I'll sit in the front. You two need to catch up."

"I can sit in the front with Garrett. That might be weird for you, Ivy." Sophia volunteers, but her eyes stray back to me.

"It's fine. I'm glad you got here safe."

I don't wait for any further prompting, slipping in behind Ivy. My knees dig into the back of her seat. They did not make this car for anyone over six feet. I get a little relief when she slides the seat up a bit, and then forget all about the discomfort once Sophia slides over into the middle seat and tucks herself under my arm. This isn't over yet, but we are getting closer and things will be better once we get that cuff off her and she has access to her powers again. Of course, that will open us up to another set of problems, but we'll figure that out when we get there. My plan right now is getting that infernal thing off of her and getting her somewhere safe. After that. I'd really like to track her uncle down and remove him from the equation altogether, but we'll see about that.

CHAPTER 23
Sophia

My eyes are glued shut, but when I open them, it's still dark and dull aches in my neck and my arm are warring for dominance. The events of the last couple of days come rushing back to me. Ferrebat, Garrett, Logan, and Ivy. I'm wrapped in a familiar woodsy scent and a pair of powerful arms, and my pillow rises and falls in a steady rhythm.

"Wake up, Soph."

I lift a sluggish hand to cover my yawn. "Where are we?"

"We stopped at a motel to get some sleep tonight. If we leave early, we should be able to make it there by early afternoon tomorrow."

"Ok." I can't stop yawning, so my voice comes out in a high-pitched squeal.

"Come on, kitty." I missed the sound of Logan's laugh, but not so much the ridiculous nicknames.

"Nope."

"What?"

"You're not calling me that." I'm too tired to glare at him. Now that I think about it, my whole body is a little achy. Kind of like I have the flu. I better not be getting sick.

"Fine, but one of these days I'm going to find a nickname that you're cool with."

"Keep dreaming. Unless it's something super fierce. We should probably call Liz to check in." Not to mention our parents, but the thought of having a conversation with either of our mothers right now is pretty unappealing.

"We should. At least we have a phone now that you're here. I'll call. You look wrecked, Sophia. Are you feeling, ok?" He tightens his arm around me when my shoulders shudder in a momentary shiver.

"I'll be fine. Probably just tired."

His look lets me know he sees through my lie, but I can't quite muster up the energy to put on a better face. He helps me out of the car, and we meet Garrett and Ivy by the front door. I'm leaning heavily on Logan.

Garrett dangles a couple sets of keys on red plastic key chains at us. "We can get to the rooms from there." I stare in defeat at the long, metal staircase that he's pointing at. I was fine yesterday. I don't know where this lethargy came from.

My foot feels ten times heavier than usual and my toe catches on the first step causing me to stumble. Logan's hands snap out closing around my arms to keep me on my feet. He helps me up the rest of the way. My stomach roils at the mildewy stench that greets us when the door opens, but I swallow the sensation down and collapse on a bed.

"Is she going to be ok?" "If I found out you did anything to hurt her, so help me!" I hear voices fading in and out around me as I'm dragged under.

CHAPTER 24
Logan

As soon as the sky lightens from navy blue to the palest of gray, I bang on the connecting door to Garrett's room to drag him out of bed and then wake up Ivy a little more gently. I got zero sleep last night. I spent it taking turns sitting in a chair beside Sophia's bed and pacing. Fear had me in its grip as she moved and cried out all night in a restless sleep. I can't imagine it was very restful.

Once every one else is up and ready to go, I lean right up to Sophia's shell of an ear. "Get up, princess. Time to go."

Her mouth moves in a cute chewing motion, and she groans before muttering. "Told you not to call me that."

A hint of a smile turns up my lips, chasing away the worry for a moment. She's still in there. "Still have to get up."

She drags herself up as Ivy walks out of the bathroom fully dressed, other than the white towel knotted around her hair.

"Can I shower first? I feel super gross."

"Of course. Let me know if you need a hand."

"I'm capable of showering myself, thanks." The words are hers, but the fire is missing from her tone. I'm used to more spunk from my girl.

Ivy towel dries her hair and starts brushing it out while Sophia is getting ready. Once the water in the shower is running, she gives me a serious look. "Is she going to be ok?"

"Yes. She has to be. It's got to be the cuff draining her. I just didn't expect the effects to come on so suddenly like this. I thought it would be a slow process."

"Me too. Maybe it works different because her powers are different. You know her Archimage powers might be stronger and therefore the cuff is feeding off her magic faster? I don't know. Just a thought. I really have no idea how this works."

"No one does. That's the problem. Because those tyrants in the past locked up or put Archimages to death, there's not a lot of research on how different they are from other Mages. We don't know enough about them."

"Yeah. Some days I wonder how Mages in the past could have been so awful and done such terrible things to each other, but then I see the things that are still going on and realize we're not so different now. We still do terrible things to each other and to the Witches. And it won't stop until people are made to pay for their crimes." Ivy's voice has risen with her passion. It's been so long since I heard her get fired up on a subject like this.

"I guess." I agree with some of what she's saying, but I'm more concerned with getting Sophia looked after right now.

"When we get this all sorted out, we can work on that agenda. With Sophia on our side, we'll be unstoppable." I don't like the fervent heat that is shining in Ivy's eyes. Is she just in this to use Sophia for her own ends? I know Ivy has always been passionate about making political waves on the magical council, but I thought maybe she'd eased up on her goals a little since they ended with her running for her life and faking her own death. I'm being ridiculous. Ivy would never use someone like that. The girl I grew up with was sweet and compassionate underneath her ideals.

"Sure. I think there are a lot of obstacles in our way before we get anywhere close to that. Getting the cuff off is only the first step."

We both fall quiet as the shrill scream that accompanies the shower running in this hole eases up. I can't wait to get this done and get home.

Sophia looks a little better when she emerges from the bathroom, but my urgency doesn't ease up.

"Ok, let's go."

Both the girls are giving me weird looks. "Were you planning on changing?" Sophia is the one to put words to the looks.

I glance down at myself. I'm a mess. I'm wearing the same dark jeans as yesterday with a wrinkled shirt, and I wince when my hand hits my hair. It's a mess too. I clear my throat. "Yeah, give me a minute."

I dart into the bathroom and clean myself up. The least I can do is change my clothes. Good thing neither of them is afraid to call me on it.

"Of course," Sophia says when I reemerge within five minutes.

"What?" I'm confused. They called me out on my disreputable appearance, so I got changed and freshened up. What did I do wrong?

"You looked like crap. Went to the bathroom for five minutes. Got changed, and that." She gestures at me.

I still don't get it. I look down at myself. I look almost the same as before. I changed the jeans out for some gray sweatpants with a dark blue athletic shirt and ran my fingers through my hair. No big deal.

"Guys." A giggle escapes Ivy and Sophia joins in. I'm happy to see Sophia has definitely perked up, but I still don't understand what they're going on about.

Garrett swings his door open before my fist lands on it. He gives me a nod and for the first time, we're on the same page. Get on the road and get out of here as quickly as possible.

Sophia is chatty and cheerful for the first couple of hours on the road. We catch up on each other's adventures. I'm still turning it all over in my head. Who gave us away?

"Did you tell anyone about the Archimage thing? Or our trip?" Maybe she let something slip.

Her mouth falls open into an 'O'. "No, but I almost forgot."

I jostle her as I bolt upright. "What?"

"Michelle. She touched me. I don't know what I was thinking about at the time, but she may have seen something to do with my Archimage powers or the cuff. I don't know how I forgot about that."

"Michelle...Lawrence. Right? She's a Psych. What happened?"

"When you were still there, she was expressing some interest in you that I wasn't down with. She almost got me to touch her when we ran into the hall the one day, but Liz stopped me and explained about her powers. The next time I ran into her, I couldn't stop it. She was definitely in contact with me long enough to see some of my thoughts."

"That's not good. Maybe I should call Mom. See if she can dig around a bit. Maybe talk to Michelle's parents." I'm worried about what she could have seen, and also how many other people she told. Our secret could be all over the compound by now if she spread it around.

"Yeah." Her soft body settles back into my side, and I'm about to ask her another question when a small snore slips from her. Good, she can rest as much as she needs until we get there.

I refuse to leave her side, so I stay in the car when we stop for a break, ignoring the red hot needles that have engulfed the arm she's resting against. I don't want to move it to disturb her rest.

"Got some snacks." Some bags of chips and convenience store sandwiches come flying at me when Garrett and Ivy get back in.

"Sophia, we've got some food." I give her a shake, but she doesn't wake up. I leave her be as we get back on the road.

I take a few bites of my cardboard roast beef sandwich before tossing it aside. I'm too wound up to eat. Sophia is shivering and muttering again like she was last night. Every small movement of discomfort from her tightens my shoulders and sets off another wave of jitters through me.

"Can you wake up? Please. You need to at least drink some water or you're going to get dehydrated." I give her a squeeze and a bit of a shake until she opens glassy eyes. How has it gotten this bad this quickly?

"Logan?" She blinks blearily at me.

"Come on. Can you drink some water, please?" I offer her my water bottle and she lifts a hand to grab it, but gives up halfway as if her arm has grown too heavy.

"Here." I lift it to her lips and tilt it back until she takes a few swallows.

"I'm tired." She drops her listless head back on my shoulder.

"Can't you drive faster?" I meet Garrett's eyes in the rearview mirror. I don't imagine his pale skin or blank eyes come from exhaustion. He's as worried as I am, and it shows.

"I mean, I can, but if we get pulled over, I can't do anything about it. I don't have any spells to sweet talk us out of that. I don't think we can afford the delay." His pained eyes flick back to Sophia again.

I sigh. He's right. It would not be helpful if he got his car seized for stunt driving. If only we had a Psych with us, they could talk any cop that pulled us over out of it, but I highly doubt any of our skills will do anything except get us into more trouble. Threatening the mundane police with fireballs or lightning is frowned upon.

"I got you, Sophia. We'll be there soon." I rub her arms to keep her warm as she mumbles again.

When the agonizing ride is finally over we pull into the driveway of the neat blue bungalow with white trim where Lena Krause lives. Our trip took us farther North, so flurries whip around us in a white sheet and a few inches of snow blanket the ground in a soft sheet of white. I pull my arm out from under Sophia, who is still in her feverish sleep, and shake it out as the feeling floods back in a rush of painful tingles. I unfold myself from the cramped backseat. I stand for a minute with the door open, hesitating about whether to pick up Sophia and bring her with us or assess the danger level first. We don't know this Mage and have no clue if anyone might have gotten to her. I find I can't leave her behind, so I scoop her up in my arms. Her head lolls onto my shoulder, but her arms slide around my shoulders, so I take that as a good sign.

Garrett heads for the front door, but I can see his right hand hovering over his hip. He's got some steel hidden somewhere, and I'm glad he's prepared for any situation. Ivy hangs back to walk with me up the path. They've cleared the snow from the driveway and walkway. She was expecting us, but we're probably early. She better be home. I don't think I can take it if I have to watch Sophia suffer any longer. The red sedan sitting in the driveway is a good sign. Hopefully this will all go down smoothly.

Garrett rings the doorbell, and we're waiting for what feels like a lifetime. I'm about to reach out and hammer on the door when it swings open revealing a middle-aged woman with long dark hair. She narrows her eyes at us for a moment until they fall on Sophia in my arms.

"Oh my goodness. Come in."

Ivy and I pile through the front door, but I jerk my head at Garrett and he seems to read my signal to keep watch outside. I don't like being defenseless in a strange Mage's house with Sophia in my arms, but I know Ivy's got my back. Garrett is not the ideal choice to keep watch, but he hasn't turned on us yet and he seems to have some sort of affinity for Sophia. He might stab me in the back if he could, but he's not going to hurt her.

We pass through the narrow front hall into a cozy family room with burgundy floral wallpaper and a large fireplace.

"Follow me. You can put her down on the couch in here." Her assortment of bangle bracelets clanks together as she gestures at the beige couch.

I lay Sophia down and smooth the damp hair off her forehead so I can drop a soft kiss on it. Her forehead is scorching.

"I'm Lena, you must be Ivy, and…?" She turns to me.

"Logan. Logan Armstrong." I don't usually like throwing my family's name around, but we are an old family with a lot of clout, so I put a little extra emphasis on my last name. I want her to know I'm not someone to mess with. Her eyes widen a touch. "This is Sophia."

"How long has she been in this condition?" asks Lena.

"It started today. She was a little tired yesterday, but she went downhill fast."

Doubt has clouded Lena's face. "And how long has she had this cuff on?"

"It's been a couple of weeks now."

Her faded blue eyes narrow behind a pair of round silver glasses. "Who put it on her in the first place?"

I exchange a look with Ivy. There is no way we're sharing details of everything that's gone down lately with this stranger. We have no idea what side she'd fall on in the let's-kill-the Archimages debate.

"We're not sure who it was. He attacked her and then vanished after he put it on and we haven't been able to track him down yet." I know this all sounds super shady, but we can hardly explain about how I got the cuff on the black market, and it got used against us by Sophia's uncle who wants to steal her powers.

Lena looks at Sophia again and I can see worry twisting her features as her eyes dart back to me. They linger with skepticism. She's wondering if maybe I'm the enemy. She seems reassured though when she looks to Ivy again.

"Please, I'm begging you, get it off her. I can't stand seeing her like this." I'll resort to begging for Sophia. No problem there. "We'll pay you whatever you want."

"I don't want payment. I'll take the cuff back, though."

I've already paid the exorbitant fee to the sketchy contact that got it for me when I didn't return it, so that's no deal breaker for me. "Fine by me. Get it off her. Please." I add that on. I'm getting to the desperate point, but I really don't want to offend the one woman who can help Sophia.

"Ok. You all should stand back a bit. Some of her magic might come out in a small burst when it's released."

Ivy takes a few steps back. "No way. I'm not leaving her." I place my hand on her leg and stand my ground.

She clucks at me. "Don't say I didn't warn you."

I watch in fascination as the woman pulls a blue crystal from her pocket and mutters some words under her breath. The crystal glows and she runs it over the hated cuff resting on Sophia's wrist. The glow transfers to the cuff and I hear a click before I'm blinded by an explosion of light and all the air is knocked out of my lungs as I'm hurled backward. Then everything goes black.

CHAPTER 25
Sophia

A burst of light startles me out of the stupor I've been in all day. I jolt up with a rush of energy flowing through my entire body. My body is tingling all over and my skin is too sensitive, as if I jumped into an icy lake.

Where am I? I drag my eyes open, and the first thing I see is Garrett running toward me. A wild energy shines from his flushed face.

"Sophia!"

"Garrett. Where am I? What's happening?"

He pulls me into a tight hug. I flinch back in surprise before peering over his shoulder to take in the rest of the room. Logan, Ivy and a lady I've never met are lying on the floor of a small room with a tv and a large assortment of plants. I'm in someone's house.

"Are you ok?" He runs his hands down my arms checking and I gasp when he gets to the Ferrebat wound. He lets go. "Sorry. Is it off? What happened?" I follow his gaze down to my now bare wrist. There's an angry red welt where the silver cuff was previously resting.

"The cuff. It's gone. My magic." I close my eyes and take an assessment. That overwhelming tingle is my magic flowing through me again. I never thought I'd be so relieved to have it back. And the bond. I find the place inside where that rests and an awareness of Logan is back. He's fine, but wait a minute. "Logan." I pull out of Garrett's arms and slide off the couch. My legs threaten to give out under me, but I push them forward.

I drop to my knees beside Logan, leaning in until his warm breath brushes my cheek, easing my mind. "Logan. Are you ok?" When he doesn't wake up right away, I sent a pulse of magic through the bond. My limbs go weak with relief when his azure eyes meet mine. The smile that spreads across my face probably looks a bit unhinged.

"Sophia." He sits up, dragging me onto his lap. His hands run up my arms and back in a continuous motion that sends shivers through my sensitive skin. His forehead drops to touch mine. He was already broadcasting his relief and happiness through the bond, so the skin contact only intensifies the sensation of our shared emotions.

I glance back at Garrett, who's towering over us with his arms folded across his chest. "Um, what happened and where are we?"

"We're at Lena Krause's house. What do you remember last?"

I pick through my foggy thoughts to see if I can untangle them. "We stayed at that stinky motel. I showered this morning, and we left. What time is it?"

"It's one o'clock. You only lost a few hours."

I blink a few times as I process the information.

A groan comes from my left and I see Ivy sitting up, followed by the lady that must be Lena Krause.

I wince under the hateful glare she gives me. "What are you?"

My eyes widen. "What?"

"You're no ordinary Mage. What kind of black deal with the spirits have you made? Get out of my house now and don't come back."

I flinch away from the anger in her eyes.

"NOW." She staggers up and grabs a long, thin metal object off the wall. It looks like some sort of weapon. Before she can do anything with it, everyone has sprung to their feet forming a shield in front of me. Garrett has a 12-inch blade in his hands, Ivy has pulled out her daggers and a ball of fire casually spitting flames balances on Logan's palm.

"Go on, Sophia. We're coming behind you." Logan says without turning his back to the Mage.

I whip my head around searching for the door in the unfamiliar house and then back steadily toward it. My three protectors don't ease up their fighting postures until we've made it safely out the front door. Lena doesn't follow us, so we settle into the car and Garrett screeches out of the driveway wheeling down the street.

We've been breaking all the speed limits for a half an hour before anyone breaks the tense silence. Logan tucked me under his arm when we got in the car and hasn't let go. As much as I crave being in his arms and back together, we need to figure out our next move. I squirm out of his embrace but slide my hand into his. I know where he's coming from. After being separated, I need the physical contact to reassure myself that we're still together.

"What exactly happened back there?" I ask, looking at Logan.

"You'd been out of it all morning. We got to Lena's house after lunchtime. She seemed nice enough and was willing to help you. She said there might be a small burst of magic when she removed the cuff. Anyway, the small burst of magic was like a giant magic bomb thanks to your extra kick of power, and it knocked us all out."

"Except Garrett." I glance up at him, but his hooded gaze is focused on the road, his mouth set in a grim line.

"We left him outside to keep watch," Ivy said.

Got it. "And that was it. She totally freaked out when she woke up. You don't think she knows I'm an Archimage, do you?"

"I hope not. I can't imagine that would be the first conclusion she would jump to, but it's possible. She suspects something's different about you, though."

"She said something about a deal with spirits or something. What did she mean by that? Like a ghost or something?"

Ivy swivels around from the front. "Kind of. There's a Nether Realm. I guess it would be kind of like what you know of as Hell. Spirits of Mages that have gone dark go there after they die. Mages have been known to make deals with them to increase their power. That's actually what we think Zeus has been doing. Traveling around through portals to the Nether Realm."

The Nether Realm. Well that's something new to research.

My skin goes cold, and I squeeze Logan's hand for reassurance when I notice him and Ivy glancing back behind us as if they're expecting a pursuit as Garrett speeds along. The realization of why would have knocked me flat if I wasn't already sitting down. "The magic. The burst of magic was like a beacon, wasn't it?" Other Mages can sense each other's specific flavor of magic and the release of my Archimage powers would have been a giant signal for anyone close enough to feel it.

Logan squeezes my hand back. "You got it. We need to put as much distance between us and that place as fast as possible."

"Any idea where we're going?" I ask.

"We should go to the cottage. Liz and I talked about it as an option before. We can hide out there," Logan says.

"That's a good idea." Ivy's voice pitches up with excitement. "I haven't been there in years."

"This isn't a leisure trip, Ivy." Disapproval tinges Logan's tone.

Her face falls. "I know, but it will still be nice to see the place."

"I knew I should stay away from you lot. You're nothing but trouble. I'll never be able to glide by under the radar again." Garrett's face is pinched with concern, and I suspect he's not as uncaring as he's trying to come off. "Where is this cottage of yours?"

Ivy reaches over and sets the coordinates into the maps app on his phone.

"Are you kidding me? That's all the way back the way we came from?"

"Yes, but it's safe. It's shielded. The Armstrongs sometimes use it for vacations, but it's also a safe house. If a major disturbance ever went down in the magical community, they could hide out there and no one could track their magic." Ivy explains this to Garrett as she fiddles with the music app until something loud and poppy comes out of the speaker.

"Why didn't you take her there in the first place if it's so safe? Some protector you are." Logan tenses up beside me as Garrett aims the dig at him.

"She had the cuff on. No one should have known about her magic. She should have been safe at the compound." Logan says the words as if he's trying to convince himself. But I can sense his feelings of guilt.

"Can you stop talking about me like I'm not here? My vocal cords haven't suffered any damage, but that might change if you guys think you can talk about me like I'm not here." Seriously, I might still technically be in high school, but I'm turning eighteen in a few months and am perfectly capable of speaking for myself.

"Sorry." Their words ring out at the same time, and I almost laugh hearing them speak in unison. I don't really have much to laugh about in my life right now.

"It's fine," I say.

Trees whip by the windows in a constant blur of greenery, buildings, and other cars until I lose track of time. The tight, anxious feeling that's been riding me since we left Lena's house eases up a bit with each mile we get away from it. The farther away we are, the less likely someone is to catch up with us. After all, they don't know where we're heading. Right?

CHAPTER 26
Logan

My shoulders ache with the knots that have formed over the last couple days of constant tension. I finally relax them as we pull into the hidden entrance that opens up onto the heavily treed driveway to my families' cottage. I enter the code, and the black gate swings open for us. We've got a state-of-the-art security system, so my parents will get a notification that we've arrived. They know we're coming here. We called to let them know, and they agreed it was the safest place for everyone at the moment.

This place is only an hour away from my family's home. It's a refuge that's been in our family for generations. It's a well-kept secret from those outside of the family other than our closest friends and has a ton of wards on it. We made it back to the area far faster than the trip to Lena's took by driving through the night. That's the bonus of having a few extra drivers and the motivation to get away from the beacon that we left behind. I hope Lena went somewhere safe. I called my father and told him to get someone out there to look out for her, but who knows if she'll accept help or not. She's not my priority, though. Sophia is.

The trip has been exhausting for all of us, but at least Sophia has gained her color back and the welt from the bracelet is fading to a pinkish tone rather than the angry red that infuriated me every time I saw it after the bracelet was removed. I'm kinda shocked the thief stuck with us, and I'm also pissed that I have to let him into my family's refuge. He didn't ditch us immediately after the incident with Sophia's magic though and put in more driving than any of us to get us here, so as much as it pains me, I can't turn him away now.

We pass through the invisible barrier of the ward, and Maple Grove appears seemingly out of nowhere.

Sophia lets out a gasp. "Wow. This is your cottage?" She uses finger quotes around the word cottage. I guess she's got a point. The place is not exactly what most people think of as a cottage. The sprawling two-story stone house sits at the top of a gentle hill as if it's keeping watch for intruders. It's highly defensible. Just one of the many things that makes it such a great refuge.

"Welcome to Maple Grove." I wave my arms in a sweeping gesture at the property.

"Figures. This is what you call a cottage." Garrett snorts.

"Whatever, man. Let's get in and settled. I don't know about you, but I'm starving." I stretch my arms over my head and release an obnoxiously loud yawn. I am actually exhausted. I can probably count on two hands the amount of hours I've slept this week. Even when I wasn't on watch or driving duty, I've been on high alert since I left Sophia at the NAMC dorm.

Turns out I was right to worry and I fully regret leaving her there.

I unsheathe a dagger and drag it across my finger causing a bubble of blood to well up from the small nick. I press my palm to the front door, causing the engraved runes to glow with a golden light, giving us access. Only my family's blood and flesh can open the door. I guess that could be taken advantage of in a gruesome way, but you'd have to get past all the other wards and tech first. I kick off my boots as soon as we enter the front door. Sophia places her backpack on the ground neatly, but Garrett leaves his hanging off his shoulder. I'm going to have to search his car later. Make sure he's not hiding something in there. I narrow my eyes at him. He shrugs and a lazy grin spreads across his face. At least I have the satisfaction that he looks exhausted, too. He did more driving than anyone. The dark bruises and drooping eyelids give me some satisfaction that he's not going to be capable of anything nefarious for at least one night.

"Who wants food before we crash?" Sophia is swaying on her feet by this point, and Ivy looks like a slight breeze could topple her. But we should probably get some sort of sustenance in us. We've been living off convenience store snacks and sandwiches. Not exactly a well-balanced diet. "C'mon." I don't give them a chance to protest and drag them along behind me into the large kitchen.

I pull open the door to the stainless-steel fridge and am unsurprised to find my parents have stocked it for us. There are a couple of pre-made casseroles sitting on the middle shelf, along with lots of ingredients.

"Lasagna?" There's an orange post it note in Mom's handwriting stuck to the cling wrap that says 'Vegetarian

Lasagna'. Of course Sophia's mom is staying with my parents, so she was thinking of her daughter. "It's vegetarian."

A couple of incoherent mumbles come from behind me, and I take that as an agreement. I dish it out and tap my foot while I wait impatiently for the microwave to do its job. When I turn around with the first couple of platefuls, I find the group of them slumped over the big pine table. Sophia's head is fully resting on her arms with her golden hair spread out around her. The other two are almost as bad with their elbows propping up their heads.

Everyone gets through at least a few bites of the meal before we give up. I toss the extra food into the compost and abandon the dirty dishes in the sink. That feels like a problem for tomorrow me. Tomorrow me will be much better rested.

I grab Sophia and my bags and lead the way upstairs. There are five bedrooms up here and Ivy bumps into me when I hesitate at the top of the stairs. I have my own bedroom, so I'll stay there. The master can stay empty, but where should everyone else go? I want Sophia to stay with me, but I don't want to be presumptuous.

"Ivy, why don't you stay in the yellow guestroom." I point to the room down the left hall across from Liz's room. "Garrett, you can stay in the blue guestroom. It's the second door on the right down that hall." I point down the right hallway. My room is the first door, so I can keep an eye on him from there. I'll notice if he tries to leave or anything. "Sophia, do you want to stay in Liz's room?" I turn to her. Everything inside me needs her to be close to me so I know she's safe, but I'm not going to put that kind of pressure on her.

Her eyes dart from Ivy to Garrett and her cheeks flush. "Can I...can I stay with you?"

I heave a sigh of relief and everything inside me finally loosens all the way. "Of course." I ignore Garrett stomping off and slide my arm through hers to lead her to my room.

"Night, everyone," Ivy calls out.

"Goodnight, Ivy," I say pointedly.

"Night." Sophia says through another yawn. As soon as we pass through the door, she stumbles over to my bed, collapsing when her knees hit the edge without bothering to remove her clothes. I'm not going there, so I toss a blanket over her and drop a kiss on her forehead. I pull her glasses off as well and place them on the bedside table. That wouldn't end while if she slept in them. I head to the bathroom to get myself cleaned up and changed. I use the ensuite in the master bedroom, so Ivy and Garrett have access to the other one on the second floor. If Sophia's going to stay with me, maybe I'll just move us in here. I have a few things in my bedroom, but since we don't stay here often, there's not a lot. I'll worry about that tomorrow.

The bed settles under me as I slip in next to Sophia. She curls into me with a sigh, and a few disjointed thoughts pass through the bond. Is she dreaming about school? Of course. Tomorrow, we can deal with the fallout from the removal of her cuff. Tonight, I need to know she's safe here in my arms.

CHAPTER 27
Sophia

"Where am I and why is my entire body stiff?" Are the first thoughts to pass through my head as I stretch out the aches. My eyes can't penetrate the darkness that surrounds me. My straining eyes can't even see the red blink of a digital clock. I fumble for the bedside table to search for my phone. No luck. Logan's cottage. That's where I am. The events of yesterday trickle back to me. Pulling up the driveway. That strange feeling of getting sucked through a wormhole as the magical barrier protecting the place parted for us. The first sight of Maple Grove. Seriously, where is my phone, though? And Logan? His cedary scent lingers on the pillow, but he's nowhere to be found.

I swing my legs over the side of the bed and realize I'm still wearing jeans from the night before. My bra is digging into my side and my ponytail is all pulled out and ratted. I can't believe I slept like this. I mean, I can, but I can't. My whole body gave up on me in defeat yesterday after the stress of the previous few days. I lean my head from side to side listening to the satisfying crack as I stretch my neck out and assess my body. Everything is a little achy, my arm is still tender and my side is sore from hitting the ground after the Ferrebat attack. Other than that, I'm good. Refreshed after I finally got a good night's sleep. That edgy nervousness that has been eating at me since Logan left is gone, and I smile when I feel the tingle of his presence at the back of my neck. He's close. That I know for sure.

A strange electricity sends a constant current buzzing through my veins. It's my magic, I'm sure of it, but it's like the volume got turned up to max. My skin is almost crawling with it. Well, that's new. Maybe it's a side effect of being pent up for so long. I'll have to look into that. I wonder if Logan's family has a library at this house. It seems to be a pretty common feature of their homes, so hopefully.

Light floods the room when I pull the heavy green curtains back and dust sparkles in the sunshine streaming through the window. There's a view of the maple grove the place is named after, but this late in the year the trees are resting for the winter, their barren branches reaching for the sky. A light dusting of frost coats the dormant grass.

I spin around at the sound of the door and my mouth falls open. All six plus of Logan is standing there, still slightly damp from a shower. Black sweatpants hang low on his hips, revealing his chiseled abs as he rubs his hair with a towel. I realize I've only ever seen him shirtless when we were training, and I was too busy trying to stay on my feet to ogle him. Even though we've shared a bed a few times, he's always been careful and considerate of me.

I drink his gorgeous body in. Muscles ripple beneath his skin as he twists around to close the door, and I catch sight of the tattoo on the back of his right shoulder. I haven't gotten the chance to study it too closely. Two crossed blades with flames licking up from the center of them. There's another one twisting up from his lower back to brush the bottom of left rib cage. I squint at the distinct five-pointed leaves crawling up the vine. Ivy. A heavy weight settles into my chest. I know I shouldn't be upset. He and Ivy were best friends and more but turns out the heart is not a very rational organ.

He turns back with a concerned look. "What's the matter?" His mouth quirks up. "Don't like what you see?" He's trying to tease me out of my sadness.

"Um." I turn back to look out at the safer landscape outside the window.

His presence heats my back as he steps in, and I lean into the soft caress of his hand like a cat seeking affection. "What is it? You can talk to me."

His eyes follow mine as they stray to the Ivy tattoo. He brushes a hand over it. "Right. You know there's only you now. You're my world. This is a symbol of my past. You're my present and my future and my forever after." His lips brush the top of my head.

The warmth of his love surrounds me inside and out and I nod. "Sorry. I know it's silly of me, but it's hard thinking of you with her. Especially now that she's here with us. I guess I'm afraid you're going to realize what you were missing."

"I'm not missing anything, and it's not silly. The thought of you with another guy…" The love coming from him twists into another kind of fire. "Let's just say I get it. I understand how you're feeling, but I'm here for you and only you."

He wraps me in a fierce hug and need explodes through me. I can't help my eyes from lingering on the expanse of bare skin on display when he pulls away.

His dark brow lifts. "No need to objectify me." He breaks the tension that hangs thick in the air with a return to his usual teasing. It's like everything got a little too intense for him.

"What?! I wasn't..." My words fall off at his sharp burst of laughter.

"I'm messing with you." An evil grin lifts one corner of his mouth, and I brace myself for whatever it is that's about to come out of his mouth. "You can objectify me any time you want."

My hand closes on the closest thing within reach on the bedside table next to me, and it's flying through the air in a stream of sparks before I make a conscious decision to throw it. A box of tissues hits Logan square in the chest, and he throws his arm up dramatically. A flash of pain hits me through the bond. I clench and unclench my fist to shake off the tingle of magic that I accidentally let slip.

"Ouch, that actually hurt. You didn't need to put magic behind it. Although I'm glad to see it's back."

My eyes widen. "I didn't mean to." My eyes dart back and forth. "Is that going to set off the magic bat signal or whatever?"

"No, you're safe. That's why we came here. Now that you have it back, you need to get a handle on your magic. You can do it here without bringing any trouble. There are so many shields and wards on this place no one can tell we're here or sense anyone's magic."

Relief floods me. "That's good." I flop back on his bed, drawing my knees up to my chest.

I wrinkle my nose when Logan drops the towel he was using to dry his hair on the floor by the door and saunters over. "What?" He catches my disgusted look and glances back at the wet towel crumpled on the floor. "Does that bother you?"

"Yes. How does it not bother you? Think of all the bacteria from the floor latching on to that warm, damp home. Then you're going to use it again?"

"Well, when you put it like that..." My eyes latch onto the muscles sliding under his skin as he bends over to pick it up. I need to go for a walk in the frosty air to cool down at this rate. "Are you ready for breakfast?" he asks as he straightens back up.

I blink my crusty eyes and pat the crazy nest on top of my head. "Um, no."

"Right, you probably want to shower first. You can use the one in my parent's room." He holds out a hand, pulling me off the bed.

His parents' room is huge. It has that expensive rustic look to it. A huge bed with thick wooden posts and a plaid quilt dominates the wall under a big window and a fireplace with a matching mantle is set into the right wall. The bathroom is where it's at, though. It's sleek and modern, with a glass walled shower that has multiple spray heads and double sinks set in a charcoal marble countertop. The enormous bathtub catches my eye with jacuzzi jets that I imagine would do an amazing job of loosening all my tight muscles and easing the aches of the last few days.

"You can have a bath if you'd rather," Logan says.

"Can I? That would be amazing."

"Of course, my cabin is your cabin. Or rather my parent's cabin." He rifles through the cabinet, pulling out some bottles and a couple of big, fluffy gray towels. "I'm going to head back to my room. I'm not up to dealing with anyone else yet. We can head down together after."

"Sounds good." I hesitate for a moment before leaning in. His soft lips meet mine for a too brief moment, and I catch a hint of worry running through him before he pulls away. My body is acutely aware of his proximity. He didn't bother to put a shirt on, so his bare chest is begging to be touched. I ignore the impulse, though, and get the taps running. The door clicks behind him, and I slide over to lock it.

I smile at the bubble bath he grabbed for me. It's filling the room with a floral scent as the water level rises and steam fills the air. I wince at the temperature when I first climb in, but my body is soon used to it and I sink into the heat, letting it embrace me in a floaty cloud of comfort.

Clean and relaxed for the first time in days, I knock on Logan's door before entering.

"Come in," he calls out. He's sprawled out on the bed when I walk in, reading a magazine with a picture of some sort of a martial artist on the cover. I breathe a sigh of relief when I notice that he's put a shirt on. He gives me a curious look. "You didn't need to knock."

"I wanted to make sure you were..."

"Sight of my bare chest was too much for you, huh?" He tosses the magazine he was reading to the floor and pats the bed beside him. "Don't worry. I got your back. I'll help you control your urges."

I whack him on the shoulder. "Should we go down for breakfast?"

"We can if you want. Are you super hungry? If not, I wouldn't mind hanging here for a bit before we go down there and have to interact with the others."

"Nah, I'm good. Sounds like a plan."

We sit in silence for a bit, enjoying each other's company, but I can't let it stand for long. There's too much going on right now. "What's the next step?"

He must catch the serious note in my voice. Or the heaviness in my thoughts because I catch a hint of teasing playfulness from him right before he leans in closer. "Like what comes after kissing? Want me to fill you in on the birds and bees? Didn't your mother teach you this stuff?"

I can't quite play along with him after he mentions my mom. The thought of her sends an ache through me. "I should call her."

"Sorry, didn't mean to bring you down. You should call her. Want me to leave you alone?" He pushes himself up, but I snag his shirt and pull him back.

"No, I'll call her later. I had some questions first."

He eases back and slides an arm around my shoulders. "Shoot."

"Well, since I got my magic back, there's been this current kind of buzzing all over me. It's like I've been electrified or something."

"Yeah, I noticed the excess of magic you've got going on." Right, the bond. "I can't be sure, but I think it might be because it was all tamped down for a while. It's like a can of whipped cream or something under pressure. All trapped in there with no outlet, the pressure built up. Now that it can escape, it's shooting out fast and furious. Maybe that's a crappy analogy."

"I get what you're saying, and it makes sense. What do you think I should do to get it under control? It's not exactly painful, but it's kind of uncomfortable."

"I think you need to practice it. You need to use it or else it could all come bursting out at the wrong moment. Like with the fireball in the bleachers."

Ah yes, the first time I consciously tried to use my magic and put a gaping hole in the bleachers at school. Not one of my finer moments. "Point taken."

"We've got a huge property to practice on here. It's perfect." Well, perfect except for the fact that I've left school and all my friends and family behind. "What's wrong?" His calloused finger tilts my chin up to meet his gaze and his wide smile falters.

"It's great. I'm glad I can work on my magic. I know how important it is. But my mom isn't here. I miss her and my friends. And I'm not going to finish my classes this semester. I know I shouldn't be concerned about that with everything else going on, but I can't help it. Before now, school was everything and now I'm drifting from one magical disaster to the next with no end in sight. It's a lot."

Understanding softens all his hard edges. "Oh, Soph. I'm sorry. I promise my parents will look after your mom. As for everything else, if I could fix it for you, I would. All I want is for you to be happy, and it kills me to see your life get messed up like this. When I get my hands on your uncle..." His dark rage takes over the despair that had been filling me. It's actually helpful. His anger is so much more useful than the sadness that was threatening to pull me under. I can use this.

"Let's go." I ignore the confusion that twists his face and dulls the rage.

"What. Where are we going?"

"To practice. I'm going to get a handle on my magic." Liquid steel hardens in my veins. Determination grips me to get a handle on my magic, so I can track down my uncle and get my life back.

"Now?"

"Yes. Come on." I grab his hand and tug at the unmoving rock that he is until he swings his legs over the side of the bed and pushes up.

"Maybe we should at least eat some breakfast first. Fuel that fire." A strand of desire cuts through the confusion as he eyes me.

"Right. Probably a good idea." I have been known to slide into hyper-focus mode and skip meals. "Let's get on it then.

CHAPTER 28
Logan

Sophia's emotions have been all over the place all morning and it's messing with me hard. The most intense thing I've felt all morning has been anger at her uncle and anyone else who would dare threaten her. I'm trying to hold on to that to keep myself intact. It would be so easy to lose myself in her feelings and I can't afford that. I need to stay on track. Yes, she needs to do a lot of training. Me, I need to track down Zeus and take him out. He's got to surface eventually, right? He wants Sophia's powers and sending minions after her hasn't worked yet, so he's going to creep out of whatever dark hole he's been hiding in and when he does, I'll be ready. That's not something she needs to know yet.

Ivy meanders into the kitchen while we're finishing up our breakfast. She stretches her arms over her head. "Morning. What's for breakfast?"

"Good morning. Whatever your heart desires. Help yourself. Seen Floppy yet this morning?"

Sophia smacks my shoulder, but Ivy looks confused. "What are you talking about, weirdo?"

I roll my eyes and sigh as dramatically as I can. "Are you going to force me to say his name? Garrett."

Ivy snorts out a laugh. "Uh no. Haven't seen him. I dragged myself out of bed merely because my stomach was loudly protesting its neglect."

"Yeah, I remember your appetite. Stuff of legends. I'm surprised you held out this long, to be honest." For all Ivy's tiny frame, she could consume an immense amount of food. Like she could always beat Trey and me at one of our dumb teenage eating contests. Any time we went out to one of those all you can eat restaurants, we'd have a challenge and, of course, Ivy always shamed us.

"You don't know me. Maybe I've changed." Her tone is teasing, but a sliver of sadness eats at me. She's right, I don't know her anymore. Ivy and Trey, they used to be most of my world and now she's a stranger and I can't spend ten minutes in the same room as him without one of us threatening the other.

Sophia reaches over and squeezes my hand, drawing my attention back to her.

"We've got to get our day going," I say.

"Already? I was thinking we all deserved a lazy day after everything that's gone down this week." Ivy's words come out in a jumble around the danish she's jammed into her mouth.

"No lazy days for me. I've got training to do," Sophia says, walking away from the sink where she rinsed our dishes.

"Training?" Ivy moans.

"No one's going to make you come, Ivy. You're welcome to if you want, but Sophia wants to get to work and who am I to argue with the Archimage?"

I get weird looks from both the girls at that one.

"Okay, maybe I'll chill this morning and then work out with you guys this afternoon."

"Great, enjoy your morning. Logan, come on."

"Yes, mom."

"Don't you dare." I burst out laughing at the dirty look she shoots me.

I'll take her to the clearing at the base of the hill behind the house. It's a nice big open space, perfect for letting loose elemental magic. Nothing to damage nearby. Maybe I'll get Ivy to work with her on her bio magic later too if she has it. I haven't noticed any signs of that one yet, but it can be a bit more subtle. I know she was already showing signs of some of the physical magic traits before she got blocked. Speed and strength were already rearing their heads. Too bad Liz isn't here. That would be a sight to behold. My sister and Sophia unleashing their bonus strength. Although Liz has been doing it for her whole life. I'd worry about Sophia getting hurt, but I also know how much Liz cares about her, so she'd be in careful hands. That doesn't matter now. Liz is safe at home with our parents and her many cats.

My winter coat mocks me, and I eye it with distaste but pull it on, along with warm gloves and a hat. Winter is the worst. I'll have to take the gloves off for some of the magic stuff. I'd hate to burn a hole in them, but I also don't relish the thought of frostbite.

The frost tipped grass crunches under our feet as we head to the clearing. Sophia's cheeks are already turning rosy red and she looks cute, all bundled up in her puffy pink winter jacket. I can think of a few things I'd rather be doing with her right now in the warmth of my bedroom, but I push those unhelpful thoughts to the back of my mind.

When we get to the clearing, she widens her stance a little as if we're going to be doing physical fighting and I don't correct her. It's not necessary, but it's fine. She might need the stability anyway with the massive amount of energy buzzing along through her.

"What's first?" she asks.

I press my lips together and spread my hands out. "We've got a lot to work with right now."

She takes in her surroundings, twisting her head to the right, then left. "What do you mean?"

"Water, right? Frost and snow. It's just frozen water. You can use that. You can use your elemental powers to control it, to change it, to mold it to your will." I punctuate my words with an example, pulling at the tingle of my powers from my core and channeling the energy into the frosted tips of the grass. I draw them up, directing the magic to change the water from its solid to liquid form. I show off a little, refreezing it and sending the icicles zipping off on either side of her with a targeted burst of air. "Give it a shot. Start small." I add the caution on to the end.

She closes her eyes for a moment, reopening them with her brow scrunched up in concentration and her mouth pursed. She pulls off her gloves and holds out a hand. Her energy is thrumming through me courtesy of our bond. If it's that bad for me, I'm not sure how she's handling it. The energy builds and then explodes in a burst. The dormant grass shoots up a few inches around us, lightning streaks back and forth from her hands, and all the frost in the clearing melts, curling into a wave that crashes down and spreads around us.

Sophia looks around wildly but can't seem to pull the erratic energy back in as it shoots off in all directions. I curse and duck as bolt of lightning singes the shoulder of my coat.

"Sophia! Look at me. Focus. Clear your mind and pull it back." I will her to meet my eyes and try to calm my own panic, so I can send a soothing wave to her along the string that ties us together.

She takes a deep breath, and her honey brown eyes meet mine. The energy recedes and the air stills. We're going to need to try a different tactic on this one. Something has changed since we were last able to practice. She had been getting a good handle on her magic before she got cuffed. Hopefully, this is just a temporary problem.

"I'm not sure what's going on. It's like I'm not in control of the magic anymore. It's got a mind of its own and as soon as I unleash my hold, it goes wild." Her arms are flying about, and her glasses are a little askew.

"Well, maybe we need to give it the release it needs and let it all out in a big burst. Then hopefully you'll be able to redirect the rest of it. Maybe there's too much all pent up in there for now."

Her look turns wary as she glances around the watery meadow. "You sure that's a good idea?"

"I'm flying blind here. I have no idea what's going on. This might work, it might not. I think it's worth a try, though."

"What if it goes wrong?" I can sense her fear. It's not good for her to fear her own powers. If she does her worst and lets it out, she'll see that it's not so bad. Hopefully. I mean, it could go really wrong. I can't let her doubt herself. I've got to be confident for both of us right now.

"It'll be ok. I'm here. You're amazing. You can do this. We haven't got any neighbors near enough to hurt. You can let it go." I inject as much confidence into my walk as I can and head over to where she's standing. I build a steel wall in my mind, so she can't sense my own fear. She doesn't need that building on top of her own. I press myself against her back. Her uncertainty is hanging in the air, so I slide my hands around her waist and drop my chin to her shoulder. "You can do this. How about you try air? Creating some wild wind should be less destructive than you know, fire."

"Okayyyy." There's still doubt in her voice.

"Close your eyes. Feel the wind on your face. Picture it picking up your hair." I lift a hand to run my fingers through the silky length but pull it back. That's not what this is about. "Now take that feeling, gather it up and send it forward. Away from us. There's nothing to damage out there, don't worry about that. Just push as much magic into it as you can." Her head nods next to mine.

The current builds and builds. When I think there can't be any magic left in her, it intensifies a little more and her body tenses against me as she sends it shooting out. The trees beside us shiver, and the boughs reach for the ground. A wave rushes through, sending the grass bending. Rocks, branches, and dirt get tossed and turned and whipped into a frenzy. The effect goes further and further out until we can't see it anymore and then it's over. Silence surrounds us. Everything settles back into the quiet still of the winter morning.

Sophia spins around in my arms, the fear in her eyes has eased up a little. "It's definitely better. That irritating buzz is gone. My magic feels closer to the level it was at before. It's still a little more intense, but manageable."

Her chin tilts up to look at me and her breath comes out in a puff. I'm about to lean in when she dances away. "What next?"

"Well, let's get back to the water thing."

Her laugh comes out giddy and her eyes are sparkling. "One problem with that."

"What?"

"The frost. I melted it."

"Right. Doesn't matter. There's water everywhere. You can pull it from the air, the ground. That's expert level difficult. It's easier to use something you can physically see, but since you managed that wind, I think you can totally handle the water thing."

"Gotcha."

I put her through a series of exercises I remember from my childhood when I was just learning to control my elemental powers. Changing the water from liquid to solid form and back. Pulling liquid from the air and the grass. Changing the liquid to its intangible gaseous form is a little harder, but she gives it a go and starts to slide back into the ease she was starting to feel with her magic before.

I call the session when sweat is trickling down her brow and her nose has gone so red she could pass for a clown. A surprising amount of energy is still buzzing through her in spite of her physical and mental tiredness. Her power is growing, and I wonder what her limit is? The rest of us Mages have hard limits. That's why we get physically fit and learn to fight that way. Nobody wants to be in the middle of a fight with a depleted energy supply. I'm not sure if that's different for her with her Archimage powers. "That's it for the morning. Great job."

She looks like she's about to protest, but then she sighs. "Definitely time to head in."

"That was amazing. You did fantastic."

Her cold nose presses into my cheek as I snag the kiss I've been angling for all morning. The flames originating where our lips meet chase away the cold as they spread through me. Our hands grasp at each other in frustration through the thick winter coats that separate us. Her tongue slides into my mouth brushing my lower lip as she gets bolder exploring my mouth. I return the favor tasting her sweetness. Everything inside me protests, but I pull back with a sigh. A small moan escapes her reddened lips, and she blinks her glazed eyes at me. That sound almost has me pulling her back in, but I fight the urge and instead pick her up to twirl her around.

"We should head back in, frosty."

"Frosty?"

"Yeah, you look like you're about to turn into a snowman."

A small laugh escapes as she rolls her eyes at me. "Nope."

Footsteps pound up behind us as we reach the back door. Garrett leans on one side of the entrance, sweat dripping from his brow. His breath comes in short pants, and he's dressed in a tight insulated shirt and running pants.

"Hey, Garrett," Sophia says.

"Hi, Sophia." He doesn't bother to greet me, and I return the favor.

She ignores the tension between us. "Did you go out for a run?"

He nods his assent.

"I'll have to come with you next time. I love running. I haven't been getting out there lately with all this craziness, but I'd like to get back to it."

"I'd love for you to join me." I consider running a bit of a futile effort, and I'd rather get my cardio elsewhere, but I'm tempted to tell her I'll join them. I resist the urge. She needs time to do her own thing, and I have nothing to worry about on her end.

CHAPTER 29
Sophia

I collapse on the mat in the home gym after a brutal afternoon session. Everyone joined us for this one. I'm getting better with the daggers, though, and I have a few more moves if I get trapped in a physical fight. I still won't be winning fights against people that have been training their whole lives, but I have a chance to do something. Run, use my magic. Every skill I have, every advantage I can get, is going to help in the long run. I need to be able to stand on my own feet and fight for myself. I won't stand to the side helpless while other people fight for me. Watching Ivy practice is an inspiration. She's deadly with a sword and quicksilver on her feet.

"Showers, then dinner," Ivy says. "I call first dibs, so I can start making dinner."

"Anyone want to drag me upstairs?" I lift a hand up on an arm that resembles the texture of jelly. I thought my body was achy before, now I'm totally fried.

Garrett bends down to give me a hand, and Logan swats it away. I'm about to protest when I'm airborne. He scoops me up and flings me over his shoulder with like zero effort. I smack at him. "Stop."

His shoulders shake with laughter. "Thought you were too tired to walk."

"Put me down you Neanderthal."

"Fine."

He lets me slide down his front and my exhaustion dissipates as every inch of my body that touches his goes up in flames. Someone clears their throat, and I step back breaking the contact as all the heat rises to my cheeks. Sometimes the rest of the world disappears when I'm around him. It's like we're in our own little bubble where no one else can touch us.

As I lift each heavy foot to clear the stairs, I kinda wish I'd let him carry me.

We part ways with the others at the top.

The smells coming from the kitchen entice me back down to find out what Ivy is cooking. Logan is still in the shower, but I'm all clean now and cozy in my pajama pants. No more exertion for me for the day. After dinner I'm going to collapse into a boneless heap on that huge comfy looking couch in the TV room. I should probably offer to help with meal prep though.

The sight of Ivy and Garrett working away together over the long kitchen counter is surprising. I guess they've been thrown together a lot recently. Something is sizzling in a wok on the stove and another stainless steel pot is bubbling away. I take a deep inhale and my mouth waters at the rich salty aromas of garlic and soy.

"Can I help with anything?" I offer. It looks like they have everything under control, but it doesn't hurt to offer.

"We've got the cooking part under control." Ivy chirps cheerfully. "Any chance you can set the table?"

"Sure," I reply. She's been so friendly and welcoming. I don't know what to make of it. I can't make the pieces of her fit together. It's been a while since Logan and her were together, but you'd think there'd be something there. Judgment of me, jealousy, even a friendly assessment of whether I'm good enough for her friend/ex. Anything other than this calm acceptance. Of course, I have no idea what turmoil might be bubbling under the surface. We never really know what's going on in someone else's head, do we? Maybe if I were a Psychic Mage... I let the thought drift away. I probably have some psych abilities, but I honestly have no desire to explore them. The thought of getting inside someone else's head is so intrusive. If it comes to that, I'll have to talk to Mrs. Armstrong about how to shield and block. Logan's taught me a few things, but she's an expert being a Psychic Mage herself.

I'm looking around for the threat when Logan comes tearing into the room wearing nothing but a pair of black track pants.

"What's wrong?"

"Someone came onto the property." His chest is rising and falling rapidly as his eyes dart around searching for danger.

I feel left out of the party when everyone pulls a weapon out of whatever random place. I guess I should start carrying knives with me even in the house? Logan nods his head to Ivy to head to the back door, and he heads for the front entrance with

Garrett. I'm left standing in the kitchen feeling foolish. What do I do now?

I'm about to go on a search for something to defend myself when a powerful sense of relief floods me. Logan calls out, "All clear." They all come back into the kitchen as if nothing happened. I have a lot to learn about this world. It's a bit disturbing that they've all grown up in this world that requires them to jump into action at the drop of a hat. Not really the kind of life I ever had planned for myself.

I release a long breath as my heartrate slows to its regular rhythm. "False alarm?" I ask.

Logan walks over, sinking his nose into my head for a moment. "It's Trey, of all people. My dad must have sent him to back us up."

"Well, that's good. The more help the better, right?" I ask.

"Sure. I'm gonna go." He waves a hand at his bare chest and heads back upstairs.

I startle back into action and open up a few drawers before I find the one with the cutlery and napkins to set the table.

The click of the front door sounds, and I narrow my eyes. Didn't Logan say only family could open the door with their blood? I'm still pondering this when a shapeless blur barrels into, me and I stagger back a few steps. Liz. Trey trails her in at a normal human speed a few minutes later.

"I missed you! So glad you guys made it here safe and sound." She spins back to me looking at my still pink wrist. "And you're free! Now that I'm here, the party can start."

Logan pauses in the doorway with a glare at his sister. You'd think he'd be happier to see her. "Liz, what are you doing here?"

Her eyes shift away. "Um, I hitched a ride." She tosses a thumb at Trey, who throws up his hands in exasperation.

"Have you met your little sister? Not an easy person to say no to. She threatened to run here on her own if I didn't let her catch a ride with me. I didn't think that would be exactly a prudent idea, so here we are."

"Trey's smart. You should be more like Trey, Logan."

"Whatever. Do Mom and Dad know you're here?"

"Not yet, but I'm sure they will soon enough." She blinks her big blue-green eyes at Logan that are a perfect match for his.

"Nuh uh. I'm not calling them. You deal with that fallout on your own." He shakes his head and walks over to the stove to snag a veggie out of the pan, swearing when it burns his hand.

"Chicken," Liz calls to his back.

He swings around with a dangerous glint in his eyes. "I'm not a chicken for not wanting to deal with the trouble my sister is stirring up again. You brought this on yourself. You can deal with it."

She only looks chastised for a moment before her usual effervescence is back. "Ok, I'll call them, but as punishment, I'm stealing Sophia away from you for the night. I'm calling it a girls' night."

I try to infuse as much doubt into my expression as I can, letting my gaze rest on Logan, then Garrett and Trey in turn. "Are you sure that's a good idea? Should we really leave these three to their own devices?"

Her mischievous smile spreads and an evil look shines in her eyes. "Yes. We definitely should. It will be good for them."

Not sure her logic is sound, but I guess we can step in if the house starts shaking on its foundation.

Dinner is amazing. Ivy and Garrett pulled together an epic stir fry. There was even tofu in there for me. Chatter around the table is pleasant and we let the deep problems disappear for the meal. Liz is a little more subdued than usual. I'm pretty sure her conversation with her parents didn't go well, but she'll snap out of it. If there's one thing Liz is good at, it's pushing away the problems of the world and living her life light and airy. I'm kind of jealous of that quality. I'm always focused and driven by something. It's always been academic stuff until now. Now it's magic. Girls' night sounds good though. A nice break. As long as it involves a couch and some relaxation, I can get back to the hard work tomorrow.

Logan and I start to clear up. "Where should Trey sleep?" Liz asks.

"Crap." Logan looks pained. "Liz, can you help Sophia clean up? Trey can stay in my room, and we'll move to the master. I'll have to change the sheets."

"I mean, he could stay in the master, couldn't he? Wouldn't that be easier?" she quirks a brow at him.

"No, it's fine."

"Mmmkay. Let's look after this as quick as we can so we can get to the serious business of girl time."

Liz isn't kidding when she says quick. She uses her speed to collect all the dishes in a blur. I'm pretty sure I'd break them all if I attempted that feat, so I stick with my regular old mundane speed, but it's still cleared up way faster than I expected.

Liz grabs my hand and Ivy's and drags us into the cozy room with the couches and the TV. I haven't explored the cottage too much since we got here, so I'm not sure where the guys are going to hang out, but I guess that's not my problem.

Once I'm safely wrapped in a cozy plaid blanket, I let myself sink into the deep couch and Liz drops down beside me. It's amazing how quickly she's become like a sister to me. I feel like I've known her my whole life.

Ivy hesitates in the doorway, staring at us for a moment. "Maybe I'll head up to my room and chill for a bit."

"No way. Come hang with us." Liz pats the couch next to her.

After another brief pause, Ivy settles into the puffy chair across from us. Liz shoos Logan away when he pops his head in.

"How's my mom doing?" I look up at Liz from under my eyelids. My calm exterior is hiding the roiling storm of guilt that's crashing through me on the inside. I've hardly talked to her since I got here. Her and Charlotte, Xavier, my other friends. I didn't talk to my brother much since he left for university anyway, but it's just one more loss. One more person I love that I've grown apart from over the last year.

Her voice gentles with understanding. "She's good, Sophia. She's settled in well with my parents and is still going to her job every day." My alarm must catch her notice. "With a guard. Don't worry, they're not sending her in alone."

"Good." At least she's safe. For now. Worry over her is a constant buzz in the back of my mind.

Liz turns a knowing look at Ivy. "How about you, Ivy? How have you been doing back here?"

Ivy's small mouth drops open. "Good. I'm good."

"This is a safe space, Ivy. You can be up front with us." Liz is really going for the kill tonight. When she said girls' night, I was picturing movies and popcorn, not intense conversation, but it's nice. There's way more to Liz than she lets people see.

"It's been...hard. Coming back here. Seeing...all of you." Her eyes dart to me and I can tell she's thinking of Logan.

"Fair enough. If you need anything, let us know, Ivy. I think we all need to get to know each other again."

The conversation veers into safer territory after that and we giggle and paint our nails as if life only exists in this cottage and there's no one out there plotting my demise. I almost forget for a few hours until we're talking about the stars, and I've gone off on a rambling astronomy rant when Liz asks me a question I'm not prepared to answer.

"When did you decide you wanted to be a doctor?"

"What?"

"You said you wanted to be a doctor, right?" Her eyes have darkened in the dim light of the crackling fire with an intensity I rarely see in them.

"Yeah. I did. Before all this." I pause to think about it. It's hard right now to remember why I wanted that. Then my dad's face flashes before my eyes. Visiting him at the hospital and seeing him tired but happy in his scrubs as he talked about a successful surgery. The excitement shining in the brown eyes I inherited from him, despite the exhaustion apparent on his face. And then the light was gone one day. It was such a waste of a life. All those people he could have helped. It wasn't long after that when I made the decision to follow in his footsteps. My heart bleeds all over again at the thought of him.

"Did you always know what you wanted to do? I've always admired people who had a direction in life from when they were kids. Me, I change my mind every other week, although I'm pretty sure I'll end up in the family business. It better be the exciting side, though. I want to be out there where the action is not stuck behind some desk. Boring."

I almost let Liz's distraction lead us away from the sensitive subject she brought up, but this feels like a crucial moment for honesty. A chance to come clean to them and myself, too. "I didn't want to be a doctor when I was a kid. I wanted to be an astronomer. Study the stars. Discover new worlds. You know?"

"That's cool," Liz says.

"What made you change your mind?" asks Ivy.

"Well, my dad. He was a doctor, and I admired him so much. He gave so much of himself to others and helped so many people. After he died, I decided to take up where he left off."

"Oh. Is that still what you want, then?" Liz gives me a curious look and I squirm under the intensity of her eyes. It's like she can see into my soul. As if she knows all my doubts and fears about this path my life has taken.

I take a deep breath to calm myself before I let the truth out in the open. "I don't think it's ever what I wanted, to be honest." Her eyes widen. "I think I did it for my dad after he died. It was a way to keep myself focused and keep my mind off his death. It was like if I did this thing for him than I wouldn't feel so guilty about still being here after he died. Like I could make up for his death by living his life." An immense weight I didn't know I was carrying around all these years lifts off my chest after the admission. Now that the words are out there, I know that they're true. I don't know what it means for my life though. I don't think the medical path was looking too promising anyway once my magic was unbound, but it's a step. A step toward figuring my new life out and getting a handle on my own desires.

"Wow. You know it wasn't your fault, right? And you shouldn't ever feel bad about being here when he isn't. I didn't know him, but I'm sure that's what he'd want for you." Liz slides an arm around my shoulder and pulls me in for a hug.

"I know, Liz. I know. It doesn't always feel like that, though."

Ivy has been silent through this exchange, but I notice tears streaking her cheeks. "I know exactly how you feel, Sophia." Right, she lost her parents too, and Garrett. There's so much loss in this house. It's amazing any of us can function on a daily basis. We've all dealt with it in our own ways.

"Ivy, come over here." I reach out for her, wanting to make a connection.

Girl's night took a heavy turn, but I don't regret it for a moment. I needed this. The truth is, the thing I've been chasing all these years isn't the thing that's right for me and I needed to face that to let go. I don't know where I'm going from here, but I've got a fresh slate.

CHAPTER 30
Logan

Guy's night last night was fine. We hung out in the games room and tried to distract ourselves from wanting to murder each other. It sounds like girls' night was a lot more intense. I kept getting alternating waves of giddiness, sorrow, and relief through our bond. It was like being on a roller coaster for me, so I have no idea how much more intense it was for her. But Sophia looks better today than I've ever seen her in spite of the circumstances. Her shoulders look lighter, as if a weight has been lifted from them. I was itching to get my hands on her by the time I joined her in bed, but she looked wrung out and there was no way I was going to keep her up.

She's ready to spend another day practicing when my dad's ringtone blasts out. I like to know when he's the one calling so I can steel myself for whatever lecture is coming.

"Hello." I try to keep the insolence out of my tone.

"Logan." He barks out. "Is everything ok there?"

"It's fine, why?" I'm confused about why he's asking that question.

"Good." He sounds relieved. "There was an attack here. Everyone is fine, but we're in lockdown, so I need you to stay there. No going into town. No going past the gate."

"What happened?"

"It was Shades. They ambushed us when Sophia's mother was coming home from work. Like I said, she's fine. We got her in the house before anything could happen, but she won't be leaving the house again until they neutralize the threat."

"Shades?" Why would the spirits of dark Mages attack my parent's house? Then it hits me hard. Zeus, the Nether Realm. We've been so busy the last few days getting the cuff removed and getting the hell away from the chaos we unleashed that I've forgotten about the portals. Zeus using them to travel around and hide out in the Nether Realm.

"It's him. Sophia's uncle. He's been using portals to the Nether Realm to get around. Ivy and I realized it after we got attacked."

"I know, son. He must have recruited or taken control of the Shades to use them as his own personal army."

It's worse than we thought. We thought he was just hiding out and traveling through the Nether, but if he's recruiting an army down there, that doesn't bode well.

"I need you to promise me you won't do anything stupid. Stay there. Keep Sophia safe. That's your job. And look after your sister. I'm not happy at all about her taking off with Trey, but it's safer for her there now, so she stays put, too. If anything happens to any of them, it's on you."

Of course it's on me. He sent Trey to help because he doesn't trust me, but the responsibility for everyone is still on me. If anything goes wrong, all the blame will land squarely on my back. It's fine. I'm used to it. "Got it. Loud and clear." I'm not sure if he catches the sarcasm dripping from my words through the phone line, but I can't really bring myself to care one way or the other.

"Good. If anything happens there, call me right away."

"Will do, sir." I disconnect before he can send any other dire warnings my way.

Everyone is hanging out in the kitchen again. I've never seen it this full. It's a big kitchen, but between Liz's energy and Trey's massive size, it looks full. I hate to be the one to bring them down while they all look so happy, but they need to hear the grim news.

"That was Dad." Liz's chatter dies down when our matching eyes meet. "Something's going down. Shades attacked our house last night." The color drains from Sophia's face. "Everyone is safe. Your mom is fine." I know that's where her mind has gone at her pallor, so I reassure her with the word and walk closer to place a hand on her shoulder. I relax a little once I'm touching her. It's like anytime I'm not within touching distance of her these days, I'm on edge. "Our parents are fine too, Liz, but the house is on lockdown. No one in or out, and we're not leaving this place for the foreseeable future." I don't mention the little point that I probably won't heed that advice for too long. No one else is coming with me, though. At least not Sophia. I'm still not sure who to bring along, but Sophia and Liz can definitely stay out of it.

"What are Shades?" asks Sophia. I can sense her curiosity now that she knows her mom is safe.

"Shades are the spirits of dark Mages or Witches. Some of them go bad. They practice dark magic, stealing power from others, death magic. That sort of thing. When they do, they condemn their spirits to live as Shades in the Nether Realm after they die." Ivy fills her in.

"So that's like hell for Mages?" I can see her brain working overtime as she processes the new information.

"Yeah, pretty much," I reply.

"And these Shades are like ghosts? Or demons?"

Ivy pipes in again while I stroke Sophia's arm. "Yes, most of them are more ghostlike, I guess. Smoke and shadows. The more powerful the Mage was during life, the more corporeal they'll be able to become. A really powerful Mage might be able to look almost human again, but those are rare."

"And what can they do?"

"They can pull magic from the Nether or the earth. They'll have varying degrees of the use of the powers they possessed when they were alive." Trey joins the conversation, rubbing the couple of days' growth that has sprouted on his chin. It makes him look older. I still keep picturing him as my friend from childhood. I wonder if he thinks of me the same way. Even though I've seen him grow up over the years unlike Ivy, the picture of him that predominates my mind is of him in his lanky midteen years.

Sophia is still trying to wrap her mind around their existence I think. "And can they wander about doing whatever they want? Is that where all the stories of ghosts come from?"

"No. They're usually confined to the Nether. Your uncle is releasing them from there. I'm not sure how. I think he's controlling them somehow. Who knows how many Shades he's got doing his bidding." This isn't something I've seen before.

Sure you hear about the occasional Mage summoning a Shade to do his dirty business, but not an entire group of them. That's a scary amount of power.

"We need to go." I wince as Sophia's chair bangs my knees when she shoves away from the table.

"We're not going anywhere." I'm not throwing my father's orders in her voice, but I'm not going to put her in danger. I don't want her going anywhere.

"My mom, Logan. My mom was there when they attacked. We have to go back." Right, of course she's worried about her mother.

"How about you call her, Sophia? You can see she's safe and we can stay put here also safe. She's not going to want you to put yourself in danger for her. I may not know the woman very well, but she's your mom, and she loves you. Her number one priority is keeping you safe."

She catches her bottom lip between her teeth and worries away at it. "Okay. I'll call her." I breathe a sigh of relief when she disappears into the next room for privacy. Her mom will tell her to stay here.

The day passes in another blur of practice. Everyone came to watch Sophia training in the morning. Liz and Ivy both gave her some individual lessons in their specialties. The only thing we don't have is a Psychic Mage to help her hone those abilities. She hasn't said anything about catching stray thoughts or getting into anyone's head, so maybe those are surfacing slower than the others. There's a nuclear amount of power pulsing within her. I can see why Mages in the past feared those born with Archimage level powers. Doesn't mean I agree with the way they dealt with them, but I do understand their fear. After all, we always fear the things we don't understand. An Archimage with that kind of power who learned empathy and concern for others would be such a powerful force they could have dismantled their carefully constructed patriarchal system. Or the alternate. An Archimage gone bad could tear apart the world. And maybe that's what it all comes down to. Those in power fearing the loss of it. Scrabbling to stay on top and keep everyone else down.

These thoughts all run through my head even as I engage with Ivy. It's great to practice my sword skills with someone who can match me. I'd never admit it to her, but her skills exceed mine. I turned Sophia over to Trey to work on her dagger throwing again, since he seems to be helping her more with that than I ever did. She's really into it and the smile that spreads over her face every time she picks up one of the knives I bought for her or gets a little closer to her target melts me a little. I don't think I'm going to be able to keep my hands to myself for another night. It's agony lying next to her in the same bed without tearing our clothes to shreds.

Ivy takes advantage of my distraction and slips through my guard. I throw my hands up. "You win."

"I know. You'll never catch up to me, Logan. Face it. You know I'm better."

"Maybe so, but I'll never admit it." I say the words, but we both know I'm pretty much conceding the point.

Maple Grove has a training room similar to the one at home. Locked away in the basement, we all work together until we're sweaty and exhausted with that burn that only comes from a good workout. Trey hasn't had too much to say since he got here, but the three of us managed to hang out without coming to blows last night, so I guess it's progress. I'm still not ready to befriend Garrett. His lips have been on my girls. There's no way his intentions are pure.

I'm getting restless here. Hiding out is wearing on me. I'm not going to be able to stay here much longer. I need to take action.

I'm going to do my best to track down Zeus, but I'm not sure who to trust my plan with. I'm not turning to Garrett. I don't trust him enough to back me up in battle, and his magical talents don't run to the type that would be useful in a magical fight. Sure, he's got training, but no magic to back it up. His tracking skills can't help us find Zeus yet since we don't own anything that belongs to him. Not to mention he's been hiding out in the Nether. I wouldn't drag my underage sister into this, so that leaves Trey, or maybe Ivy. Trey seems like the most likely candidate. Even though he's my father's lackey I don't think he'd rat me out to him at his point. I'll have to pull him away for a chat later. We need to work out a plan. I'd like to head out tomorrow even if the thought of leaving Sophia behind tears at me. She snags my gaze when she gets a good throw in and claps her hands with a bounce on her toes.

CHAPTER 31
Sophia

It was movie night. Liz and I got outvoted, so we ended up watching some action-comedy thing. It was pretty funny. There's been a strange tension emanating from Logan all evening, though. It's been hitting me in waves even as I snuggled into the crook of his arm. I'm relieved to be this close to him. Something's going on in that head of his and I don't trust it. He's plotting. I thought we were past all the secrets and lies, but apparently that's not the case.

He's still aware of me. As if he's been waiting for it, he leans in close to my ear the minute a yawn overtakes me. "Are you ready for bed?" His breath tickles my cheek and blows a few strands of loose hair back. It sends a shiver through me. The good kind.

"Yeah. I'm ready." And I am ready. I'm still tired. The last couple of days have been physically and mentally taxing. I went to bed last night completely drained, but tonight there's another strange energy riding me. I need to be close to him. All the tension of the last week has caught up and I need to feel his lips on mine and his hands on my body.

He must catch the lust pulsing through me, because his eyes darken and he jumps up, pulling me along with him.

"Night everyone." He calls out without a backward glance as we leave the behind the curious glances of our friends. That's what they are now. Our friends. Our second family. I've grown so close to this odd assortment of people over the last little while. A chorus of good nights follows us out the door.

"Keep it down. I don't need to be scarred for life." Is the parting shot from Liz. Trust her to try to dampen the mood. It doesn't work though. A pulse of heat is burning through me and I'm not even sure if it's mine or his or a combination of the two. All I know is that I don't even want to wait until we get to our room before I get my hands on his bare skin.

He pulls me into his body, kicking the door shut as we pass through and we're both immediately tangled around each other. I try to yank at his shirt because I need to get my hands on his bare skin like yesterday. He obliges by yanking it over his head. I pull mine off and he stills my hand.

"You don't have to do that, Sophia." His voice has drops to a gravelly whisper, and I can see the need in his eyes contradicting his words.

"I know. I want to."

The air soothes my fevered skin when I pull my shirt over my head. I don't know what it is, but tonight feels important. Like it's the culmination of weeks of tension that's been building between us. I know we have so many other things to worry about, like how we're going to track down and neutralize the threat of my uncle, but that's one of the reasons this moment matters so much. We don't know what's going to happen tomorrow, so we have to enjoy today while it lasts. Each moment is a breath of air that will be gone in what is a mere millisecond in the existence of the universe.

We fall back on the bed, and my hands run up the heated skin of his back. His well-honed muscles slide under my touch. Our mouths crash together, and I run my hands through his hair, tugging him closer. Flashes of his thoughts pass through my mind as our bare skin joins us together even closer, and I can see myself through his eyes. It's a weird but good feeling. I wonder if he can do the same for me. I trace a finger over the tattoo imprinted on his back, and he shivers at my touch with a low groan. There's a heady power to that. The ability to move him that deeply with a single touch.

There are still too many clothes separating us, and I push at his sweatpants, trying to get them off. He pulls back a bit. "Wait a sec, Soph."

I place a hand on his rough, stubbly cheek and look into his eyes. "It's fine. I'm ready. For you. I want this."

A shadow passes behind his ocean eyes, darkening them with something. What is it, guilt? I seize the thread of the bond and try to sink into his mind the way I have a couple of times unconsciously when we were close. A barrier slams into place blocking his thoughts from me, and it's like he dumped a bucket of ice water over my head, dousing the flames.

I untangle myself from his limbs and look him in the eyes. "What are you hiding from me?"

He lays there with that guilty look in his eyes and rubs the back of his neck but doesn't reply. He doesn't want to lie to me, but he also isn't into sharing whatever is going on in that head of his. Well, if that isn't a mood killer, I don't know what is. I was about to share the most intimate thing with him, and he's hiding something from me.

"Good night, Logan." When I roll over to get up and brush my teeth, he pulls me back in close, kissing the top of my head. I sigh and relax into him for a moment before pulling away again.

"Going to brush my teeth. If you feel like sharing, shoot. If not, I'm tired and need to get to sleep." His silence speaks for itself, and he lets me slip out of his arms this time.

Ideas race through my head as I brush my teeth and I dismiss each one. I can't think of anything he'd want to hide from me unless...he's planning on leaving. How many times has he said he's going to track down Zeus? He couldn't possibly be planning on doing that without me, could he? Yes, yes he could. That's what he's hiding. I thought we were a team. I thought we were in this together, but he's still trying to protect me. My skills might not be there yet, and my magic is still a bit of a wild card, but I need to help finish this thing. I need to be there and if he can't see that, then he doesn't know me very well.

He's staring at the bathroom door with a pained look on his face when I emerge. My gaze slides down to the sweatpants I didn't manage to get him out of, and I can tell why he's uncomfortable. Too bad for him. I plop down on the bed. "You're planning on leaving. Without me." It's a statement of fact, not a question.

His eyes squeeze shut, but he still doesn't respond. "I thought I blocked my thoughts from you." There it is. His response all but outright admits that I'm right.

"You did. Good job. Just because I can't read your thoughts doesn't mean I can't tell what's going on in that head of yours."

Still nothing from him. He's not even going to try to deny it. "Well, what was your brilliantly thought-out plan? Do you even remember what happened last time you left me behind?"

His face goes an ashy gray at the reminder that I got attacked at the compound and on the road with Garrett when he left without me. "You're safe here."

"No, we're safer together. And since you're not telling me about this amazing plan of yours, I'm going to assume you were winging it. Never a smart idea."

"We can't keep living like this. Constant fear, never knowing when our lives are going to get upturned. Trapped at this cottage, not allowed to leave or see our families."

"Yeah, I agree. That's why I need to come with you. And we need a plan first. All we know is that Zeus has been hiding out in the Nether Realm, and he has a bunch of creepy Mage ghosts at his disposal. That's it. You running off without a way of tracking him down or fighting him when you get there is stupid and it will get you killed and I can't take that because...I'm falling for you, Logan. Or maybe I've already crashed to the ground at your feet. I'm yours and you're mine and we're in this together. We can do this, but we need to do it as equals. You and me. Plus, maybe that group of random weirdos we seem to be stuck with now."

He snorts out a laugh and turns to me with an apology in his eyes. "You're right. I know you're right, but all this inaction is killing me. I want to get out there now and do something about it. And the thought of you being in danger. I can't tell you what that does to me. It doesn't change what I know about you. You're fierce and strong and way smarter than me, obviously. But you're right. We should think this through first."

"Of course I'm right. I'm the brains of this operation. You should know that by now."

"Well, I do know that. What does that make me then? The brawn?" His mouth twists in a sardonic grin and he flexes his arm. It sends a thrill through my gut, but I push it aside.

"You're the beauty, of course." I tease him.

"Not possible. You're the most beautiful thing on this planet."

I smile. "Just this planet?"

"Yeah, don't get greedy. I'm sure there are some hot alien chicks out there in some other galaxy."

I laugh and snuggle back into his side. The frenzied need might have dissipated, but this comfortable intimacy is good too. I lay my head on his shoulder and slip into a deep sleep.

CHAPTER 32
Logan

"It's planning day!" I announce to the motley crew gathered in the kitchen at breakfast time. My mouth pulls down in a frown when I don't see a certain golden head. "Where's Sophia?" An awareness of her tugs at the bond, and I know where she is before Liz even speaks.

"I think she found the library," Liz says. "I'm pretty sure she could find a book after the apocalypse. Actually, you know what? She'd live in a library after the end of days. Probably a smart idea. You can't eat books, but they will tell you how to grow anything or use any sort of weapon. She'll outlive us all."

And welcome to random thoughts from my sister. "I'm sure she would. Anyone know if she ate anything before she lost herself in our book collection?"

They all look at each other. "No, she didn't. I was here when she came down." Trey's the one who replies.

"Okay, I'll drag her out of there for some sustenance."

I head into the small study/library and a minor flare of anger flicks at my brain when I see Sophia and Garrett's blond heads bent over some books. Her laugh bubbles out at something he says, and the anger twists into jealousy. I want to be the only one to make her laugh like that. That's a dumb thought, but sometimes you can't stop the things that pop into your brain. I know other people will make her laugh. I don't want it to be him, though. His lips have touched hers even if only briefly. Unfortunately, I had to witness it, so the image is seared into my brain forever.

"What's up?"

Satisfaction soothes the angry beast inside when her whole face lights up at the sight of me. That's better. "We did some reading on Shades and the Nether Realm. I told you it was planning day." That she did. I didn't realize planning day was going to involve reading books, but I guess most things do for Sophia, so it makes sense. It certainly hasn't hurt us so far. She was the one who tracked down the Mage that removed her cuff.

The smile on Garrett's face is tight at the interruption. Good. "You should get something to eat, my queen."

She rolls her eyes at me. "Really?"

"You didn't like princess. I thought you might want a promotion."

"Nope. Try again."

"Oh, I will. Don't worry about that. I'd go with bookworm, but worms are slimy and creepy. I could never compare you to one of those."

"Maybe so, but they're also useful. They make soil more nitrogen rich and promote plant growth."

"Of course they do. Still slimy, and you are many things, but slimy isn't one of them."

"I'm gonna grab some breakfast," Garrett says, standing up and returning a book to the shelf. His eyes slide from me to Sophia and then back again as he exits.

"Oh, you're still here. Hadn't noticed."

"Logan, you don't need to be such an ass all the time."

"But you like my ass." I turn around to display it for her. A giggle escapes, even though her mouth is turned down in disapproval. There it is. That laugh is all mine.

"Can I finish reading this one?" She looks at the book with a longing that almost makes me jealous again. That would be completely ridiculous, though. I can let myself be a little jealous of a floppy-haired thief whose lips have touched hers, but a book is going too far.

"Nope. You need food or you'll waste away, and I'm not carrying you around all day. I don't have time for that."

"Fine, but I'm coming back here after."

"I hope you at least learned something useful." This library is smaller than the one at our house, but it's still got a decent collection. My family has been collecting books for decades, centuries maybe. Not sure what would happen if something happened to us and a mundane was the first person to gain access to one of our houses. They'd think we were pagans or something. Magic isn't a religion though, it's a skill or talent you're born with or you learn to control. It's all around us all the time, the mundys just can't wield it. I certainly don't envy them that. Sometimes my father's rules and the role set out for me is stifling, but I can't imagine my life without magic. It's also what brought me to Sophia.

Sophia is gracious enough to not call me out on my plan to take off, but she points out the need to do something. We can't wait here for the inevitable attack. Or for someone we love to get kidnapped again.

We linger in the kitchen after breakfast. There's plenty of room at the big table for us all to sip coffee and lounge while we figure out a plan of action.

"The biggest problem is that we don't know where Zeus is. Even if we had something that belonged to him, Garrett can't track him in the Nether, so how do we draw him out?"

Ivy's gaze darts from Sophia to me and back. "You're not going to like this..."

Steel hardens my face, and I send all of my disapproval into one look. "Then don't say it."

"But, Logan. It might be the only way."

"What?" Sophia asks.

"He's looking for you, Sophia, right? So you might be the only one who can draw him out."

"You want to use me as bait? This idea got tossed around the last time we were trying to get to him."

"And the answer was no last time, too." I'm not even contemplating this one. Everything inside of me rebels against the idea of putting her in danger on purpose. After all, I was tied to her with this bond to protect her. It's more than that now, though. I would sacrifice anything for her at this point.

"And look how well the alternate option turned out last time. Liz got taken instead because she was trying to make a deal with someone shady. It's not using me as bait so much as going out into the open. We're planning on doing that anyway, right? Going out to face him down. This way, we'd be able to pick a location to square off with him. It would give us a tactical advantage, right?" Sophia takes hold of the idea and runs with it, nodding her head and using her hands to emphasize her points.

"She has a point, man. We can find a solid, defensible location, get ready, and then she can release a tiny hint of her power. Just a taste. See if it draws him out." My fingers are itching to close around Trey's throat as he nods along with her plan. "This could work."

"Yeah, draw out Zeus, his Shades, and who knows what else her power might attract. Anything or anyone could show up." I try to tamp down the anger and fear to reason with them.

"What's your plan?" Sophia tilts her head in challenge.

The problem is I don't have one. No plans. No ideas on how to track him down. He's like a ghost himself in the Nether Realm. Existing beyond our ability to track him. "I don't know." I bite out in frustration and slam my hand on the table. There are no good options here.

"Okay. Let's revisit that," Garrett says. "Why don't we talk about the rest of the plan? How are we going to fight him? What about the Shades? Sophia and I were doing some research this morning to see what we could come up with. It looks like your elemental powers will be the most useful against them. Ivy's plant control could be good for slowing Zeus down and for any of the corporeal Shades. Daggers and blades will only work on anything that's solid."

"So what's your purpose here, then?" I level Garrett with a stare. He doesn't have any useful magical skills that will help in this battle, and physical training will only go so far.

"I've got some spells up my sleeve. That's one of the things Sophia and I started researching this morning. And then if anything goes wrong, I'll get Sophia out of there fast. The last thing we want is for her to get captured, right? That would be bad for everyone." The hard mask he wears on his face all the time softens when he looks at her. I clench my fist tight. It will piss Sophia off if I punch him.

"Fine. Did you figure anything else out we can do, general?" I turn to her.

"There are some spells to send Shades back to the Nether Realm and slam a portal shut. They're pretty intricate. Not sure if we have time to master something like that, but we can try." She continues to amaze me with how much she's learned about magic in such a short period of time.

"Sounds good." Anything that will help sounds good to me at this point, no matter how far out the idea is.

"When are we going?" I've been trying to ignore the constant drumming of Liz's fingers on the table during our conversation. She hasn't contributed anything, but her energy is off the charts right now.

"I think we can get ourselves together and pick a location by Friday, maybe. That gives a few days to plan and prepare. What do you think, Trey?" I think this might be the first time I've asked for his opinion since he showed up to help guard Sophia and the look of surprise that crosses his face acknowledges that fact.

"Uh, yeah. I think that'll work. The sooner the better is probably good, but we don't want to run off unprepared."

"Good. I need to get away from this place." Liz springs up from the table and bolts out the door so fast you'd think the chair was on fire. She's probably going for a run to get rid of the excess energy she carries around. I'm used to her, but the others look a little floored by her abrupt departure.

"What's the plan? Other than Liz, obviously, we should all work on something. I'd like to keep researching the Shades and the spell to send them back. Someone needs to find a suitable location for the showdown."

"I'll look after that." Trey's deep voice rumbles out.

"And then we need to prepare. We can all pack a few of our own things in case we get stuck overnight somewhere, but we need to make sure we have food, weapons, and any other necessities. Who's going to be in charge of that?"

Sophia is making notes in a pink spiral notebook in her precise handwriting. I never thought organization would be so hot, but here we are. I guess it's all part of the package. The smart, sassy, booknerdy package that is all her.

"I've got weapons under control." I pull a chain out from under my shirt. The key to our weapons cabinet dangles from it.

"And food?" She prompts.

"Sure. I've got food too. I'll get Ivy to help."

She slams her notebook shut. "Perfect. I'm going back to the library."

My eyes fall on Trey. I don't have too much to do yet, so maybe I'll talk to him about scouting out a location. Then I'll see if I can drag Sophia out of her books to get in a little magic training. She shouldn't neglect that now that we're so close to taking action.

CHAPTER 33
Sophia

The book weighs me down as I hug it to my chest. The aged sheets of paper feel like they could crumble under my touch, and I don't want to ruin the ancient manuscript. I don't really want to take it outside, but I don't think it would be the best idea to practice this spell in the house, especially not now with my unpredictable powers. Sometimes they seem to be inaccessible and sometimes they come roaring to the surface when I'm not expecting it. An image pops into my head of flames licking at the ancient tome until it's a pile of ash kicking my heart into overdrive.

I hesitate on the front porch. The wind is whipping snow flurries around in a chaotic whirlwind. Steady hands land on my shoulders as I duck back inside and collide with someone. I lift my chin up to see who I crashed into and my eyes meet a pair of eyes that look almost green in the eerie grey light coming through the door.

"I'm so sorry, Garrett."

His eyes fall on the spell book I'm clutching to my chest as if it's a life preserver. "It's all good. What are you up to?"

"I wanted to practice this spell we found, but I thought it would be safer if I did it outside. I can't take this book out there. It's going to get destroyed." My hand strokes the cover that's so worn with age it feels like silk under my fingertips.

"Don't they have a work shed out back? Maybe we can borrow that if there's enough room in there."

I don't know why I didn't think of that. "Great idea. I'll go ask Logan."

I place the book down on a side table and bounce off to the kitchen where Logan and Trey are still at the table. Their dark heads are bent over a laptop and a sense of tentative camaraderie floats through the bond. It's so good to see them getting along that I hate to interrupt.

"Um, Logan." I keep my tone soft. I'm almost afraid that if I speak too loud, I'll startle them back into animosity.

Logan looks up immediately, and the warmth of his love brings a smile to my face. "What's up, Soph?"

"I was wondering if that shed out back would be big enough to practice my spell."

"Definitely." He pushes up from his chair and rummages through a drawer in the kitchen. I almost laugh when I see the junk drawer full of every conceivable bit of nonsense. There's everything in there, from elastic bands to batteries. A snorted laugh escapes when he pulls out a hot pink lanyard with a key dangling from it. There's a triumphant grin on his face.

"Got it. Want me to come with you?" His steps eat up the ground until he's close enough to feel the heat emanating from his body.

"No, I've got this. You and Trey look busy." I twirl a strand of hair around my finger. "I'm actually going to take Garrett. He knows a lot about spell casting, you know. Witchy thing."

His lips press together. He's probably trying to stop himself from saying something he'll regret. "Ok. Be careful."

I give him a smile, but when I turn to walk away, his hand closes on my elbow and he spins me back around, straight into his arms. His head tilts, and he leans down, capturing my lips in a tender kiss. I push up onto my tiptoes, molding my lips to his. The tip of his tongue darts out to trace the curve of my upper lip and my teeth capture his full lower lip.

We break apart at the jarring sound of a throat clearing.

Heat spreads up my neck as I catch sight of Trey over Logan's shoulder. "Sorry, Trey."

"S'all good."

"I'll see you later." Logan's low chuckle follows me as I manage to make my escape this time.

"Lo…later." I slam a hand over my mouth as I leave the kitchen. Did I almost just say the L word? Not the time or the place for that.

Garrett is waiting patiently for me when I get back to the front hall, but he's got a black garbage bag in his hand this time.

"Planning on murdering me in the shed and disposing of my body?" I quirk an eyebrow at the bag.

"Nah, there's plenty of time for that. This is for the book. Keep it safe from the snow and wind. I thought you'd want to wrap it up yourself."

An appreciative warmth swells in my chest that he was so considerate. Of course I want to make sure I wrap it up and keep it safe. If I was going to trust anyone with it, it would be him. I know he has a similar reverence for books as I do.

We tumble through the door of the shed, escaping the brutal wind that was threatening to lift me right off my feet. The interior is immaculate. A neat row of locked cupboards line one wall and a massive wooden work table sits off to the side. Other than that, there's a shiny riding lawnmower and a snowblower perfect for the long driveway. I twirl around in the large empty area that dominates the middle. "This is perfect."

Garrett leans on the wall with his eyes fixed on me.

"It's not even too cold in here." Looks like the work shed is insulated. Fancy.

I lay the book on the work table and the sweet musty smell of old books sends a smile to my face when I flip to the spell. Garrett snags the bookmark I used to mark my place before I can stop him.

"My weapon of choice for the zombie apocalypse is unicorns?" I stifle a laugh at the confusion all over his face as he stares at the cartoon image of a unicorn with a zombie speared on its rainbow horn.

"Um, Xavier got that one for me. He designed the image and ended up having a whole set printed for my sixteenth birthday. T-shirt, bookmark, tote bag, the works. He's not known for his restraint." My stomach does an uncomfortable flip at the thought of how I left things between us. I miss him so much, but it's better this way. Safer if he keeps his distance.

"Okay then." It looks wildly out of place when he puts it down on the table next to the book.

I memorized the words of the incantation this morning in the library, but now I need to practice them with power. I don't know how we're going to tell if they're working without opening a portal to the Nether, but since that's clearly not an option, I guess we'll have to hope it works. The lack of certainty makes me uncomfortable. I like everything planned out and under control, but I'm trying to at least learn to manage my anxiety at the uncertainty that plagues me at every turn these days.

Garrett backs up a few steps as I start reciting the Latin words. I looked up the pronunciation and every, so they come out crisp, clean and precise. I don't feel anything. No tingle of power stirring within me to weave itself into the words.

"Sounds good," he says.

"Yes, but I don't feel anything. There's no magic to it. I don't know what I'm doing wrong."

"Maybe you're concentrating too hard on the perfection of the words and trying to control the magic. I can't say that I know what it feels like to be a Mage with all those powers bubbling within you." A longing look passes over his face. "But when I pull power from an object or a natural phenomenon to use in a spell, I have to let go and allow the power to well up into the words. Coax it to me, not force it." His hands move in time with his words as he tries to describe the feeling. "That probably doesn't make sense."

It actually does make sense. Now that I think about it, my magic comes most naturally when I let it take over, something that's hard for me. I'm always trying to tamp it down or control it. "No, it does."

I close my eyes as I recite the words again. This time I don't try to force the magic into the words. I can feel it deep down, perking it's ears up like a curious puppy. I let the buzz travel through my veins. It's almost there when I reach the end of the incantation, but my jaw is still tense. I think I've been a little afraid of my powers since they all came flooding back and I knocked everyone out at Lena's house.

"You can do this, Sophia. Just let go." His familiar voice is soothing and I realize he's come to be someone I trust. In spite of everything that's gone down between us, I trust him.

I try one more time. Concentrating on relaxing my muscles from my tightly clenched jaw to my shoulders that I didn't even know had been creeping up toward my shoulders until now. I let my mind go to my blank white space that I escape to before a stressful event and it comes. I can see the golden glow of magic infusing the words with power in my head.

The familiar tingle of magic surrounds me in a cloud, and I know I did it.

"Yes!" I jump up and down, clapping my hands together. "I got it."

Garrett sweeps me up in a hug, spinning me around. "You did. You totally got this." His voice goes husky as he drops me and breaks away. "Sorry. I didn't mean to…"

I'm flustered. "It's fine, Garrett. You didn't do anything wrong."

"Maybe not, but I wanted to." He paces the room.

"Oh, uh." I don't know what to say to that. Garrett and I tried the dating thing when I thought he was a completely different person. We had a hard restart when he picked me up and start on this wild journey with us Mages, but I thought we were both firmly on the friendship page.

"It's fine. You don't need to worry about it. I know you don't feel the same way and even if you did, I would never let anything happen between us. I'm no good for anyone."

"That's not true, Garrett. I know you're a good person. You came to help me and you've stuck with us throughout all this craziness. You're facing down Zeus with us."

"That doesn't change all the things I've done. I'm not a good person, Sophia. Helping you out now doesn't erase all the bad stuff."

My heart aches for him. He's been through so much. I know he essentially became a thief for hire after his family died, but he lost everything. It's no surprise that he lost himself. "Doing bad things doesn't necessarily make you a bad person, Garrett. I know you're not a bad person. You never would have come when I called if you were. I know you're not evil and you wouldn't hurt someone."

His eyes go wild and he drops his hands on my shoulders, staring deep into my eyes. "But that's the thing. I did hurt you. Taking that job from Zeus. I've tracked people down before, but they were bad people, criminals. I knew they were going to be punished, but I never let myself think about those details. You were just another person to track down. When I first met you, I didn't know what to think. You were all sweet and innocent. I went along with it until you got kidnapped. Then I dropped the contract. I should have disappeared from your life then, but I didn't. I stuck around trying to figure out if there was another way you could be useful to me."

My stomach clenches. He was angling to use me. Like Logan thought. "You're only here to use me?"

"Not anymore. That was before. Now I'm only here to help. To make up for everything I did to cause you harm."

"You don't have to be here if you don't want to. Nobody's keeping you. Don't let your guilt force you to stay and make amends."

"That's not it. Ever since I picked you up to track down Logan and Ivy, I knew I wouldn't go back to my old life. I'm not going to steal anymore. I'm going to help people. I'm in this until the end."

I mull his words over in my head, feeling the truth in them. I nod at him. Curiosity tugs at my brain. I need to know why. I've never been good at figuring out people's motivations. "Why did you start stealing in the first place? I guess it was hard to make ends meet after they died, but wasn't there anyone you could turn to?"

His shoulders slump in defeat. "That's the thing. My parents had an insurance policy and savings. I never needed to steal. At first I tried to go on living my normal life, but I flunked out of school and wore out everyone's sympathy. I don't know why I did it at first. Maybe I was hoping to get caught, but after that first job, I finally felt something other than pain. The adrenaline rush, the fear. It was exciting. It broke through the numb shell and let me live again. At least some sort of life. It was the only time I felt something…until I met you."

My eyes widen. I don't like where this is going.

He pins me under his gaze. "I care about you, Sophia. As more than a friend, and I know you don't feel the same way. And I know I don't deserve you, but who knows what's going to happen to us in a couple of days. We might not all make it through, so I needed to tell you how I feel."

"Garrett…I care about you too. Just not in that way. But you deserve someone who returns the feeling. You are worthy of love."

His touch is electrifying as he runs a thumb over my jaw, chucking my chin like a weird relative. His hand trembles as he pulls it away, but he doesn't take it any farther. That's how I know he's not a bad person deep down. He respects me enough not to push it even though I can see the need in his eyes.

"Saying it doesn't make it true." He backs away as if he has to put some space between us.

"No, it's true because it's a fact. I don't say things unless they're solidly based in evidence. I've seen your actions and I know you're a good person. You're going to have to accept that. And we're all coming back from this unharmed. We have to." I infuse as much confidence into my final sentence as I can, but I know I just contradicted myself. We might not all come out of this unscathed. It's going to be dangerous, and any number of things could go wrong.

CHAPTER 34
Logan

After snagging a quick kiss from Sophia, I head back to the kitchen. Trey has pulled out a fancy-looking laptop. I'm sure it's from the magical council, so it will have all the bells and whistles, including a serious firewall and anti tracking software. The Mages might not move at the speed of light to keep their personal views up to date, but they've definitely learned the art of keeping their information safe in the technological age. It's one reason they're still so fond of books, but even Mages use cell phones and the internet.

"Hey, Trey. How's the search going?"

There's surprise behind his eyes when he looks up at my friendly tone of voice. "Good." His reply comes out cautiously.

"Mind if I help?" I stay back with my arms crossed over my chest, ready for his rejection.

"Sure."

"What you got so far?" I swing a chair around and lean in close to check out the screen.

"We obviously need somewhere that's easily defensible and far enough from mundanes that there won't be an exposure risk.

I nod. "What are you thinking? Empty warehouse?"

"Yeah, I thought about that. But it'll be a logistical nightmare if it has too many entrances and windows."

I nod. He's right. Our numbers are limited. We need somewhere to keep Sophia safe so she can get her spell ready in case everything goes to Hades and we need to send him back to the Nether Realm fast. We need to catch Zeus unaware and get him locked down fast. I have no idea what magic he has going on right now, but if he doesn't have time to bring too many friends to the party, we might be okay. "What about a house? An abandoned house somewhere."

"I thought of that, but again, our vision will be limited. Too many blind spots. I was thinking maybe an abandoned storefront? Big glass front windows, no second floor and limited entrances. We'll be able to see him coming, but as long as it has some places to hide, maybe a back room, we claim the advantage."

"That's a great idea."

The comforting tingle of the bond announces Sophia's presence before her words. "Um, Logan."

I can't stop a huge smile from spreading across my lips when I see her. "What's up, Soph?" Missed my opportunity for a new nickname.

"I was wondering if that shed out back would be big enough to practice my spell."

"Definitely." This drawer is a hot mess. My mother is such a neat person, but she has a tendency to be a bit of a closet slob.

"Got it. Want me to come with you?" I kind of hope she says yes. I don't know why I didn't think of the shed before as a rendezvous spot to get away from all the prying eyes in this house.

"No, I've got this. You and Trey look busy. I'm actually going to take Garrett. He knows a lot about spell casting. Witchy thing."

I slam my lips together to avoid saying something she won't like. I trust her, and she trusts him. "Ok. Be careful."

I can't resist giving her a reason to think about me in, so I clasp her elbow and spin her around for a kiss. She leans into it and the world fades away as I get lost in her warmth.

I send some daggers at Trey when she pulls away at the sound of his throat clearing.

"Sorry, Trey," she says.

"S'all good."

"I'll see you later." I call out laughing as she boots it out of the room like her shoes on fire.

"Lo…later."

"Wow, dude. You're falling hard, aren't you?"

"I think it's reasonable to say that I've fallen." There's no point in denying it.

"Okay then. Can you think of anywhere close enough that might work? The only issue would be to find an abandoned store that's isolated from mundanes." I appreciate that he accepts my statement about Sophia and leaves it alone.

"Yeah, so a standalone store or a plaza that's still under construction or abandoned." I'm mulling locations over in my head, but not coming up with anything.

"Right," Trey says. "Great idea." His fingers fly over the keyboard. "Look at this. There was a planned community outside of Pinecrest that got abandoned by the developers when they ran out of money. That would be perfect." Pinecrest is only a couple of hours' drive from here. That would work.

There's an article about the development and he finds a site where someone has posted pictures of abandoned places. A chill runs through me at the photos he flips through of sanitariums and schools. The schools are the worst. There's something so creepy about deserted schoolrooms. When he gets to the ones of the development, there are photos of houses in various stages of construction and a strip mall full of empty storefronts.

"That one." My finger jabs at a store on the end of the strip that's completely finished with an intact window. "Can you zoom in?" Looks like there's a long counter set near the back that would be perfect to use as a shield. We'd definitely have the upper hand there.

The picture blurs a bit as he zooms in, but you can clearly see a long counter at the back.

He squints at the screen. "That would totally work. We should drive out there today to check it out. Make sure it's safe and no one is squatting there."

Trey's hand smacks mine in a high five and I think it's the first time I've touched him not in anger in years.

"You're on. We should wait until after lunch and then we can head out there.

I'm rooting through the cupboard for a snack when Ivy walks in. "Hey, guys. How's it going in here?"

"We found the spot," Trey replies.

"That's great. Where is it?"

She sits down beside Trey and he shows her the site we were scoping out. I'm pouring myself a glass of water when the fern beside the sink stirs. Its tendrils perk up and I swear it must grow an inch or two. I glance back at Ivy. She must be leaking a little magic.

Trey and I chatted on the car ride and got caught up on everything we've missed in each other's lives. We've missed out on a lot, so it's good to reconnect. I'm impressed with how quickly he's moved up the ranks of the MED. He was always driven and ambitious, though.

Sophia wasn't thrilled she couldn't come with us, but it's better she stays there safe until she has to emerge as bait. That thought sends an icy dread through me, but I know it may be the only way we can tempt her uncle out of hiding. At least we'll be in control of the situation. We'll have the upper hand. Liz stayed behind to help her with her magic, so that eases my mind.

It looks promising as we park and get out of the car. A blanket of untouched snow covers the parking lot and walkways with a white blanket. Looks like nobody is in and out of this place. A lockbox is hanging from the door handle. I take one more glance around. When I'm satisfied the place is still a wasteland devoid of mundanes, I pull some magic to send some water at the box. As soon as it hits, I freeze the water, cracking it open. Trey's hand flies out to catch it before it hits the ground.

He pulls the key out of the mangled box. "Flashy much?"

"What would you have done? Gotten a sledgehammer out of your trunk? Nobody is around. We're fine."

The neglected lock clicks open with a groan of protest and we ease into the building.

We both start coughing as we kick up the thick layer of dust on the floor and it shoots down to our lungs, coating our throats.

Once we've recovered, we make our way in further at a sedate pace. The place is perfect. There's a lot of dust but no dangerous construction debris. There's room to crouch down behind the long counter, but no other furniture for our enemy to hide behind. A set of swinging doors behind the counter leads to a storeroom in the back. Other than a bunch of empty metal shelves, a big industrial sink, and some cleaning supplies, there's nothing back here. The perfect place to sequester Sophia so she can get her spell ready. I picture that conversation. Yeah, that'll go well.

"Looks perfect, right?" Trey asks.

"It's great. This is definitely the place. We should probably give it a sweep so we don't all die of dust inhalation before we even get a chance to fight him."

"You have a point."

The sun is hanging low in the sky by the time we finish cleaning the place up and walk out into the freezing cold. It wasn't warm before, but now the temperature has dropped to bone chilling levels.

I wait until we're on the road. "Look, man. I'm sorry," I say.

Trey's head swivels to me, but I avoid meeting his gaze, concentrating on the road instead. "For what?"

"For everything. What happened with Ivy, and pushing you away. I know it wasn't your fault. It was me. I felt guilty."

I can feel his eyes piercing with me. "It's ok. I get it. I know why you acted like such a dick." I dart a look at him. "I never blamed you. Not really. Maybe for stealing Ivy in the first place, but I know she was never yours to steal. She made her own decision."

Deep stuff dealt with, we go back to light banter for the ride home.

CHAPTER 35
Sophia

The last few days have passed way too fast in a blur of reading, training, and fighting. I've been too tired and still kind of annoyed with Logan for thinking it would be a good idea to ditch me here, so we haven't had a repeat of THAT NIGHT, but I've been gnawing on my cheek all day thinking about it. We're going to be leaving tomorrow. Who knows what could happen? I don't even want to think about the possibility, but this is going to be dangerous. One of us could get killed. The thought of Logan getting hurt shatters me, but it's a real possibility. I think I need to let go and enjoy every minute with him. I know I'll regret it if I don't.

Resolve in place, I put the book I was reading back on the shelf and head out to find him. I'm pretty sure I've got the spell down one hundred percent, but it's only a backup, anyway.

Hopefully, I won't even need to try my hand at random magic spells that most people spend years perfecting.

I almost don't want to intrude when I catch sight of him and Trey sitting at the kitchen table polishing some already shiny swords. None of the usual heat and distrust is lurking beneath the surface. They look like what they would be if circumstances were different, a couple of old friends sharing a moment. I've noticed they've started to let go of the tight grips they've had on old resentments for the past couple of days. Maybe they've been thinking along the same lines as I have about how precious life is. It's nice to see them reconnecting either way. I know how close they were growing up and that much friendship is a shame to waste.

The tingle at the back of my neck hits me, and I realize Logan probably knows I'm standing here. As if he heard my thoughts, he turns slowly toward me, sweeping his gaze from head to toe before pushing up from the table and reaching over to slap Trey on the shoulder.

My feet leave the ground as he swoops me up, smacking a kiss on my forehead. He's been careful around me as if he knew I needed the space.

"Wanna go for a walk?" I ask, sliding a hand into his.

"For sure. Catch you later, man."

"Later, Logan." Trey studiously fixes his eyes on the blade he's buffing beyond perfection.

We bundle up and head outside. I need to have him to myself right now, which is a tall order around this house with everyone in residence.

"Anywhere in particular you want to go?" he asks as the cold air slaps me in the face when we step out the door. The air has that fresh, bracing scent of winter and it snowed again last night and actually stuck to the ground. There's only a couple of inches, but it covers the ground in a pristine white blanket and coats the trees in a layer of icing like on a gingerbread house. I eye the maple grove, but there's no privacy to be had there with the branches barren for the season. A little farther out, there's a small patch of evergreen trees with branches drooping under the weight of the snow.

"There." I point toward the little patch of trees.

"Your wish is my command." He lifts my pink mittened hand to his mouth for a kiss, spluttering and pretending to spit out a mouthful of fuzz from it.

"Uh huh." I roll my eyes at his antics.

He pushes aside some branches for me, and a shower of chilly flakes tickles my face. There's a little clearing in the middle. It's like a different world in there. Like we're in the middle of our own personal snow globe. The layer of snow and surrounding trees around us muffle the noise. This place is quiet to begin with, but this is another level of silence.

The peace and isolation give me the courage I need to lean in and grab the side of his face. I didn't count on the slipperiness of my mittens, though, and they slide off his face. I let out a giggle. Clearly, sexy is not my natural state of being.

He seems to get the point. He reaches behind my head and his gloves seem to have more traction because he pulls me roughly against him, cutting off my giggle as our lips meet. The chill that was setting in goes up in flames as he nibbles on my lower lip and scrabble to get a hold on his back. I should take the mittens off, right? This is worth a little frostbite.

"Maybe this was a bad idea," I say with a gasp.

"Not a chance. This was the best idea." He swallows any further comments that might slip out as we get lost in each other.

After what feels like a year and a second, all at the same time, he drags himself away from me. "You're shivering. We should get back inside."

"I'm fine." I lie. The heat from his kisses is great, but it's not actually keeping me warm in reality. Frostbite apparently is not cancelled out by lust.

"I mean. We're both probably going to need showers to warm up, so no one will miss us if we disappear for a bit." My favorite smirk is back. The one that's full of desire.

"Fair enough." I shiver at the promise in his voice.

Logan showers in the other bathroom so when I emerge from the ensuite in nothing but a towel he's in a pair of sweatpants that look soft enough to touch and he's drying his hair.

As he tosses his head back his abs ripple. His mouth drops and heat darkens his eyes when he catches sight of me.

I'm clutching the towel to me with one hand, but the other reaches out to run along the silky skin that stretches over the well-defined muscles of his chest. He shivers under my touch before closing a hand around my wrist.

"I know I said we'd have alone time, but we don't need to do anything."

I place a finger over his lips. "Logan. We don't know what tomorrow is going to bring. I want to be with you. I don't want anything getting in the way this time. No fights, no intrusive sisters or friends. Just us."

That seems to be enough convincing. He crushes me against him, hands tangling in my damp hair as we get lost in each other.

Goosebumps rise as he runs his hands over my smooth skin. I return the favor until we're both aching. When I reach lower he stills my hand.

"Not yet."

My eyes flick up to him under my lashes. I thought he wanted this.

"I'm ready. I want to."

"Not here. Not now when we're about to head off tomorrow morning for a dangerous battle."

"Right. That's what I'm saying. I want this before we go. I don't want to wait to see what happens tomorrow." I plead with him.

"That's exactly why not. You deserve everything. And I'm going to give it to you. When we don't have a knife hanging over our heads. Not to mention some time to ourselves without my sister in the next room."

My eyes drop closed. I know this isn't happening now that he's dropped the sister card.

"Fine, but once this is over, you're mine."

"I'm yours already. Always and forever, princess." I don't even reprimand him for the princess. I'm too happy to be snuggled in his arms warm and safe.

CHAPTER 36
Logan

We're gathered together at the breakfast table, all tense shoulders and forced jokes. My sister is the only one who seems genuinely unperturbed by our plans for the day. I keep shooting glances at Sophia to make sure she's ok. She sends me small smiles and nods in spite in spite of the grim atmosphere.

After breakfast, we pack up the car and Logan, Garrett, and I take Garrett's car, and the others pile into Trey's SUV. I don't even mind Garrett driving, since it means I can hold Sophia close for the entire drive. I'm not letting her go until I absolutely have to.

The foreboding feeling of dread worsens with each mile we get closer to the abandoned store. As we agreed on, we park one car out front and the other behind the storefront. This leaves us more escape routes if things go sour, and I have a bad feeling in my gut things are going to go sour. Sophia was eerily quiet on the ride other than looking up the store and area on street view. It was helpful but not what I'd expect from her.

"Come on, Soph. Time to go."

A fiery passion lights up her eyes as she climbs out of the car. She wraps her arms around my waist, and I pull her in close. Her head turns up for a kiss. It goes from soft to desperate in seconds.

"This is not goodbye, Sophia." I tell her firmly, willing it to be true.

We're approaching from the front. Trey's car is going around the back to cover that entrance.

We approach the store with caution. It looks undisturbed from yesterday. The fresh blanket of snow that fell last night has covered our footprints and there are no new ones. I can't see anything through the big front windows.

Sophia trails me through the front door and Garrett follows behind her, keeping alert for any signs of life. Our feet don't stir up as much dust after the sweep we gave it yesterday, but the place still has a musty odor that intensifies as we make it behind the front counter. The plan is for Sophia to release a bit of her magic and then stay in the backroom with Garrett to work on the spell while we wait for Zeus to show up.

The backroom is undisturbed, and we let Ivy and Trey in. I grab Sophia's hand and give her a nod as I give it a squeeze. I can feel her magic stirring as she pulls it up. A flicker of flame forms on her palm, lighting up the place. The flame builds into a small fireball, and she smiles until it keeps growing and her eyes go wide with panic.

"Look at me. Look at me, Sophia. You got this. I squeeze her hand one more time. Her brown eyes flicker behind the flame of her fireball and her pupils dilate as she focuses on me.

I can feel her panic easing and the fireball diminishes along with it until a loud roar sounds from the front of the store, and a sharp sulfuric stench hits me.

Her magic flares back to life as I whirl around, pulling out my knives. That was too fast. How could he have tracked her this quickly?

Shades start spilling through the swinging door in the backroom. We're swarmed, and I can't see past the shadowy figures surrounding us. They quickly surround us in a mass of black shadows we can't see past.

A handful of Mages also emerge from through the swinging door. Flashes of erratic lightning and fire blind us, and I have to let go of her to whip up a frenzy of wind that blows all the Shades back. The wind blows aside the wall of shadow, giving us a temporary reprieve from the shadows.

"Garrett, get Sophia out the back." I call out. He grabs her hand, but the Shades have surrounded us and there's no clear path to the door.

The battle rages around us and I'm surprised the floorboards are holding us up as we dart around. I'm using my fighting skills as much as possible to avoid tapping out of my energy reserves or setting the store on fire, but the Shades keep coming and kicking them does nothing except throw me off balance and give me a chill when my foot sinks through their smoky figures. They disperse and keep coming. Flames are crackling on my palm. The fire disperses the shadowy figures into dust and my wind keeps them back, but we've still got Mages coming at us. We're outnumbered.

I can feel Sophia's Archimage powers humming in the air, outstripping the rest of us as lightning and fire shoot from her hands. I send a bolt of lightning at one of the Mages that creeps behind her and he falls to the ground convulsing.

My heart sinks when Sophia's uncle emerges from through the door with a knife to her friend Xavier's throat. There are bruises on his face and a wound on his forehead is trickling blood.

A strangled scream comes from Sophia and I reach out for her, but she blurs out, slipping through my grasp. My heart sinks, but a couple of Mages come at me, and I whip out two knives to throw at them, not checking to see if they've landed before I spin into a low kick at the female Mage who comes at me from the right.

"I love you, Logan!" The call comes from across the room and when I look up again, Sophia has run straight into the arms of the enemy. I'm so mad at her right now I can't even process the words she said to me for the first time. Her uncle releases her friend's neck from his knife grip, but he doesn't let Xavier go, dragging them both toward the back door. I freeze in terror long enough to get swarmed by shades until I can't see her anymore. I try to run after them, but there are too many things going on around me and knife slices through my right arm with an agonizing burn.

I shake it off and sprint through the swinging door into the front of the store. As I make it through, I spot the reason for the seemingly endless stream of Shades. A whirling black whirlwind has formed in floor right in front of the door. It's an oily black mass of shadows that emanates a soft roar as it spits out Shades. It's a portal and Zeus is edging closer to it with Sophia and Xavier clutched in his arms.

CHAPTER 37
Sophia

The store is a mass of confusion, dark shadows, and bright flashes of light. I didn't hesitate for one second when I spotted Zeus holding a knife to Xavier's neck, but even after I turned myself over to him, Xavier is still white and shaking in his other arm.

"Let him go! You have me. Please." I beg him as lightning crackles along my skin.

"And I will, niece. As soon as I've got you safely out of here, he's free to go."

"Now. Let him go now." All of my anger, fear, and pain intertwine with Logan's in an overwhelming mass of emotion. My magic is sparking from my skin, rumbling inside me like a predator waiting for the right moment to pounce on its unsuspecting prey. It's been a lot to deal with ever since I got it back, but now I'm actually scared of it. I have no idea if I can control this fury lurking deep inside me. What scares me even more is I don't know if I want to control it.

"You don't get to make demands." His brown eyes look sinister in the grey light punctuated by occasional flickers of lighting and flame from the Mages. A ball of fire forms on the palm of his smooth hand and I eye it in disgust.

"Who did you have to kill for that power?"

"No one you know. Although that Lena you led me to gave me a nice jolt."

My heart sinks. Lena. One more person I led straight into the arms of this evil man. One more person whose blood is on my hands.

I thought he was going to lead us to the black hole by the front door that's spewing out a steady stream of black smoke that reassembles into vague human shapes once it's out. They're overtaking my friends. They can't die because of me, too. I don't know what to do. Logan's pain sears through me, and I almost double over.

Logan and Garrett burst through the door, surrounded by dark shadows and battling a pair of Mages. I cry out when I spot the blood pouring down Logan's right arm. I gather the crackling lightning that keeps sparking off my skin and send two bolts at the Mages who are battling with my guys. The unsuspecting Mages collapse, leaving Logan and Garrett with just the Shades to deal with. He drags me not to the portal but to a jagged hole in the front window. I struggle in his arms until I catch sight of Xavier's eyes wide with terror. My magic is too wild, too intense. I'm afraid I'll hurt my friend if I tap into any of the dangerous power currently building inside.

He hustles me out the door, and I blink at the sunlight that hurts my eyes after the intense darkness. If he wasn't still dragging Xavier behind him, I'd make a run for it. I'm surprised my friend is still on his feet after all that. He shoves me toward the road, but the fight spills out after us, and Liz zips around the side of the store, scooping me up and pulling me away from Zeus. I reach out for X and try to escape her grasp. I kick and claw at her, but she holds me tight. Zeus's eyes dart from me to Xavier and then he shrugs before sending a ball of fire right at my friend's chest.

Everything inside me turns to ice as Xavier's lifeless body falls to the ground as if it's in slow motion.

"Nooooooo." I let loose a bolt of lightning at Liz, and she drops me. My knees hit the icy ground hard before I scramble up and run back toward X.

I put my ear to his mouth and look at his chest. There's nothing but a blackened hole where his heart used to be. His huge, wonderful heart. My best friend. "No, no, no, no, no." My chest aches as my heart shatters into a million pieces. This is my fault.

I wrap my trembling arms around his shoulders and pull him in close, cherishing the last of the warmth that's already seeping from his body until he's nothing but a cold, lifeless shell of the person he was. The same as I am now. I'll never be warm again.

A deep rage replaces the painful ache, and I look up at the battle still raging around the abandoned plaza. Zeus has been drawn into the fight, and Liz, Logan, and Ivy surround him. Liz keeps darting around him in a blur and landing the occasional blow, while he exchanges balls of fire with Logan. Trey and Garrett are still in the thick of it with the Shades, and it looks like they're losing.

This needs to end before someone else dies. I need to end this. All the rage boils and bubbles inside me until I feel like a can of pop that someone has shaken. I concentrate on the words of the spell I learned with Garrett. There's no way I can target my magic to hit my uncle without taking out one of my friends, so I'm going to have to use the spell to drag him back to the Nether. Our plan lies in shambles around our feet anyway.

It's like the fuse has been lit on the rage that's been building inside me since I watched that ball of fire take my friend from me. The magic comes crackling to the surface and I feel like I'm electrically charged. I concentrate on the words of the spell, and a cloud of energy forms around me. I release the tight hold I've had on it. I shove a little extra force into my words, and let go sending it into the dark void.

The oily darkness spins faster and faster into a hypnotizing nightmare as it sucks the Shades back into it. The others keep fighting, but the roiling whirlwind starts dragging everyone else back toward it. My eyes widen as I realize my friends are losing ground to the sucking hole that's decreasing in size by the minute. The Mages that have fallen in the fight are the first to go down.

Zeus and my friends continue to struggle. I push my legs toward them to help. Liz is holding her ground, and Garrett has thrown up some kind of magical barrier that he and Trey are leaning against. Ivy has huge vines twisting all over her body to fight the pull of the portal, but my eyes widen in horror when I see Logan and Zeus losing ground to it.

My uncle meets my gaze with brown eyes that share an eerie similarity to mine, gleaming with fury. Hatred twists his face as he drops his eyelid in a wink and grabs Logan's arm before leaping backward into the abyss that's barely large enough for them.

Black spots dot my vision as I skid to a halt at the edge of the void that snaps shut as I reach it. A hollow emptiness replaces the warmth of the bond. My knees crumble beneath me, and I drop to the ground, pounding my fists on the pavement until someone gently pulls me up.

The magic stirs again in a restless buzz, like there are ants crawling all over my skin. Rage lights me up, melting the arctic wasteland inside me. The power builds and builds and I let it. I hear someone call my name and I'm distantly aware of sirens wailing in the distance, but I ignore it all to lose myself to this anger. All this time I've been wasting energy holding it in, and it's effortless to let it go. It's amazing. It comes rushing out of me in a tidal wave and the sky lights up in a blinding flash. A deafening roar hammers my ears as the entire strip of stores. I throw an arm over my face as rubble and glass pelt me in painful hits and slices.

A firetruck comes screaming up along with a couple of police cars and an ominous white van. A magical enforcement team spills out in their black uniforms with the distinctive red crest. It must be a team of Mages and Witches, so we're in the clear from the notice of mundanes.

As red, orange, and yellow flames lick away at the building, The MED team approaches us with caution.

I lie there limp until someone helps my drained body up.

After a blur of getting checked over by the medics, we have to go through the entire story. The tears finally come when I tell them about Xavier and Logan. There's nothing but a sea of guilt and numbness inside me. The tears are just there. My brain is a fog grief and exhaustion.

"We're going to take you back to HQ. You'll need to share your story with everyone there." A stranger in a uniform takes hold of my elbow. I want to shake it off, but I've got nothing left.

"Can't we go home for the night?" Liz pleads. Her natural exuberant state is gone, and she looks like a wilting flower with her teal dipped hair hanging limp and sweaty in her face. Cuts and welts mar her face and hands. I saw her fight with Zeus. She must have used all of her reserves. "We'll come back in the morning to share our story again. Our parents will make sure of it."

"I'm sorry, miss. You have to come with us. We'll send someone to pick up your vehicles and you can drive home after."

"Okay."

I'm physically aware of Liz's hand closing over mine, but it's gone so numb I don't feel it. By the time we're seated in the van, I'm shivering so hard my teeth are chattering.

"She's going into shock. Can we get a blanket?" A panicked voice sounds far away, like I'm hearing it through a tunnel. A woman hands Liz a blanket and she settles it around me. She grabs my chin and tilts my head until I'm looking into her eyes. I drop my lids to avoid the pain it causes to look into her eyes that match his so perfectly. "Stay with me, Sophia."

"You promised, Liz. You promised we would be alright." Her whole face crumples.

"I know. I know I did. I'm so sorry. I'm so sorry."

"It's ok. It's not your fault. It's mine."

"No it's not. It's not your fault. You can't take that on yourself."

"I'm tired."

"Don't fall asleep." She slides onto the bench seat next to me and pulls me in close. Her warmth at least eases the chill that's taken over, but the numb hopelessness remains.

CHAPTER 38
Sophia

The drive back to the NAMC compound is somber. I imagine this team came from a closer location, so I don't know why they're taking us all the way back there. I should probably call my mom, but I don't know if I can muster up the energy.

I hear Liz's soft voice mumbling into her phone me. She'll tell my mom what happened. As long as she knows I'm physically ok, it'll put her mind at ease.

"We have to go to the compound first to answer some questions, then we'll come home."

Liz listens to her response.

"Please don't. I have no idea how long we'll be, but I'll let everyone know about your invitation, and I'll call you when they let us go."

She pauses again.

"I really don't think that's a good idea right now, Mom. Sophia's not so good right now. Mentally. Physically, I think she's fine."

She's wrong. I'll never be fine again. My friend is dead because of me. The void swallowed my heart, and I don't know if he's alive or dead. I can't even think of the blood streaming down his arm as it dragged him away from me. I'm completely hollowed out.

"Always." She says. "I love you, Mom."

"Hey, Sophia. You still with me." I turn my head toward her, but I don't even see my friend.

When we get to the compound, a guard leads us down a long white hallway. I've never been inside this building. "Take those three into room five." He gestures at the second guard, pointing at Ivy, Trey, and Garrett. "You two come with me."

Liz practically carries me into the room. Another guard joins us across the table.

"Tell me everything that happened. Beginning to end," one guard says.

Liz fills him in on the entire story. I'm vaguely aware that he occasionally directs a question at me, but I can't get out more than the odd whispered yes or no.

I'm not even aware of the tears that start flowing when he asks about Xavier until they drip onto my hands.

"And then she blew up the entire strip?" He looks skeptical.

"Yes."

They get up and leave us sitting there.

After what feels like hours, the guards return with a council member and another guard, giving the small room an edgy crowded feeling. "Take her. That one can go." Someone's hand grips my upper arm.

"No. What are you talking about? You're not taking her," Liz cries out.

"She committed a crime. She leveled a building in a mundane neighborhood in broad daylight. You know we must hold her accountable."

"It was self-defense. There were Shades swarming us, and Zeus had opened a portal to the Nether Realm. She saved everyone. Not Xavier or Logan. Would you want all that getting out into the world?"

"So you say. Where's your proof? The MED team saw no evidence of Shades when they arrived. I've never heard of multitudes of them gathering anywhere."

"If you try to take her, you're going to have to go through me. Where's my father?"

"He's not here. This is happening. If we have to go through you in the process, we will."

The door bursts open and Mr. Armstrong appears. "Let her go." The commanding tone in his voice allows for no protest, and the steely grip on my arm tightens for a brief moment before releasing me.

I'm barely aware of the car ride back to the Armstrong's house, but I finally notice something when we get back.

"Where's Garrett?" I ask.

"They locked him up, too. Apparently, his Witchy heritage was crime enough to hold him." Liz's pretty face twists with disgust at the kind of system that would do that.

I whip around in my seat. "We have to go back. We have to get him." I unsnap my seatbelt and open the car door to jump out as it still rolls up the driveway.

"I'll deal with getting him released tomorrow. I needed you out of there," Mr. Armstrong says. "If they'd kept you there tonight, I would never have gotten you out. There's something going down at the council. Lawrence has swayed some of the members over to his side and they're planning a coup."

I blink at him. "If you don't help us get him out tomorrow, I'm going in myself." I don't care about the consequences. I can't lose Garrett, too. I wish I could go back right now, but I know I'm useless. I've got nothing left. It's like I have the cuff back on again. I'm completely void of the tingle of magic. I drained it completely when I took that place down.

My mom is out the door and has her arms around me before we're halfway up the walk. Her soft lavender scent surrounds me, but it isn't accompanied by the usual comforting feeling.

Mrs. Armstrong pulls Liz and Ivy into her arms, but her face crumbles for her missing son.

I'll get him back. If it's the last thing I do, I'm getting my heart back. My only fear is what Zeus will do to him before I get there.

THANK YOU READERS

Thank you so much for taking the time to read my debut series. You can follow me on Twitter, Instagram, Facebook, or TikTok to see what craziness is going on in my author life. Visit my website **nicoleaoliverauthor.com** to get these links or sign up for my newsletter. Hint, my newsletter subscribers get all the latest news first in addition to bonus scenes, freebies, and giveaways.

Finally, if you loved this book please leave a review on Amazon, Goodreads, or wherever you buy your books. Reviews mean so much to us indie authors.

ACKNOWLEDGEMENTS

I can't believe I'm no longer a debut author. It's been a fantastic journey publishing my first two novels within a year. I couldn't have done it alone, though.

Thanks so much to my amazing family. From my husband who always supports me and shares his home office when I'm off work, to my twins who are my inspiration to live my dreams. Even with the "Nobody cares about that except Mama." comment. I might let you all read my books. One day.

We all need women in our lives who lift us up and encourage us every step of the way. Thanks, Steph for being my cheerleader. I love you.

To all my Starbucks fam. Thanks for those of you who bought my first book. It's probably better if you never talk to me about it.

To the Greater Hamilton Writer's Association. It's been fantastic to find a group of local authors to meet with and I can't wait to see what the future brings for the Book Crawl and the literary community.

I definitely could not have done it with the help of my Beta Readers, Editors, and ARC Reviewers. Thanks so much to my cover designer Emily Wittig. I still have no idea how you turned my random jumble of ideas into the perfect covers.

And to all my Book Besties on TikTok, Instagram, and Facebook. You're all amazing. I've found such an encouraging community of authors and readers. You all inspire me to continuously learn, grow, write, and read.

ABOUT THE AUTHOR

Nicole A Oliver is a Fantasy author from Hamilton, Ontario, Canada. A voracious reader, Nicole has always loved becoming lost in magical realms. She loves to travel, but she believes there is no better substitute than getting lost in a book world when that's not possible. Her passion for the genre and the power of words led Nicole to aspirations of becoming an author early in her life.

Nicole, her husband, and her two biggest fans, her twin son and daughter, love to hike and always have their eyes open for magical creatures when they do. During the day, Nicole indulges her love of coffee and fuels her writing by slinging mugs of java. Her family enjoys putting their heads together over jigsaw puzzles, spending time outside, and trying out the fares of local restaurants. Nicole is a horse lover and will admit to imagining herself as a fierce warrior heading into battle whenever she is lucky enough to get to the barn.

Rational Magic is the second book in the planned Archimage Trilogy, and Nicole's first series.